Jinxing of the Witch

Crypt Witch cozy paranormal mystery series - book 13

K.E. O'Connor

K.E. O'Connor Books

JINXING OF THE WITCH

Copyright © 2022 by K.E. O'Connor

ISBN: 978-1-915378-11-8

Written by: K.E. O'Connor

Chapter 1

"If I have to look at another seating plan, I may let Frank get his wish to kill Aurora." I grabbed the huge mug of coffee in front of me and took a swig.

Rhett Blackthorn chuckled as he leaned across the table and caught hold of my hand. "You'd never do that to Aurora. Didn't you once tell me she's been planning her wedding since you were kids?"

"She has, which is why she's panicking so much. Her wedding has to be perfect. Even though she has a wedding planner, she's still running around doing everything herself."

I caught Patti's eye as she stood behind the counter in Sprinkles and gestured at the huge tray of warm dark chocolate brownies she'd brought out from the kitchen.

She waved a hand in acknowledgement and grinned. "How many do you want, Tempest?"

"Do you want one?" I asked Rhett.

"Sure. It's hard to beat brownies from Sprinkles."

I lifted up two fingers at Patti, and she nodded. I turned back to Rhett. "I'm glad you could meet me at the last minute. I needed a break from all the wedding talk."

"It's less than two weeks away," Rhett said.

"Yeah, Aurora tells me that every five minutes. You'd think she was the first person to get married. And she spent all that money hiring Marisa, and she's barely used her wedding planning services. Marisa's been getting in touch with me, asking if there's anything she can do. How am I supposed to know?"

"Because you're the only bridesmaid and the bride's older sister." He lifted my hand and kissed the palm. "Everything will be fine. Aurora and Lex will be blissfully happy. And everyone else will eat too much and dance for too long on the day."

"That's the plan. So long as Aurora's head doesn't explode from stress before the big day. And it will be a big day. All those people who've said they're coming. It's the whole village and then some." I shuddered.

Patti walked over with our brownies and set them on the table. "How are you two lovebirds?"

"We're perfect, thanks," I said.

"You'll be planning your wedding next, after Aurora and Lex have had their moment." She raised her eyebrows at Rhett. "When are you making an honest witch of Tempest?"

He pushed his dark hair off his face. "Um..."

I shook my head and grinned at him. "I'm honest enough. And we're fine as we are."

Patti opened her mouth to say something else, but a customer called her away. "Oh, I've got to go. Just so you know, I make a wonderful triple decker brownie cake that would be perfect for a wedding. I can customize it. Whatever you like."

"We'll keep that in mind," I said as Patti hurried away.

"It's not a terrible idea," Rhett said.

"I agree. A triple decker chocolate brownie cake would be awesome."

He huffed out a laugh. "We've been together a while."

"And we work fine like this."

"You wouldn't be tempted if I suggested we elope? We could do something discreet, just a few close friends and family members."

My heart did a happy flip at the thought of marrying Rhett. "You know what my family is like. Nothing's low-key and discreet with them. And I'd have to invite everyone, or I'd never hear the end of it. And if Aurora discovered we were planning a low-key wedding, she'd collapse with shock, then take over and order harpists and cherubs before I could stop her."

Rhett broke off a piece of brownie and held it out to me. "I'm just putting it out there. You know, testing the water for when we're grown up enough to take the plunge."

I took the bit of brownie he held out. "One day. Let's get through Aurora and Lex's wedding first."

His gaze flicked to the window. His eyes widened, and he pushed back his chair, a grin spreading across his face. "Aidan's here."

I looked out the window. An enormous converted truck painted black with red and yellow flames along the side rumbled past.

"Remind me again who Aidan is?"

"He's only the best bike repair specialist I've ever met. If he doesn't know something about a bike, then it's not worth knowing. He's in high demand and is on the road all year round. I haven't seen him in eighteen months. My ride's long overdue one of his special services. All the guys have booked in for a tune-up."

I vaguely remembered Aidan coming to Willow Tree Falls a couple of years ago. "And the timing couldn't be better, since Gideon and his gang are arriving soon."

Rhett's mouth twisted to the side. "Magic is shining on us. The Tusks have been prodding for a while to get their claws into the village. It's not happening, especially not after I race Gideon and show him who's in charge." He looked over at me. "You're coming to the race? I need my good luck charm by my side."

"Of course. I'm looking forward to it. Give me a group of testosterone fueled bikers with an attitude over an over-hyped bride-to-be who can't make a decision over what music to play at her wedding."

"Is one of those brownies for me?" Wiggles trotted over, his tail in the air and the sandy fur on his head looking messy, like he'd been rummaging somewhere he shouldn't.

"Where have you been hiding?" I said.

"I was out back, checking the trash. Patti often leaves interesting finds out there. It's important not to leave food out, or it attracts rodents."

"Or a hungry hellhound with a bottomless pit for a stomach," I said. "If you've been eating the trash, you won't want any brownie."

He placed his front paws on the table. "There's always room for brownies."

"I'm heading out to see Aidan," Rhett said.

"You go. Have fun with your bikes. I'll catch up with you at the race." I kissed Rhett goodbye and laughed as he almost ran out the door.

"The Willow Tree Falls biker gang will roast the Tusks." Wiggles hopped onto Rhett's vacated seat and snuffled the plate the brownie was on. "I don't know why they're wasting their time coming here."

"Because Gideon Blazeheart has an ego bigger than the sun. And although he denies it, I know he's got his beady eyes set on taking over around here. We don't want that."

"Definitely not. I can't have Rhett and his gang leaving the village. You'd follow him, and you know I can't leave."

"I'd never chase after a guy like a lovesick teenager," I said. "But it would make things tricky. It's never going to happen, though. Since Rhett's been in charge of the gang, everything's calmed down. The rivalry disputes take place on the other side of the barrier. He's good for the village. We don't want him going anywhere."

"From the gooey look on your face, you really don't. You've got it so bad for him."

"Don't you start. Patti was just on about us getting married." I sipped more coffee.

"If you do, can I be best man? No, that's too much responsibility. Don't you have to do something with the rings?"

"You have to keep them safe," I said. "And Rhett would choose his best man."

"I can't be a bridesmaid. I don't suit girly colors. I could organize the stag do. Head up the entertainment." His ears flipped up. "No, I'll be in charge of your catering. I know all the best food places around the village."

"If we ever get married, and that's a big if, it'll be something small. No massive banquet or enormous cake."

"Then what's the point in getting married?" Wiggles said. "It's all about the food, isn't it?"

I scrubbed my fingers through the fur on his head. "Some people think it's to do with declaring your love and then sharing that happiness and commitment with everyone."

Wiggles scarfed down the brownie, while I sat back and finished my coffee. "I'll get you to change your mind. We'll have a giant banquet at your wedding."

The door to Sprinkles crashed open. Aurora raced in, her blue eyes wide and her cheeks bright pink. "There you are! I've been looking everywhere for you."

"What's the problem?" Aurora had been appearing in front of me, looking stressed out almost every day for the last month.

"Something terrible has happened. It's a disaster." She scooped Wiggles off the chair, slumped down in the seat, and buried her head in his fur.

Wiggles squirmed in her grip. He was never fond of cuddles. "Is there a delay on the wedding cake being ready?"

"No, the food is fine." Aurora lifted her head. "Not that it matters. I can't believe what I heard from Marisa this morning."

"Has she done something wrong?" I pushed my brownie over to her. "Eat this. It'll make you feel better."

"I'm too tense to eat." Aurora grabbed the brownie and took a large bite.

"Take a few deep breaths, eat the brownie, and then tell me what the drama is. We'll fix it. We've fixed all the problems you've come across so far."

She stuffed the rest of the brownie in her mouth and chewed furiously before swallowing. "You won't fix this. It's a nightmare. A message has gone to all the guests saying the wedding's been canceled." She dropped her head back on Wiggles.

"Wow! Why would you do that?" I asked.

"I didn't! I knew nothing about it until Marisa contacted me. She kept apologizing and asking if it was something she'd done."

"That makes no sense. Maybe Marisa got a message to cancel a different wedding and mixed you up with someone else she's working with."

"No. I met with her, and she showed me what she'd received. It said: *Aurora Crypt and Lex Fontaine's wedding is canceled. Guests are to return all gifts and not attend the service or evening celebration.*" Aurora let out a sob.

I raised my eyebrows and looked at Wiggles. "Aurora, I don't want to worry you, but you don't think Lex did this, do you?"

Her head shot up, and a single tear tracked down her cheek. "No! He's head over heels in love with me. He has been since the moment he saw me."

"He took a while to get around to proposing," I said. "Could he have gotten cold feet, and this is his cowardly way of breaking things off? Just so you know, if it is, I'll happily kill him for you."

"Me too," Wiggles said. "That's a jerk move."

"Oh! That's sweet of both of you. No, Lex wouldn't do this." She tipped back her head and blinked her eyes. "And on the off-chance he is involved in this mess, I'll be the one killing him."

I chuckled. "You'd never kill anybody."

"Someone will wind up dead over this disaster." She leaned forward, squashing Wiggles against her chest. "And I can't believe Marisa simply sent the message without checking with me. She knows I'm committed to getting married. And yet the second it looks like it's off, she's dashing around telling anyone who'll listen."

"This wasn't her fault," I said. "Somewhere along the way, wires were crossed. Unless..."

"Unless what?"

"You don't think it was Marisa who did this, do you? After all, you've turned into a massive Bridezilla. Even Mom's avoiding you."

She swatted my arm. "I'm not, and she isn't. I need my wedding to be perfect, especially after what happened in my last relationship."

"Yeah, it's hard to forget the psycho old guy who turned you into a Stepford wife with a tainted spell and then hid you in a statue," Wiggles said.

Aurora sniffed. "I have to make sure people forget my previous fiancé turned me into a stone dragon."

"You were a dragon for a tiny amount of time," I said. "And you made a really great dragon."

"You did," Wiggles said. "I'd have happily peed up you."

Aurora's forehead wrinkled. "I've maybe been a teensy bit full on when it comes to my wedding preparations, but it's nothing Marisa hasn't handled before." She sighed dramatically and then waved at Patti. "Hey, Patti. We need a large box of your mixed brownies to go."

"Coming right up," Patti called back.

"We're going somewhere?" I said.

"Yes! We have to undo this mess and make sure my guests know the wedding is back on. I can't have an empty ceremony and no one dancing at my reception. The villagers will think I'm unpopular. It'll be a terrible start to married life."

"It could be a blessing in disguise. After all, you have got two hundred and fifty people coming."

"I want everyone I know to be there, so they can celebrate with me. And they won't be there if we don't fix this right now." She stood and set Wiggles on the ground. "You're my bridesmaid. You must help."

"Okay, I'll grab the brownies. You head to your store and get a list of everyone we need to contact."

She leaned over and hugged me. "I knew you'd sort this out. Don't be long. We have lots of people to speak to."

"Wait! Can't we just send them a message?"

"No! They have to hear directly from us that this is a mistake. I don't want anyone to miss out."

I groaned as Aurora raced out the door, her blonde hair flying out behind her. This wedding rescue mission would take all day.

I headed to the counter, collected the dozen brownies from Patti, and paid for them.

"Is everything okay?" Patti asked. "Aurora looked stressed."

I glanced around. "Did you get a message saying her wedding had been canceled?"

"I did. I was so shocked I didn't know what to do. I would have come over and said something, but I didn't want to bother her. Is it off?"

"No. It's definitely on. Keep it in your diary."

"That's a relief. I've been looking forward to their wedding for ages," Patti said.

I looked at the fresh cinnamon rolls and iced buns on the counter. "Make me up a batch of those to go as well. This challenge will need sugar and plenty of it."

No matter how hard I tried, there was no escaping my sister's wedding.

Chapter 2

I rolled my shoulders and stretched out my arms. I glanced out the window to see the darkness had long since chased away the sunshine.

Aurora walked out of the back room in her store, a smile on her face. She was carrying a tray of chamomile tea and a plate with the last of the iced buns on it.

"I'm feeling so much better. Everyone's been contacted. They all know the message about the canceled wedding was a misunderstanding." She set the tray down and poured out the tea.

"Most of them didn't believe the message was real," I said. "And why would they? It's all you've talked about for months."

"I'm just glad this mess has been sorted. Still, I wouldn't mind having another look at the place settings for the dinner. Have you got time?" Aurora was already reaching under the counter and pulling out a large rolled piece of paper.

I jumped up and backed away to the door. "No, it's getting late. I need to check in at Cloven Hoof. It'll already be open, and the team will be wondering where I am."

The door behind me opened. I turned to see Lex Fontaine hurry in.

"Hey, Tempest. I heard from my beautiful bride that you've helped save the day." He hurried over to Aurora, wrapped his arms around her, and gave her a big kiss.

"I can confirm the crisis has been averted," I said.

There was a loud crash and two high-pitched hisses from the back room. Wiggles, Sox, and Charlie bowled out in a blur of magic sparks.

Wiggles jumped to his feet and shook out his singed looking fur. Sox and Charlie, who were no longer the tiny fluffy kitten familiars they used to be, jumped on his tail. They were almost as big as Wiggles and had several more months of growing to do.

"What are you three doing?" I said.

"I was showing them a spell," Wiggles said. "They're not getting the hang of it."

"Did it involve fire?" I plucked a piece of something charred and smoking off his back.

"Of course. My magic is fire based," he said. "But these two are more into playing than spell casting."

Sox's eyes narrowed, and Charlie's whiskers bristled.

"We'll have to get them their own playroom in the castle," Lex said. "They're proving to be quite a handful."

"They're adorable." Aurora kissed the end of Lex's nose. "They're the perfect familiars."

Sox and Charlie slunk over and curled around Aurora's legs, purring and twirling their black fluffy tails around her.

She picked them up and kissed them.

"Hey, Lex." Wiggles strolled over to him. "How about you grant us three wishes? After all, we're almost family. You must do that all the time for your family."

Lex tugged at his shirt collar. "No, I never do that. If I share my gifts with family members, it gets complicated. My wishes are only for those who need them."

"We really need them," Wiggles said. "I've been trying to get Sox and Charlie to talk. That's my first wish. It would make life easier if I wasn't trying to decode cat body language. As you can see from the scratches on my nose, it doesn't work out in my favor."

"Wiggles, we've had this conversation several times. Lex won't grant you any wishes," Aurora said. "Besides, you need his lamp before he'll grant you anything."

"So hand over the lamp," Wiggles said. "I don't see the problem. My second wish would be for an unlimited supply of doughnuts to arrive at my door every morning as soon as I wake up."

"My wishes are only to be used for good," Lex said.

"I see nothing bad about that wish," Wiggles said.

"Your waistline would," I said.

The sound of low rumbling engines had me turning to the window at the front of the store. A dozen low rider motorbikes cruised past, the engines emitting a throaty, rich purr.

Wiggles, Sox, and Charlie raced to the window and stared out.

"The Tusks have arrived," Wiggles said.

We joined him and watched them cruise past. The riders were dressed in black leathers and didn't wear helmets. Gideon Blazeheart was at the front of the pack, his long dark hair streaming out behind him, and a silver slash of lightning on the back of his jacket.

"I've never been to a biker race," Lex said. "Do you have them here every year?"

"No, they take place all around the world," I said. "We've hosted them a few times. Auntie Queenie was in the Dead Tree Witch gang the last time there was a race in the village."

"Those bikes are impressive," Lex said. "I wouldn't mind one."

"You could always wish for one," Wiggles said.

Lex chuckled. "Maybe not. From the looks of them, they're not ordinary bikes. The wheels aren't touching the ground."

"They're anything but ordinary," I said. "Any normal vehicle coming into Willow Tree Falls will develop engine faults. The magic around here plays havoc with them."

"Wow! The bikes are propelled by magic." Lex gave a low whistle. "I'm very tempted."

"No, they're dangerous," Aurora said. "Don't you dare get on one before we get married. I'm not having my new husband injured for our honeymoon."

"I'll be on my best behavior," he said. "But after the honeymoon, we could look into getting one. It could be fun to go out on the open road."

"Where would we put Sox and Charlie?" Aurora said.

"We could get them a sidecar," Lex said.

"That's hardly the bad guy biker image you want to portray," Wiggles said. "You could get a couple of saddles on the back. They'd fit in there."

Sox and Charlie jumped on him, making their feelings on that idea clear as they bit his ears.

"Are you worried about Rhett taking part in the race?" Aurora bent down and pulled the cats off Wiggles before they could inflict any damage.

"No. I'm certain he'll win. Rhett knows every inch of the roads around the village. There's no way anyone can beat him."

"We'll have to go tonight and watch the races." Lex said. "It'll be fun."

She wrinkled her nose as she settled Sox and Charlie over her shoulders. "I'm not sure. We should stay here. There's so much we need to do for the wedding."

"What else needs doing, my sweet? Now that business over the message has been cleared up, everything is in hand," Lex said.

"There are several things I need to double check. And I was about to take a look at the seating plan," Aurora said.

Lex cast a desperate look my way. "We could do with some fun. A wedding shouldn't be so stressful."

I decided to throw him a lifeline. "Aurora, Rhett will be offended if you don't show up. And the races tonight are just friendlies, so it won't be too intense. You have to come and lend your support."

"Let's go," Lex said. "Everyone will be there. We don't want to miss out."

Aurora's gaze went to the discarded seating plan. "I suppose half an hour off won't hurt."

I gave Lex a discreet thumbs-up. "The race starts at the end of Mom and Dad's road, and I'm hosting a party for the bikers at Cloven Hoof until midnight. We're gathering there and then walking to the race."

"We'll be there," Lex said. "I wouldn't miss this for the world."

"Great. But I have one condition," I said.

"What's that?" Aurora was reaching for her seating plan.

"No more wedding talk. Tonight is about letting your hair down and enjoying yourself. All the wedding stuff will be here tomorrow. Tonight's a chance to forget your worries."

"What if I have a really important question I need to ask you?"

"It'll wait till the morning," I said.

"Lex, you'll back me up on this." Aurora turned to him. "Our wedding must take priority."

"And it will. But your sister's right. Party tonight, wedding tomorrow." He kissed her forehead.

She gave a sigh but nodded. "Okay, but I'm only doing this because I love you both so much."

"Love you too, sis. Now, I'd better get going. I'll see you at Cloven Hoof later." There was no way Aurora could stop herself from talking about the wedding, but maybe the bikes would distract her for five minutes. I lived in hope.

"Excuse me. Coming through." I tried to nudge my way past one of the Tusk bikers and a curvy redhead who were making out by the side of the bar.

The woman giggled as she spotted me. It was Moon Fairfax. She worked the occasional shift in the Ancient Imp when Petra was short-handed. Moon dragged her guy away and into the crowd on the dance floor.

I set the tray of lemon drops on the bar and blew out a breath. These bikers sure knew how to drink. Not only that, but it looked like almost everyone in the village had joined in the fun. I didn't mind. The more the merrier in Cloven Hoof on a party night like this.

Merrie and several other bar staff raced around, taking orders and topping up drinks.

The music was pumping, the dance floor was crowded, and so far, the bikers had behaved themselves.

The music changed, and people cheered as an upbeat song came on.

Abruptly, the atmosphere altered, and people turned to the main door as it opened.

Gideon Blazeheart strolled in, looking like he owned the place.

I took an instant dislike to him and his arrogant strut. This was my bar.

Eleven giant leather clad guys broke off from the crowd and joined him. They were all tall, moody looking, and some of them had impressive facial hair going on.

Rhett appeared by my side with Ian Blaine, one of the more mean-spirited of his biker gang. "It's time to make the introductions. Let's ensure Gideon and his cronies know who's the boss around here."

"You mean me, right?"

He kissed my cheek. "You're the boss of my heart, baby. That's all you need to worry about."

It was a super cheesy line, but it worked. "Have fun. I don't much fancy tackling that ego."

He winked at me before strolling over to Gideon. The crowd parted around them. Everyone seemed to be holding their breath to see who would make the first move.

I gestured Merrie to cut the music. Things were about to get interesting.

Gideon's sharp gaze ran over Rhett, and he pursed his full lips. "So, you're the head of the Willow Tree Falls gang?"

Rhett nodded. "Are the Tusks enjoying their visit to my patch?"

"So far, we're underwhelmed."

"Your recent behavior suggests otherwise." Rhett glanced over his shoulder as his own gang surrounded him.

I smacked my lips together. The testosterone in the air was palpable. I sipped more lemon drop.

"I don't know what you're talking about," Gideon said.

"I've heard the rumors. People report back to me when someone puts out feelers about acquiring this territory."

"You shouldn't listen to rumors. Although I wouldn't mind experiencing the power of the stone circle in this place." Gideon stroked a hand down his chest.

"As a guest, you're welcome to visit the stones," Rhett said. "So long as you don't abuse our hospitality, there'll be no problems."

"Me and the guys never abuse hospitality," Gideon said. "Boys, go get some drinks. Let's make friends with the locals."

Rhett nodded at his own gang, and the two groups dispersed toward the bar.

"Get ready for trouble," I said to Merrie. "And keep an eye on how much they're drinking."

"You got it, boss," Merrie said.

I turned back to see Rhett with his hand on Gideon's shoulder. Their heads were together, and I couldn't hear what they were saying, but from the look on Gideon's face, he wasn't impressed.

Rhett dropped his hand and nodded. After a second, Gideon returned the nod. His gaze cut away from Rhett and landed on me. He grinned and winked.

I arched an eyebrow and looked away. He wasn't an unattractive guy, but I was more than happy with the biker I had.

Rhett and Gideon broke apart, and Rhett headed over to his gang. His confident strut made my stomach flutter. It was clear who was the boss when it came to the bikers.

I'd just collected some empty glasses when I turned and almost walked straight into Gideon's chest.

He caught hold of me. "Steady now. I don't want you falling at my feet. Although that could be fun. I'm Gideon Blazeheart. You must have heard of me. And you are...?"

"The owner of Cloven Hoof," I said.

His black eyes sparkled as his gaze slid over me. "You're Tempest Crypt. I've heard good things about you. Thanks for the welcome party tonight. That's real civil of you."

"My pleasure. What have you heard about me?"

He leaned closer, his breath tickling my ear. "Is it true you have a demon inside you?"

"You'd better believe it. And he's prone to bursting out without warning, so you should back up." I pressed a hand against Gideon's chest and pushed him away.

"A witch with her very own demon to command. You must be powerful. I'd love to explore that power. We should go somewhere, just the two of us, and get the sparks flying."

"Nope. You're not my type," I said.

He caught hold of my arm. "I'm only being friendly. I hope to see you at the race later tonight. Will you be cheering me on?"

"Is there a problem?" Rhett appeared by my side and wound a hand around my waist.

Gideon scowled and stepped back. "You're the reason she's not interested in me?"

"It's not that. Tempest simply has excellent taste," Rhett said.

I suppressed a grin. "It's fine. Gideon was just introducing himself. He knows I'm not available."

"Everyone's available for a price."

Rhett growled, and I bared my teeth at Gideon. This guy was a piece of work.

"A price?" I shot him a sharp smile. "What do you have in mind?"

Gideon's grin was predatory. "How about winner takes all?"

Rhett moved away from me and stood in front of Gideon. "What are you talking about?"

"I'm talking about Tempest," Gideon said. "If I win the race against you, I get to take her out on a date."

"No way," I said. "I'm nobody's prize."

"She's not," Rhett said. "Gideon, you're out of line."

"Tonight's races are supposed to be friendly," I said. "No one is betting on anything."

Gideon's top lip curled. "I bet you can be real friendly when you want to be."

He'd gone too far. "Rhett will destroy you when you race each other."

Gideon briskly rubbed his hands together. "That's my kind of race. So, how about it, Blackthorn? Let's go outside and see what you're made of?"

Rhett growled. "It's on." He pressed me close to his side. "I'll win this race for you."

I wasn't one for swooning, but what's a girl to do when she gets a promise like that?

Chapter 3

I bundled out of the club with everyone else. Even Frank was stirring as the large group of partygoers and bikers headed to the race site.

"What have I missed?" he muttered inside my head.

"You haven't missed anything." I kept my voice low to make sure no one noticed me talking to myself. "You're just in time to see Rhett teach an egotistical biker a lesson."

"Sounds dull. Wake me up when something exciting happens." His energy had barely prickled up my spine, and it died away just as quickly.

I wasn't reassured by his disinterest. My ability to control Frank's outbursts had been shaky at the best of times these past few months. When I got angry, it always stirred him up. And this atmosphere wasn't helping me remain cool, calm, and collected. Everyone was itching for a fight. And it looked like Rhett and Gideon would give it to them.

"There you are." Granny Dottie grabbed hold of my hand.

"Hey, Gran. How's it going?" I kissed her cheek.

"Fine. This is so exciting. It's been a long time since we had a biker showdown in the village."

"Gideon deserves it," I said.

"I saw him talking to you in the club. He was being very familiar."

"That's why he deserves it. I didn't know you were in Cloven Hoof. I didn't see you in there."

"I stopped by for a quick drink. I was waiting for the races to start. I was coming over to talk to you when I saw Gideon. Then Rhett intervened and sorted things out."

"He'll sort everything out," I said. "Gideon overstepped the mark. It's time to teach him a lesson."

"This is just like the old days when your auntie was in the gang," Granny Dottie said. "It was so much fun. And you can't beat riding a bike. I'll never forget those days when I used to sit on the back of your grandad's bike, the wind in my hair, and my skirt blowing up around my thighs. Oh, and the rumble of that big bike between my legs. It got my heart pounding."

"That's too much information, Granny," I said.

She chuckled and patted my cheek. "There's always room for a knee trembler on the back of a bike."

I grimaced and covered one ear. "Enough!"

The crowd was approaching the start of the race site. My mom, Dad, Auntie Queenie, Aurora, and Lex were already there.

Wiggles bounded ahead and met up with Sox and Charlie. They jumped on his back and bundled with him in the dirt.

Aurora waved when she spotted me. "Over here!"

I kept hold of Granny Dottie's hand as we hurried over.

Aurora's eyes were wide as she took in the scene. "I just saw Rhett go past. He looked angry."

"So he should. Gideon's just challenged him," Granny Dottie said. "And he wanted Tempest thrown in as part of the winnings by the sound of things."

Aurora gasped. "How exciting. Two men fighting over you."

"I don't want any men fighting over me," I said.

"Oh, hush, of course you do. It's good to get a boost to the ego and know you're desirable." Granny Dottie kissed Grandpa Lucius on the cheek.

A tall guy with a mass of shaggy blond hair and enormous shoulders strode past, pushing a large black bike. A skinny girl with bright red hair limped along behind him. She was dressed in stained overalls and had a toolkit in her hands.

She slowed as she spotted Wiggles and the cats. "Oh, they're cute. Hello, little ones. Are you here to see the race?"

Wiggles wagged his tail. "That's right. It's the first time for these two." He tilted his head at Sox and Charlie.

The woman's eyes widened. "You talk! And you have lovely red eyes. They match my hair. Are you a miniature hellhound? No, you can't be. You're way too cute to be a devil dog."

"I may be small, but I've got a lot going for me." Wiggles blasted out a small plume of flames.

She set down the toolbox, pulled an oil-coated rag from her pocket, and wiped her hands on it before petting his head. "That's so clever. You are a terrifying hellhound."

Wiggles accepted the pet she gave him. "This is Sox and Charlie. They're my... foster kids."

She knelt in the dirt and tickled the cats under their chins. "Do you talk, too?"

"They will one day. It's a work in progress," Wiggles said.

The woman finally looked up at me. "Oh! Sorry! I'm an idiot. I love animals. I'd have a dog of my own, but Aidan has allergies." She stood and stuck out her hand. "I'm Maddie Vixen. I work with Aidan on the bike repair truck."

I shook her hand. "Tempest Crypt."

"Is this your dog?"

"Yep. Well, he likes to think of himself as his own dog, but we hang out together."

"He's sweet." Maddie sighed. "I wish I could have a dog."

"You should tell Aidan to get his allergies sorted," I said. "You can't beat the smell of dog drool on your pillow or fur in your morning coffee."

She laughed. "I know, right? I'll have to make do with lots of strokes with this lot while I'm here."

"Maddie! Catch up. I need those tools." The guy with the blond hair was gesturing at her.

She grabbed the toolbox. "Gotta go. Enjoy the race." She limp-walked away.

"I like her," Wiggles said. "I wonder how she feels about cake for breakfast."

"I bet she loves it," I said.

"The bikers are getting ready for the first race," Mom said. "You'll want to see Rhett off."

Rhett and Gideon sat astride their bikes. In front of them was a long straight lane that led to the barrier of Willow Tree Falls. With no other traffic on the roads, they were assured a clear path.

The buzzing crowd pressed in on either side of them, everyone eager to see the race begin.

I hurried to Rhett's side and touched his arm.

He looked over at me and winked before revving his engine.

"You've got this," I said. "Show Gideon who's in charge around here."

"He won't know what's hit him by the time I'm done with him." Rhett pulled me in and gave me such a passionate kiss that everyone in the crowd was cheering by the time we pulled apart.

My cheeks were flushed as I stepped away, a smile on my face.

I re-joined my family, my heart racing almost as loudly as the bike engines.

Moon Fairfax walked in front of the bikes. She must be more involved with the bikers than I'd realized if she was starting the race.

She raised her arms and cocked her hip before looking around at the crowd and waiting until the noise died down and all eyes were on her.

"That one reckons herself as something fancy," Granny Dottie muttered. "A biker groupie. You get them everywhere."

"That was me a minute ago with Rhett," I said.

"Nonsense. You're his girl. He needed a lucky kiss to secure a win." She fanned her face. "Although that was some kiss."

I grinned, but my attention was glued to Rhett.

His eyes were fixed on the road in front of him. This felt anything other than a friendly race. Both bikers meant business.

"Are you boys ready?" Moon tossed her hair over one shoulder, exposing bare skin and a crimson bra strap.

They each raised a hand and revved their engines.

She flashed a smile at someone in the crowd then dropped her arms, the signal for the race to begin.

The bikes raced away. The crowd surged into the lane, cheering and yelling.

Wiggles, Sox, and Charlie were at the front of the crowd, chasing after the bikes, their little legs a blur of movement, and sparkles of magic flying off their fur.

A flutter of something soft and white passed by my face. Dazielle descended from the sky. Of course, the head of Angel Force had to spoil the fun.

She shook out her wings and scowled at the crowd. "I should have known you'd be at the center of this trouble, Tempest."

I hurried past her, keen not to miss the race. "Not now. I need to see Rhett win."

Dazielle strode along beside me, tutting and scowling at the jostling crowd. "There's not supposed to be any bike races in the village. This is a peaceful place."

"It's not a real race. And you don't want the Tusks thinking they can take over. Trust me, having Rhett in charge of the bikers around here is a good thing. You should be on his side and cheering him on."

"I warned him about this," Dazielle said.

I glanced at her. "Rhett? What did you say to him?"

"That he wasn't to encourage Gideon or anyone else to get involved."

"Dazielle, the bikers have been racing each other for hundreds of years. It's not going to stop now." The roar of the bike engines faded. "This is important."

"It's also illegal. And it's not happening on my watch."

"It is. Get used to it. Now, I need to go congratulate my guy on winning his race." I dashed past her and pushed through the crowd, eager to get to the front and see Rhett's victorious return.

I'd just reached a gap when sparks of jagged light flashed into the air, close to the magic barrier.

Wiggles appeared out of the gloom, flanked by Sox and Charlie. His eyes were glowing red, and smoke plumed out of his mouth. "He cheated! I just watched Gideon blast Rhett off his bike."

"That cheating, deceitful warlock." I ground my teeth as I raced along the lane. "Is Rhett hurt?"

"I didn't see. But he was going fast when he was blasted by Gideon," Wiggles said. "He shot into a hedgerow."

Gideon's bike cruised into view, and he crossed the finish line. He sat astride his bike, a smug smile on his face and one hand raised in the air as his gang congratulated him.

"Oh no, you don't." I launched myself at Gideon and sent him flying off the back of his bike. His ride crashed to the ground as we rolled in the dirt.

"Hey, calm down, hot stuff. If you wanted a tumble with me, you only needed to ask." His hands gripped my shoulders.

"You cheated! You were seen. You knocked Rhett off his bike." I growled in his face and sparked fire magic on the tips of my fingers.

"Tempest, what are you doing?" Dazielle appeared by my side, a flurry of feathers and indignation.

"Gideon hurt Rhett." I shook Gideon by the collar of his leather jacket. "If you've injured him, I'll rip your head off."

Gideon chuckled, but a spark of fear appeared in his eyes. "Get this witch off me. Angel, do your job."

Dazielle's blue eyes narrowed. "Is this true? Did you attack Rhett?"

The crowd had gathered around us. Gideon's guys were at the front, not looking happy to see their boss pinned to the ground.

"No! Rhett lost control when we were racing." Gideon smirked up at me. "He must be losing his touch. It's time for Blackthorn to step aside and let a real man take over."

"Tempest, let him up," Dazielle said.

I curled my fingers into Gideon's collar. "He's not going anywhere. Where's Rhett?"

"I'm right here." Rhett limped out of the gloom, pushing his bike beside him. He had dirt down one side of his face, and blood was trickling from a wound on his head.

"Did Gideon do that to you?" I asked.

Rhett scowled at Gideon before flicking a glance at Dazielle. "I'll deal with this."

Dazielle pursed her lips. "If a crime was committed, you need to report it."

Rhett's gaze fixed onto Gideon. "There's no crime to report. I'll sort it."

"You can do what you like," Gideon said. "And I'm more than happy being pinned down by this beautiful witch. She's getting me excited, pressing herself against me. She must be missing out on something from her current squeeze."

"You're disgusting." I rolled off him and jumped to my feet. "You were seen using magic on Rhett."

Gideon got to his feet and brushed down his jacket. "Yeah, by who?"

"Me and my awesome foster kids." Wiggles strode into view.

Gideon snorted a laugh. "No one will believe the word of a fat dog and his weird fluffy sidekicks."

Sox hissed, and Charlie slashed a paw in the air.

"I'm not fat!" Wiggles puffed out his chest. "I'm big boned. And I saw you, loser."

"Dazielle, are you going to arrest Gideon?" I said.

She looked from Rhett to Gideon. "Rhett, do you want to press charges?"

The crowd around us grumbled and shifted, the bikers sizing each other up as the tension grew.

"No, it's fine," Rhett said.

"If I let this matter drop, it ends here," Dazielle said. "No more fighting. That goes for all of you."

"Rhett knows when he's been beaten." Gideon tried to sling an arm around my shoulders, but I shrugged him away.

"Watch yourself," Rhett said, his voice a low rumble in his chest.

"I don't know why you're unhappy. You made the deal. Winner gets the girl. And I definitely won this race. Tempest is all mine," Gideon said.

Rhett dropped his bike and raced at Gideon, but he was a few seconds too slow. I slammed my hand against Gideon's chest and blasted him with a knockback spell.

Gideon yelped and landed in the dirt ten feet away.

There was silence for a few seconds, then the crowd erupted as the rival bikers clashed, fists, magic, and curse words flying.

"Stop this at once, or you're all under arrest." Dazielle flapped from one fighting group to the other, pulling people apart and failing to maintain order.

I was stalking toward Gideon, ready to give him another piece of my mind, when Ian Blaine launched out of the crowd and jumped him. They crashed to the ground, and hot magic sparked between them.

I looked around for my family, wanting to make sure they were okay. The situation felt dangerously out of control, with spells shooting in all directions. I was relieved to see Aurora standing to one side with Lex. They were looking after several people who'd sustained injuries. Dad was tackling a couple of bikers, pulling them apart and forcing them to calm down. From what I could see of Granny Dottie and Auntie Queenie, they were helping but also firing off shots of magic while they did. They enjoyed a good rumble when they got the opportunity.

Someone heavy slammed into my back and sent me to the ground.

Anger burned inside me. And with that came the unwelcome feel of Frank stirring. His energy coiled up my spine and tickled the back of my neck.

"I thought I told you to tell me when things got exciting," he said.

I pulled myself upright and rubbed my bruised knees. "Not now. Your help isn't needed."

"You always say you never need me, but I seem to come to your assistance more and more."

"You call it assistance. I call it a problem." I dodged a blast of rogue magic that shot out of the fighting crowd and looked around for Rhett.

"How about you let me out?"

"In return for what?" There were always conditions when it came to Frank's help.

I pulled apart two warring bikers and blasted a guy from the Tusks in the chest, sending him sprawling.

"Five minutes with your sister, and I can stop this right now," Frank said.

"You're not even getting five seconds with her. Back off, Frank." I spotted Gideon in the crowd. He was bloodied, bruised, and looking furious. Good, that was no less than he deserved.

"How about three minutes?" Frank said.

"Nope. Get lost." Despite fighting him, Frank's power grew inside me. I was losing control. The frenetic, chaotic energy was only making things worse. He was feeding on the rage of the crowd and loving every second.

I caught Lex's eye and waved at him. "Get Aurora out of here."

He raised a hand. "We're okay. She wants to stay and help people."

"No! It's Frank." I pointed at my chest. The crowd wasn't the problem. I was.

Recognition dawned on Lex's face. He'd seen enough of Frank over the time he'd been with my sister to know I wasn't messing around. "We'll go right away." He tugged on Aurora's arm and whispered in her ear.

She looked around, panic on her face. She saw me and walked closer, but I waved her away.

She hesitated. I could see the indecision on her face. Aurora always wanted to help people and often put herself at risk when she did so. But this was one risk I wasn't letting her take. She was no match for Frank.

I shoved a biker out of the way as I watched them leave. It was only when she was out of view that I could relax an inch and unclench my teeth. One disaster had been averted.

The second I let go of my control, Frank's energy poured over me. My vision clouded red, sweat broke out on my forehead, and an intense, dark, jagged energy spun through me, heating my veins and making the tips of my fingers tingle.

Even though I hated Frank, he came with a handy side order of incredible power. I could still be injured when he was in control, and he had no care for my safety, but when our energies combined, we were a force to be reckoned with.

I knocked out two Tusk bikers as I slammed into them. Jagged spikes of black energy poured from my fingertips and covered another fighting bundle of bikers on the ground.

They recoiled from the energy and scurried away on their hands and knees.

"Tempest, what are you doing?" Dazielle was suddenly in front of me, hovering several feet off the ground, her wings extended. "Get control of Frank."

"Out of my way, angel." The words slurred out of me. Frank's voice was deep and made me sound like I'd smoked thirty cigarettes one after the other.

"I can't do that. You're a danger to everyone. Tempest, I know you're in there. Get control of your demon."

I raised my hands. Sticky, foul smelling magic dripped from my fingertips. I pointed them at Dazielle. "Last warning."

She covered herself with her wings and spun upward. Frank's dark magic missed her by an inch. She swirled over my head as I strode through the crowd, smashing into fighting bikers as if they were nothing more than annoying flies. And that's all they were to Frank. He was having fun.

Gideon stood to one side, yelling orders, but he was no longer taking part in the battle he'd started. He was a coward.

I shot toward him, magic sparking on my fingertips and Frank's hot energy driving me on. I had to destroy him.

"Yes, crush that insect. You'll make him pay for interfering. Willow Tree Falls is ours." Frank snarled and fired heat through me.

"Yes! He'll never get in my way again."

A hard, muscular body slammed into my side, and I smashed to the ground.

I rolled over, hissing curses and sparking magic at whoever dared stop me from achieving my mission.

"Tempest, calm down." Rhett's voice was low and urgent in my ear as he forced me to stay still.

"Get off me. You have nothing to do with us. You're not important. We will kill you if you don't leave us alone." Frank's voice roared out of my mouth, and I saw red. Anger, rage, and a hatred I'd never experienced before flooded through me.

Rhett yanked me to my feet and pinned me against his chest. "Get control. You don't want to hurt anybody. It's Frank. He's making you do this. You have to stop. Everyone's at risk if you don't."

I squirmed and bucked in his arms and soon broke free. I pointed a finger at him and snarled. "You're dead."

A flurry of white wings surrounded me. I was spun into the air and gagged as I inhaled the sickly sweet angel scent of vanilla and sugar. Angels disgusted me.

The wings opened as three simultaneous blasts of ice cold magic shot into my chest.

I gasped and threw back my head as the pure, intense magic coursed through me.

Frank roared in my head. "No! You Crypt witches won't stop me. I'll have my revenge. I won't be pinned down and told what to do."

I forced my head up, my vision blurry. A gasp of relief shot from my lips as I saw my mom, Granny Dottie, and Auntie Queenie pulsing magic into me. I focused on them. They were my lifeline. They were bringing me back to sanity and dragging Frank into his cage.

My gaze flicked to Rhett, and I let out a deep, mournful sigh. I'd never hurt him. He was always there for me. He stuck by my side no matter how weird or crazy things got with Frank.

I gathered my energy, inhaled a modicum of control, and clenched my fists. "We're done, Frank."

He roared his protest in my head, but slowly, inch by painful inch, his power slid down my spine, until he was nothing but an angry growl in the back of my head.

I lifted a shaky hand. "I'm good. You can stop now."

Dazielle's wings clamped around me as the magic blasts faded, keeping me from falling and breaking a bone. She held me close as she lowered me to the ground.

"Tempest, we need to talk about Frank," she muttered in my ear.

I tried to get out of her wings as we landed, but she had me in a painfully tight grip. I was going nowhere. "We don't. I'm dealing with him."

"You definitely aren't. That was too close. People could have been killed." She finally let me go, and I staggered away.

I scraped a hand down my face and glanced at her, guilt shifting through me like a tidal wave. She was right.

I looked around and let out a sigh. The fighting was over. Several people were limping away, and the bikers had gone.

Mom wrapped me in a warm, soft hug. "Is everything okay?"

I hugged her with one arm and reached a hand out for Rhett.

He took it and gave it a squeeze, letting me know everything was good between us. This wasn't the first time he'd tangled with Frank. It wouldn't be the last.

"You good?" he asked.

I nodded. "Yes, that's enough fun for one night. I'm exhausted. Let's go home."

Chapter 4

"Wake me in about a week." I stuffed the pillow over my head and snuggled deep under my duvet.

Wiggles caught hold of the pillow and tugged it away, exposing my head. "I'm hungry. You've been in bed for hours."

"I'm not leaving my bed ever again."

"Last night wasn't that bad." He slumped on his belly and stretched out his paws. "Nobody got killed."

"Only because I have a family of awesome witches who stopped me when Frank was in control. I couldn't do anything to stop him. He'd have killed everyone who got in his way. And he planned to kill Rhett." I shuddered at the memory.

"You'd have figured something out."

"I got lucky last night. I'm safer here. I can't hurt anyone if I don't leave my bed."

"You're feeling sorry for yourself. A box of triple chocolate muffins, a huge coffee, and a shower, and you'll be back to your old self."

"Nope. It's not happening."

A knock on the apartment door had me groaning.

"I'll go see who it is," Wiggles said. "Maybe they have food."

"Don't. I'm not seeing anyone."

Wiggles returned a moment later. "It's your mom. You have to let her in."

I flopped onto my back and stared at the ceiling. Last night had been out of control crazy. More accurately, I'd been out of control crazy. It could have been the excitement and magic buzzing around that stirred Frank into a frenzy, but I hadn't felt him this strong for ages.

Wiggles nudged me with his nose. "Your mom's waiting. And I smelled food. She's brought us something delicious. You can't deny me my treats. It's animal cruelty."

I slid out of bed as another knock came on the door. "I'm coming." I hurried to the door and cracked it open.

Mom raised her eyebrows when she saw me. "I figured you might be in hiding."

"I'm not safe to be around."

"You haven't been safe to be around since you came into your powers."

"That's not reassuring."

"It should be. It's what makes you such an impressive Crypt witch. I'm not going anywhere. If you close the door on me, I'll keep talking until you let me in."

Wiggles nudged past me. "Come in, Cora. Tempest is neglecting her hellhound care giving duties."

Mom smiled down at him. "You do look famished." She tapped the lid of the white box she held.

There was no use arguing with these two. I stepped back and eased open the door.

Mom walked into the kitchen and looked around. "I've got muffins and some of Patti's amazing cherry and chocolate scones." She set everything out on the counter and switched on the kettle.

I perched on a stool, feeling like a guilty teenager who'd been caught out after curfew.

She patted my cheek as she hurried around the kitchen, pulling out plates, pouring coffee, and then settling on her own stool. "How is our less than charming demon this morning?"

"Frank wasn't happy about being forced down last night. I expect I'll pay for it at some point." I picked up a scone and pulled it to pieces.

"I'll have that if you don't want it. I'm about to faint with hunger." Wiggles headbutted my leg.

Mom hopped up, filled Wiggles' bowl with food, and left a muffin on the side.

He raced over and got stuck in.

She returned to her stool and took a sip of coffee. "Is Frank still causing you problems?"

"He is."

"And he's been like that since your father returned?"

"Yep."

Mom was quiet for a moment. "You don't think it's your father's magic stirring up Frank, do you?"

"No offense to Dad, but he's not that powerful. It can't be that. I did wonder..." I glanced at her. We'd not really spoken about this.

"Go on. What's on your mind?" she said.

"I wondered if Dad had done a deal with Frank after I swallowed him. I was young when Frank attacked Aurora. He should have destroyed me, but he didn't. Not long after that, Dad vanished."

She shook her head. "No, I'd have known about that. You're a powerful witch who has the ability to tame a demon. Frank made the biggest mistake of his cursed life when he picked on this family."

"I guess so."

"I know so." She ate a piece of muffin. "Do you have control of Frank now?"

"He's rumbling around in the background, the same as always, but he has no interest in coming out." I tipped back my head. "I probably need a break from Willow Tree Falls. I haven't had many assignments that have taken me out of the village for a while. Frank likes a day trip. But the demons seem quiet. No one is interested in trying to destroy the world."

"Which is never a good sign."

I sat up straight. "You think they're up to something?"

"Demons are always looking for ways to cause trouble. But no, I've not heard anything that has me worried." She placed a fresh scone on my plate. "Besides, I like having you around. Both my girls are home where they belong. I don't like it when you leave. Everything seems better when we're all here."

"I like hanging out here, too." We ate our breakfast scones and muffins quietly for several minutes. I was already feeling better.

"The family is all back in the village. It makes me happy," Mom said.

"Is everything okay with you and Dad, you know, since he came home?" It was weird talking to my mom about this situation. Dad had been back in the village for months, and sometimes, it seemed just like the old days. It was as if he'd never left.

"Oh, we're getting there. Most of the time, it's good. We've both changed, but we're not having any troubles we can't manage. He's still the same kind-hearted rogue I fell in love with all those years ago. And he's so looking forward to giving Aurora away at her wedding."

"Yeah, that'll be good." I stuffed the scone in my mouth, working up the courage to make my next suggestion. "About the wedding. Given the whole Frank situation, I'm not sure I should go."

Mom lowered her mug. "Why not? You have to be there."

"I don't. Do you think Aurora would mind if I backed out?"

"Tempest, she'd be devastated. You know she would. You can't let her down."

"I'm not doing it because I hate the dress she's making me wear. I'm doing it because of the killer demon lurking inside me. What if Frank gets out of control like he did last night?"

Mom narrowed her eyes. "He wouldn't dare. Not with the whole Crypt witch coven there."

"He might. I didn't expect him to burst out and attack the bikers. I usually get a warning, so I can put on the brakes."

"You were distracted. Rhett had fallen off his bike, and Gideon was strutting around like a prize peacock, trying to lay claim to you."

"I usually know Frank's looming, though."

"You're worrying about nothing."

"Frank isn't nothing."

"We'll figure it out," Mom said. "You have to be at the wedding."

"But Frank gets jealous when Aurora is around other guys. He wants her all to himself."

"He can want all he likes. He's never having her."

"Yeah, but the message doesn't go through his thick demon skull. What if I get there on the day, and he rears up and slaughters every member of the wedding party?"

"It's not happening. You underestimate your power over Frank. Yes, he's a strong demon, and you two are tightly bound, but that doesn't mean he can be in charge whenever he likes. I've never seen you doubt your powers so much. Should I send you off to witch finishing school? Give you a reminder of how strong you are?"

"Witch finishing school? That's a thing?"

Her warm smile soothed me. "It could be. I'll have to look into it."

I rubbed my forehead. I'd always been sure of myself. I was so used to dealing with Frank. We'd come to an uneasy alliance a long time ago. Things were different now. Things felt deadly.

Mom rested a hand over mine. "We'll get through the wedding. I'll keep an eye out for Frank and make sure he doesn't play up. But you have to be Aurora's bridesmaid. She'll never talk to you again if you don't show up on the day."

"She won't talk to me again if the demon I live with runs riot and spoils her big day."

"Trust yourself. And we'll be there in case you need extra support. Just remember, you can always ask for help."

"Thanks, Mom. You always know the right thing to say."

"That's what moms are for. Now, let's finish breakfast, and we'll have no more talk of you not attending your sister's wedding."

"Got it. Did she tell you about the weird message that went out, saying the wedding had been canceled?" I bit into my scone, feeling a hundred times happier.

"She did. It was strange. Aurora had no idea who sent the message."

"I reckon it was the stressed out wedding planner who messed up. Marisa has aged ten years since she started working for Aurora. My sister may look cute, but she's terrifyingly stubborn when she wants something."

"Poor Marisa. I'm sure it was an accident. Aurora wants me to drop by her store soon. She's panicking about the seating plan. Has she said anything to you about what's wrong with it?"

"She's said way too much about it. I'm keeping out of that minefield. The plan is fine. It was fine the first time we looked at it, and it was fine the fiftieth time."

Mom finished her coffee and stood. "If I go, you won't go back to bed, will you?"

"No, I'm feeling better."

"Wiggles, make sure Tempest gets showered and dressed." Mom smoothed down my hair and kissed my cheek. "I'd better get off. Aurora will start looking for me if I'm late."

I followed Mom down the stairs and opened the main door of the club to let her out. "Tell Aurora I'm sorry about last night. I hope I didn't scare her."

"She's not worried. Well, she was worried about you, but Lex saw her safely away."

I gave Mom a hug and watched as she walked off. She turned as she reached the end of the lane and waved at me.

I raised my hand, turning my head as a flash of movement caught my attention. There was someone standing by a tree on the other side of the lane. They seemed to be watching me.

I narrowed my eyes and took a step out the door. They instantly vanished.

Was someone watching the club? I waited a moment to see if they'd reappear, but there was no sign of them.

I shut the door, locked it, and headed upstairs to finish breakfast.

Wiggles was perched on my stool. There were no muffins left. He looked up, crumbs covering his whiskers. "I left you the scones."

"You're so thoughtful." I moved the plate out of his reach before he snagged a scone.

"Now you're out of bed, what are we doing with the rest of the day?"

"I need to check in with Rhett. I almost killed him last night. I have to make sure there are no hard feelings."

"It's not the first time you've almost killed him. You've blasted him on his butt dozens of times since you've been together."

"I have not. I can count the number of times on one hand." I finished my scone and coffee. "I'll grab a shower, then we'll head to his place."

Half an hour later, we were strolling to Rhett's apartment. I knocked at the door and waited.

Wiggles snuffled around a new metallic sculpture of a giant toadstool that had appeared outside his front door. In his spare time, Rhett made works of art out of pieces of scrap metal. He'd once made a sculpture of me and Wiggles. My gorgeous biker boyfriend was amazing with his hands.

I peered through the window but didn't see any movement. "I bet he's at that bike truck. He said he had his bike booked in for a tune-up."

"I know where that is," Wiggles said. "I saw it parked last night when we were at the race. This way."

We headed back into the village, passing the stores, and out toward the forest.

Sure enough, a large black truck was parked. One side of the truck had been lowered, creating a sloped entrance ramp. Inside was a huge workspace, full of tools and several motor bikes.

The woman we met last night, Maddie, looked up from a bike she was leaning over. She was dressed in a black overall, her red hair scraped off her face. She lifted a hand. "Hey, have you got a bike that needs looking at?"

"No, but I'm looking for someone. Rhett Blackthorn? Has he brought his bike in yet?"

"Hang on a second. Let me look at the sign-in sheet. I haven't had a second to myself since we got here. All the bikers want our attention."

"Rhett said your work's popular."

She waved us up the slope. "I'm glad I saw you, actually. I found something this morning that's perfect for your dog." She peered at a sign-in sheet in front of her and nodded. "Rhett's booked in, but his bike's not here yet. He should be here anytime, though, if you want to wait around."

"Only if we won't get in the way," I said.

Maddie grinned and looked around the workspace. "It's organized chaos. It works for me and Aidan."

"What did you get me?" Wiggles trotted over. "I'm a big fan of anything food related."

"Oh, it's not food. Let me get it out." Maddie slid open a drawer and rifled around for a few seconds. She pulled out a small black collar with silver studs. "I found this and immediately thought of you. What do you think?"

Wiggles sniffed the collar. "I like it. Put it on me."

Maddie unclipped his red collar and slid on the thick, black one.

He strutted in front of us. "Do I look like a rough, tough biker hellhound?"

Maddie tipped back her head and laughed. "You look great. I can see you on the back of a bike, the wind in your fur as you tear along the highway."

"It's a good look on you, Wiggles." I looked over at a huge wall of trophies and medals. "Who do those belong to?"

Maddie glanced at the trophies. "Most of them are mine. Come take a look." She walked to the shelves. "I loved to race. I'd be out most evenings, testing the bike and fine tuning it. I competed most weekends. I'd travel all over the place to take part in a race."

"You must be really good to win all these," Wiggles said.

She tapped her leg and frowned. "Not anymore. I got in an accident and messed up my leg. It was so bad, even with a couple of operations and some seriously heavy magic thrown at me, the injury never fully healed. I'm lucky. I can still use my leg, and I get to work with bikes every day, but I miss it. There's nothing like the thrill of winning a race."

Bike tires screeching outside and someone yelling had us turning to look out the truck.

"You did it! Admit it."

I strode to the ramp. That was Rhett, and he sounded furious. Maddie was right behind me, as was Wiggles, as I hurried down the ramp.

Rhett had Gideon by the collar of his leather jacket and was yanking him off his bike.

"Hey! What's going on?" I raced over.

Rhett growled in Gideon's face. "Ian's dead. And this jerk killed him."

Chapter 5

I grabbed Rhett's arm. "What happened to Ian?"

Rhett growled in Gideon's face. "He was run over and left for dead by this guy."

"Be careful what you say, Blackthorn." Gideon bared his teeth. "Have you got proof to back up that accusation?"

I also wanted to know the answer to that question.

"It had to be you," Rhett said. "Ian was bragging last night about punching you. He told me you threatened him. You said you'd get back at him."

Gideon snorted. "If you're talking about the guy who jumped me when my back was turned, I wouldn't waste my time getting rid of him. He's no threat."

A swirl of gray smoke spun around Rhett as his magic sparked in the air.

"Rhett, take a breath," I said. "Did you see Gideon do something to Ian?"

He slid a glance my way. His face was contorted in anger, and just peeking out was his grief. He cared deeply for every member of his biker gang, even the ones always getting in trouble, like Ian.

"You were there last night," he said. "You saw the fighting. And Ian was right in the middle of it."

"But did you see Gideon kill Ian?" I said.

"It doesn't matter what I saw. I know he did it."

Gideon jerked out of Rhett's grip. "Like I said, you've got no proof. I wouldn't even know where to find him. Not that I'd bother trying."

"It was you. You ran him over with your bike. You left him for dead," Rhett said.

I winced. That was a horrible way to die.

"I've sent a message to the angels." Maddie ran over. "I don't know if that was the right thing to do, but things seemed tense out here."

"This is gang business," Rhett said. "The angels don't need to be involved."

"I'm sorry to say they do," I said. "If Gideon murdered Ian—"

"I didn't kill the guy. You're not pinning this on me," Gideon said.

"People saw you fighting," I said to him. "That gives you a motive for wanting him dead. You wanted to get your own back."

"I fight with a lot of people. They don't all wind up dead," Gideon said. "Anyway, why are you so interested in this, witch? Are you defending your boyfriend because you don't want to see him get hurt?"

"You need to stay out of this, Tempest," Rhett said. "I'll deal with Gideon."

"I'd like to see you try." Gideon sneered at him.

"Rhett, this isn't the way we handle things," I said.

"Ian deserves justice. You know what the angels are like. It'll take them months to deal with this."

"And you know what I'm like." I rested a hand on his tensed bicep. "I'll get to the bottom of this quickly. We'll figure out what happened."

"I already know what happened. We've got the killer right here."

Gideon straightened the collar on his leather jacket. "Are you getting a witch to fight your battles, Blackthorn? Have you lost your touch? You lose a gang member, and now you have a girl doing your dirty work. Wait until I tell everyone. You'll be an even bigger joke."

"Wiggles, get him," I said.

"My pleasure." Wiggles opened his mouth and blasted a jet of sulfurous fire at Gideon.

He yelped and batted at the flames on his jacket.

"That was just a warning shot," I said. "Don't leave this village, Gideon, until we find out what happened to Ian."

"You can't make me stay." He glared at Wiggles, who belched at him. "And keep that disgusting thing away from me. It should be put to sleep."

I sparked magic on the tips of my fingers. "Say that again, and we'll both show you what we think of bullies."

Gideon scowled then turned and hurried away.

"We shouldn't let him go." Rhett's narrowed eyes were focused on Gideon.

"The angels do have their moments of being competent, especially when I steer them in the right direction." I turned to Maddie. "What did you tell them when you made contact?"

"I wasn't sure what to say." Her anxious gaze shot from me to Rhett. "I said there'd been a fight, and someone was dead. I told them Gideon could be involved."

"That's good enough for now. They won't let Gideon leave until this is sorted." I looked back at Rhett. His hands were clenched by his sides, and a muscle in his jaw was flexing. "Where's Ian's body?"

"It's close to where we raced last night, on the edge of the woods. Near the old wishing well," Rhett said.

"Maddie, get in touch with the angels again and tell them that location. We'll meet them there."

Maddie nodded and hurried away.

I took hold of Rhett's hand. "We'll sort this. We'll find out what happened to Ian."

He shook his head. "I'm supposed to look out for the gang. This shouldn't happen. Ian's always been a hothead, but I didn't think he was in any danger last night. We were all wound up after Gideon cheated in the race. Maybe Ian went back to teach him a lesson. I don't know."

"We'll find out what went on soon enough. Let's go deal with Ian, first." I tugged on his arm, and after a few seconds of hesitation, he started walking.

I kept a tight hold on him, the tension radiating off his body making me twitchy.

Wiggles trotted along beside us. "It should be Gideon who's dead by the side of the road. That guy is a massive jerk."

"He's also a coward," Rhett said. "He likes to start fights and run away from them, leaving other people to deal with the mess. Did you see him last night? He was standing by the sideline barking orders but not getting involved. He's always been that way."

"Have you known Gideon long?" I said.

"He's been on the scene for years. But he's a minor player. I used to think he was all mouth, but now he's killed Ian, maybe he's got bigger ideas."

Just as we arrived at the forest, Dazielle and Dominic descended from the sky in a flutter of huge white wings.

Dominic gave me a cheery wave. "Hey, Tempest."

"Hi, Dominic." It could be a lost kitten, a triple murder, or a dodgy spell turning people green. He was always smiling.

Dazielle strode over to me. "What's this about a fight and a body?"

"It's Ian Blaine," I said.

She pursed her lips. "That troublemaker."

Rhett scowled at her. "He wasn't a troublemaker."

"I've had to warn him about his dubious activities at least once a month since he joined your gang," Dazielle said.

"You won't have to worry about that anymore," Rhett said. "You need to arrest Gideon Blazeheart. He killed Ian."

"You saw this happen?" Dazielle said.

"No, but it was him."

"Let's take a look at the scene before we start arresting people," Dazielle said. "Cassiel is on her way. She'll do an examination of the body, then we can find out who did this." She turned and strode ahead of us with Dominic.

I hung back a few steps with Rhett. "I know you must be hurting but keep calm. I'll make sure Dazielle does the right thing. I'll help with the investigation."

He blew out a breath and rolled his shoulders. "Thanks, Tempest. I've let the gang down, though. This is my responsibility."

"No, it's not. You're a great leader. They won't blame you for this." I walked alongside him as we headed into the forest.

We were only a few meters inside the trees when Rhett pointed ahead of him. "Ian's just up ahead."

The angels had stopped and were looking down. Dominic turned, a grimace on his face. That was never a good sign.

Dazielle's wings fluttered out around her. "This is unfortunate. No one deserves to die like this."

Rhett muttered under his breath, his hand squeezing mine. "You don't want to look at him. It's not a pretty sight."

I hated looking at bodies. I had no stomach for it. I never knew how Cassiel could be so calm when it came to autopsies. Hunting for clues, interrogating suspects, figuring out who was lying, that wasn't a problem. Show me the actual victim, and I turned into a marshmallow.

I risked a quick peek past Dazielle's wing. Ian was laid out on his back. There were marks across his torso and legs where a bike had been repeatedly driven over him.

My stomach protested, and I stepped away. "Did you find him?" I asked Rhett.

Dazielle turned to face us. "I'm also interested in hearing that answer."

Rhett nodded. "Everyone was supposed to be meeting up. We have another race planned for tonight."

"Which you don't have permission for," Dazielle said.

"That's not important right now," I said.

She frowned but then nodded at Rhett. "Go on. You were having this meeting. Where was that?"

"In the woods. We've got several sites we use. Everyone turned up except Ian. We were joking around, saying maybe he got lucky last night. But even though he breaks the rules now and again—"

"All the time," Dazielle said.

"You're not helping," I muttered.

Rhett lifted a shoulder. "Whatever. Ian was dedicated to the gang. And he never missed a meeting. We waited for a while, but he didn't show. Then Drake said he'd been talking about getting back at Gideon. It got me worried. After we'd discussed tactics for the race, I took a walk to find the Tusks and see what they knew."

"The forest is a big place. How did you conveniently stumble over Ian?" Dazielle said.

"There was nothing convenient about it," Rhett said. "I noticed bike tire marks in the dirt leading into the forest. They shouldn't have been there. None of the bikes went into the forest last night. We stuck to the racing lane. So I took a look. I wondered if someone had run off the road and been injured. That's when I found him."

"And you went straight to Gideon and accused him of killing Ian?" Dazielle said. "You should have reported the crime. You've alerted a potential suspect and given him a chance to fake an alibi."

"You know about it now," Rhett said sullenly. "And this is biker gang business. The angels shouldn't even be involved."

"If a murder's been committed in Willow Tree Falls, we will be involved," Dazielle said. She glanced at me. "Although a liaison between the two groups would be appropriate. Tempest, I trust I have your support?"

"I'll be supporting Rhett," I said.

Dazielle huffed out a breath. "You need to support the discovery of the killer." She lifted a hand as Rhett opened his mouth. "Of course, we'll look into Gideon's whereabouts once we know the time of death. Your suggestion he could be involved is valid. I witnessed a number of fights at last night's illegal race. Gideon was directing most of them. But I'm not charging anyone until we have evidence."

"That'll take too much time," Rhett said. "Gideon needs to be taken down now. He's a scumbag, and he's sneaky. He'll get out of the village before you do anything."

Dazielle shook her head. "I've sent two angels to keep an eye on the Tusks to make sure they don't do anything. They're not going anywhere. You need to keep calm, Rhett. You can't take justice into your own hands."

"I can when it's a member of my gang who's been killed," he said.

"Then you'll end up behind bars, and your gang will be adrift without a leader. Don't do anything foolish," Dazielle said.

Rhett glowered at her then looked away.

"Since you're here, you can tell me where you went after the fighting broke up," Dazielle said.

Rhett stuffed his hands into his jeans pockets. "Why do you want to know that?"

"Because I need alibis for you and all your gang."

His head shot up. "It wasn't anyone in the Willow Tree Falls gang. We all liked Ian."

"He was a troublemaker who broke the rules. That would have put your gang in jeopardy, and it would have annoyed other members, possibly even you. Tell me where you were last night. What happened after the race ended?"

"That's none of your business. I protect the gang. I keep them in line. You should be asking Gideon these questions. Go do your job." Rhett stepped forward and jabbed Dazielle in the shoulder.

"Keep it cool," I said. "You're angry about what happened to Ian, but you shouldn't—"

He wheeled on me. "I'm raging mad. And we're wasting time."

I grabbed his arm and pulled him close. "Rhett, you need to take a step back. You were friends with Ian. You're not thinking clearly. Dazielle's right. Everyone who knew Ian needs to be spoken to. Not because the angels think they're guilty, but they could have seen or heard something that gives them a clue about who killed Ian."

"Thank you, Tempest." Dazielle lifted her chin. "I see that some of the time you've spent with me is making you think like a detective."

"Zip it," I snapped at her. This wasn't about following protocol. This was about keeping Rhett's temper in check. He was hurting and angry, which could make him do something stupid. Something that could get him in a lot of trouble.

"There's Cassiel," Dazielle said. "You two can go for now. I'll speak to you later." She walked away as Cassiel landed a short distance from the body.

I caught hold of Rhett's shoulder and turned him to face me.

His blazing gaze met mine. "This has to be Gideon. I don't get why the angels are being so stubborn."

I looked back to see the three angels surrounding the body. "Let's get out of here. It's not doing you any good seeing this."

He sighed, and his shoulders slumped. "Fine. But I'll get revenge on Gideon. Whatever it takes, I'll make him regret ever coming to Willow Tree Falls and messing with my gang."

I let out a quiet sigh as we left the scene. Knowing just how stubborn Rhett was, I had no doubt he'd follow through with his plan if I didn't find the killer quickly.

Chapter 6

I walked with Rhett in silence for several minutes. He was fiercely protective of his gang, and if I wasn't careful, he'd be the one behind bars for murder.

"Let's go to the Ancient Imp for a drink," I said. "We'll find a quiet corner and talk about this."

"What's there to talk about? Gideon did this."

"So, let's find the evidence to prove it. The angels are watching his every move. He's not going anywhere."

"I should have killed him when I had the chance," Rhett said.

I stopped walking and yanked him round to face me. "No, that's not you. You're not a killer. You're angry, and it's making you lash out. We'll make sure Gideon pays for what he's done. But what if it wasn't him? What if you kill him and the angels discover somebody else murdered Ian?"

Rhett scraped a hand through his dark hair. "Who else could it have been? It's so obvious it was him."

"Let's get a drink and take a few minutes to think this through." I tugged him toward the pub.

Once we were inside, I grabbed an iced tea for me and a beer for Rhett. We settled at a table at the back of the pub where no one would hear us.

Wiggles wandered off to hunt down food.

Rhett grabbed his beer and downed half of it. His gaze went out the window. "Gideon must have surprised Ian. He chased him down and ran him off the road."

"Let's go back a few steps. When was the last time you saw Ian alive?" I said.

His eyes narrowed, and he downed more of his beer.

"I'm not asking because I think you're guilty of anything, but we need to establish a timeline to figure out what Ian did after his fight with Gideon. I was there, so I know things got physical between them. Then what?"

He huffed out a breath. "We left the race together. Most of the guys had their bikes with them. We ended up back at my place. We hung out there for a couple of hours before everyone drifted home. The guys needed to blow off steam after the brawl, so it seemed the safest place for them to do that."

"You mentioned Ian was talking about getting even with Gideon."

"You know what he was like. Ian had a big mouth and a quick temper. The others were winding him up as well."

"Could he have gone after Gideon?"

Rhett tipped back his head. "He'd had a lot to drink last night. He left his bike at my apartment and walked back to his own place on the other side of the village. That must have been when Gideon found him."

"Do you think Gideon was lying in wait for Ian? How would he have known where to find him?"

"I don't know. You'll have to ask him that. Maybe Gideon was cruising around and spotted Ian. He rammed him with his bike while no one was about."

"Could the Tusks have followed the gang back to your place?"

"Where I live isn't a secret. It would have been easy for Gideon to get his cronies to follow us. Then he just needed to pick the right time to get Ian." Rhett ducked his head. "Did you see his legs?"

"They were messed up. Ian must have fought back."

"He wouldn't have been able to if he'd been knocked out," Rhett said. "I didn't move him when I found his body, but there was blood on his head. Gideon could have run him down with the bike then whacked him. He dragged Ian into the forest and finished him off."

"Why run him over with a bike?" I said. "Why not use magic? Gideon could have taken Ian down with a knockback spell then blasted him with something toxic."

"Gideon likes to get physical with people. You know, leave his mark."

"Had they met before last night?"

"Only in passing," Rhett said.

"It's an odd choice of murder weapon. Killing someone with a motorbike isn't the easy option. And the bike would have been damaged. Ian wasn't a small guy."

"Our bikes are almost indestructible. And they run on their own magic power source. They can take on anything and come out the other side with only a few dents. This killing is about Gideon throwing his weight around and proving a point."

We sat in silence for a minute.

"You need to take a step back from this. I'll work alongside Dazielle. We'll make Gideon our priority. We'll bring him into Angel Force and question him."

"It's a waste of time. He'll only lie to you and get his gang to cover for him."

I arched an eyebrow. "Yes, that's the trouble with these biker gangs. They always look out for each other."

"What's that mean?" Rhett snatched up his beer and finished it.

"It means I need you and the gang to be open. You need to talk to the guys, get them to tell the angels anything they saw last night. They could have clues that point to the killer."

"Why bother? We look out for each other. The gang sticks together. They'll understand this was Gideon."

"Do you stick together even if a member of the gang is a killer?"

He scraped back his chair and glared at me. "Ian's death has nothing to do with my gang. Whose side are you on?"

"No one's side. I'm looking out for you. We both want to see Ian's killer brought to justice."

"So go get your angel pals to arrest Gideon Blazeheart."

"Rhett, they won't do that until they have evidence. You shouting and yelling and demanding he gets arrested won't make this move any faster. If anything, Dazielle will dig in her heels. She can be incredibly stubborn."

"She should walk away from this investigation. And so should you. I'll deal with it."

"No, you won't."

"Are you going to stop me?"

I threw my hands up in the air. "I shouldn't have to. I've already said we'll look into Gideon first, but I need you to cooperate. I need the rest of your gang to cooperate, too. Go speak to them. Most of them won't have heard what's happened to Ian. You need to be the one to tell them."

He jerked his chin up, some of the pain and rage on his face fading. "Yeah, I will. You're right. The gang has to be my focus right now."

"But don't tell them Gideon did this. Once they believe that, any useful information they have will disappear. They'll be focused on Gideon as the killer."

"Because he is the killer."

I clenched my hand around my glass. "Tell them what happened and ask them if they saw anything unusual. Maybe one of them walked part of the way back with Ian. They could have seen the bike that killed him go past. They may have even seen who was on it."

Rhett's gaze flicked over me, and his expression hardened. "You seem to be more angel than witch these days."

"I'll ignore that, since you're grieving and angry."

He shrugged. "It doesn't help that you've got that weird mark on your forehead. The angels have you on their side, no matter what you tell me."

I pressed a finger against the mark I'd been given by a higher angel on a recent investigation. "It's never bothered you before that I help the angels."

"Because it never got in my way until now. If you weren't working with the angels, you'd help me hunt down Gideon. You'd probably be the one to fire the killer shot when we found him and beat a confession out of him."

"That's enough. I don't kill people who are innocent."

"Gideon Blazeheart has never been innocent. He's got decades of causing trouble behind him. We'd be doing the world a favor by getting rid of him. Not so long ago, you'd have agreed with me on that."

"Not so long ago, you'd have never suggested something like that. Maybe we've both changed."

He jabbed a finger at me. "You definitely have."

"There you are." Aurora raced over to the table, her hand covering her mouth. "I've been looking everywhere for you."

Rhett stood. "I'm leaving. I've got things to do."

I jumped up from my seat. "Rhett, don't do anything you'll regret."

He glowered at me. "I'll see you around, Tempest." He turned and stalked out the door.

I sighed and shook my head. That was the last thing I needed, Rhett on a vigilante mission.

Aurora grabbed my arm. "You have to help me." She was still covering her mouth.

"Not now. I've got a few problems of my own. One of Rhett's gang members has been found murdered in the forest. Rhett's on the hunt for the killer."

Aurora looked over her shoulder. "Oh! Poor Rhett. I'm sorry about that, but this is a huge problem. It can't wait."

"Why are you covering your mouth?" I said. "Have you got a cold sore?"

"It's so much worse than that. You have to come with me."

"Aurora, I've got a murder to investigate and a boyfriend I need to stop from being an idiot."

"From the look of him, Rhett could do with time to cool down. I've never seen him so mad."

"Which is why I need to go after him."

"Please, five minutes. You have to come to the store. This is really important. Life changingly so." Her voice was muffled by her hand.

"Five minutes. Then I go after Rhett." I called Wiggles out from under a table, where he was sneaking chips off the floor, and we left the pub.

Aurora kept her hand over her mouth as we walked back to her store.

"Tell me what's going on," I said.

"You need to see this for yourself," she said.

I kept glancing at her, but she kept one hand firmly in place, so I couldn't see her lips.

She gestured me into her store after unlocking the door. "It's on the counter."

Wiggles trotted in. "Hey, what's wrong with Sox and Charlie?"

The two cats sat on either side of a large white box. Their fur was puffed up and their ears flattened.

Sox hissed at the box.

"What have you got in there?" Wiggles placed his front paws up on the counter.

"That's the problem," Aurora said. "It arrived this morning. I thought it was a gift."

"Is it safe to open?" I peered at the box.

"Nothing will jump out when you open the lid," Aurora said, "but it's definitely not safe."

I flipped the box lid open. Inside was a delicious looking chocolate cake with cream ganache. A large slice had been cut out of it.

"I don't see the problem." I picked up the card by the side of the box. "To Aurora, here's a small gift to celebrate your upcoming wedding. This cake has been made just for you. Enjoy." I turned over the card. "There's no name. Who sent it to you?"

"Someone who hates me." Aurora gave a muffled sob from behind her hand.

"Are you worried about gaining weight before the wedding?" I asked. "Is that the problem?"

"No, it's not that."

"I can help you out with the cake," Wiggles said. "You won't gain an ounce if you let me eat it."

"No! And no one's eating any more of that disgusting cake." Aurora slammed the box lid shut.

"I still don't understand," I said.

She lowered her hand, tears in her eyes. All around her mouth, the skin was stained purple. She poked out her tongue, which was also purple.

"You ate a piece of the cake and it did that to you?" I said.

She swiped away tears. "I thought it was someone being lovely. They wanted to celebrate my upcoming wedding. I tried a small piece, but it was so delicious that I had two bits. It was only when Charlie growled at me and ran away that I realized something was wrong. I looked in the mirror and almost fainted when I saw the purple around my mouth."

"Why would someone put a spell like that on this cake?" I said.

"Because they don't want me to marry Lex." She grabbed my hands. "Tempest, you must help me. My marriage is jinxed."

"Aurora, it's not jinxed, but this is weird. Do you know what kind of spell is in the cake?"

"I thought it was a simple color change spell. But I've tried several reversal spells and nothing's made this budge." She gestured at her mouth. "I'm a fright. I can't get married looking like this."

"Have you tried a dark purple lipstick to hide it? You could go for the gothic look on your big day if it hasn't faded by then."

She whacked me on the arm. "Take this seriously. Someone is targeting me. First, a message goes out about the wedding being canceled and now this jinxed cake. I'm telling you, someone doesn't want me to walk down the aisle and marry Lex."

"I'm sure it's not that."

"What else could it be?"

"Aurora, chill out. I'm sorry you have a purple mouth, but I can't help. Ian Blaine's been murdered. That's got to be my top priority."

Aurora collapsed on the counter and sobbed. "You don't want me to get married either. You think I'm being ridiculous about wanting to spend the rest of my life with one guy. But I love Lex. We deserve to be happy. Someone doesn't want that. Someone is after me. What if they do something more serious the next time?"

"It's a mean trick, but it's childish rather than devious." I looked in the box again. Was someone really after my sister, or was this a simple mistake? "How do you feel?"

"Devastated. Like it's the end of the world. My life is ruined."

I just about managed to stop from rolling my eyes. "I mean, are you feeling sick or dizzy? If someone really didn't want you to get married, they'd have done something deadlier than turn your mouth purple."

She grasped her stomach. "Maybe I've been poisoned. Not that you'd care."

"Of course I care. But I'm also aware there's a killer on the loose in Willow Tree Falls, and Rhett wants him dead."

"Oh, go! You're no use to me. Some sister you are. The next thing you'll be telling me is you're not coming to the wedding."

I grimaced. I'd been thinking just that. She'd hit me right in the weak spot. "Stop crying. I'll help. Let's see if we can find a spell to reverse the staining. I'll make some tea, and you pull out the spell books. But I can't stay long. The angels can hold things together for a while, but they've got two sets of gang members to question. I'll have to help them soon."

Aurora flung her arms around me and kissed my cheek. "You're the best sister in the world."

"Yuck! Get off me with your gross purple mouth."

She kissed me again. "Let's fix my face. Then we can figure out who sent me this disgusting gift."

Chapter 7

I chewed on the last piece of pizza delivered by Mystic Mushroom, and looked at the short list of names Aurora had written down.

Three hours had passed. So much for a quick solution.

Wiggles was asleep in the corner with Sox and Charlie, and we were no closer to finding out who had it in for Aurora.

"Are you sure you can't think of anyone else who'd want to stop you from getting married to Lex?" I asked.

She leaned on the countertop and tapped a finger against her chin. "Honestly, no. Everyone loves us."

"There are only two people on this list, and one of them is dead."

"I had to put Lex's ex-wife on the list. After all, she did come back from the dead once. Maybe she's returned again."

I looked at the second name. "Mrs. Fontaine. I thought you two got along?"

"I always worry that Lex's mom doesn't think I'm good enough for him."

"Has she said anything to make you think she doesn't want the wedding to go ahead?"

Aurora picked up a mirror and stared at her reflection before scowling and placing it down. "She'll definitely have doubts about me now. Nothing we've tried has gotten rid of this purple stain."

"The color of your mouth shouldn't affect the way your soon-to-be mother-in-law feels about you," I said. "How about we try a conceal spell again? I saw the color fade when you used it."

"I've done a dozen spells. I'm exhausted. My magic needs to re-charge. This hideous spell isn't budging."

"You could still try the purple lipstick option."

"I'm not going gothic for my wedding," Aurora said.

"It's being held in the grounds of an enormous, creepy castle. A goth look would fit right in."

"No! Go grab me that spell book by Maeve Irish off the top shelf. There are a few things I haven't tried in there."

I strolled over, grabbed the spell book, and returned to the counter.

Aurora took it from me and flipped through the pages. "I've been wondering about someone else who could have done this."

"Like who? Why isn't their name on this list?"

She glanced at me and quickly looked away. "Could it have been Frank?"

I jerked upright. "Why would he do this?"

"Because he's been so difficult recently."

"I'd know if he was involved," I said.

She bit her bottom lip. "You are having a few problems with him. You can't always keep him under control."

"You think he took control of me, figured out a spell to change the color of your mouth, put it in a cake, and sent it to you? That's not Frank style."

"He definitely doesn't want me to get married."

"I don't disagree. But he's much more slash, burn, and destroy than sneaky tricks. And he doesn't have total control over me. I'd have known if he tried something like this." I was eighty percent sure I would, anyway.

"You're right. But I must consider all the options." Aurora stifled a yawn behind her hand. "I could be overthinking this. Maybe the ingredients in the cake were off."

"I've never known a dodgy egg to turn someone's mouth that color," I said. "That's magic. And it's powerful stuff since neither of us have been able to shift it."

She yawned again. "I'll find the solution. There's a reversal spell for almost anything."

"You should get some sleep. What time were you up this morning?"

"Too early. I had to check everything was on track with the wedding flowers. It's so hard to get hold of the woman dealing with them."

"She's probably avoiding you. How many times have you nagged her about the flowers?"

"I never nag. I just need to make sure everything is right. I could do with an early night, though. And I could wake up in the morning, and this horrible spell will be gone. Maybe it's only temporary."

"Let's hope so. I need to get going." I checked the time and grimaced. It was getting late. Cloven Hoof would soon be open and need my attention.

"We can work on this tomorrow," Aurora said. "I'll come by your apartment."

"No can do. I'll be focused on solving a murder," I said.

She huffed out a breath and jabbed a finger at her mouth. "You should focus on helping your little sister."

I shook my head. Sisterly guilt could only be manipulated so far. "I'll help when I get the chance. Drop by the apartment, tomorrow. Just don't come too early."

We said goodbye. I woke Wiggles, and we headed out the store.

He shook out his fur and stretched. "Where to now?"

"We're overdue a visit to Angel Force. I need to find out what Dazielle's been up to. They may have already arrested Gideon, and it'll be case closed."

We walked through the village and over to the large white building housing the angels.

The reception was empty, and there was no one on the desk, so I strolled through the back, looking for Dazielle.

The place was surprisingly busy, considering the late hour. Lots of angels were bustling around, carrying heaps of papers and looking nervous.

I strolled over to Dazielle's office and tapped on the door.

She glanced up and frowned. "Oh, you're here. That's just what I need."

"I'm happy to see you too." I walked over to the seat by the desk and dropped into it. "What's going on? Have you got a lead on the case?"

She glanced out the door. "I've got an audit due. And a bunch of murderous bikers in the village is the last thing I need getting in the way."

"It is a tragedy when you're forced to solve crimes rather than push paper around your desk and tick boxes."

She didn't lift her head from the file she was reading. "Was there something you needed?"

"I'm here to offer my help on Ian's murder. Fill me in on what you've done so far."

She shut the file and turned her attention to me. "I've been giving it some thought. I'm not sure you should be involved in this investigation."

"Why not?"

"You're not impartial. Your involvement with Rhett will make you biased. I don't want you to conceal evidence."

"I wouldn't do that."

"Would you conceal evidence if it showed Rhett was guilty?"

I pursed my lips and glanced at Wiggles. He was sneaking up on a plate of sandwiches. "I'll do my best not to mess this up. And it looks like you're desperate for help. Besides, we're practically partners these days."

"Which doesn't exactly answer my question."

An angel hurried into the office and dumped a pile of folders on Dazielle's desk. "This is for the first quarter. I'll bring the rest in a moment." She hurried out.

Dazielle rested a hand on top of the files. "I could do with an extra body around here."

"And I do know most of the bikers. They're more likely to talk to me than you."

"That's true. I've spoken to each member of Gideon's gang. None of them are talking."

"That's not a surprise. They'll cover for each other. How about Rhett?"

"He's being just as shifty. I've had the angels speak to his gang members. They were unhelpful."

"They're all pointing the finger at the Tusks?"

"You got it. Each gang is blaming the other. And Gideon claims to have no interest in Ian."

"Which we know isn't true. They were fighting yesterday."

"Which means he's on the top of the suspect list. But while both gangs close ranks, there's not much I can do."

"Let me see what I can find out. But I'm telling you now, this has nothing to do with Rhett."

"Remember what I said about you being impartial," Dazielle said.

"I guarantee he'd never hurt a member of his gang."

"Are you his alibi for last night? If so, I can discount him from this investigation."

"Shucks, I'm flattered. You'd really believe me if I gave you an alibi for my boyfriend? You trust me that much?"

"You're not funny, Tempest."

I grinned at her. "I have my moments. I wasn't with Rhett, though. He said he went back to his apartment with the rest of the gang so they could blow off steam after the fight. He needed to make sure everyone had their temper under control."

"That's more than I got out of him. He said it was none of my business."

"I'll talk to Rhett again, and his gang members, see if anything shakes loose." I sat forward in my seat. "Has Cassiel had a chance to look over the body? Has anything useful come out of the autopsy?"

"Not that I know of. We can drop by and see what she's found out. I need a break from this audit madness." Dazielle pushed back her seat and stood.

I grimaced. "You could just fill me in on the details once you've poked the corpse about."

"Are you feeling squeamish, Tempest?" She arched an eyebrow at me.

"Cassiel is always so good with the bodies. I don't like to tread on her toes."

"Follow me. If you're a part of this investigation, you can't pick and choose the bits you want."

I dragged my feet as we walked out of her office and into the small lab at the back of the building Cassiel used for her work.

I hung back at the door as Dazielle strode over to Cassiel, who was on the other side of the room. There was a body laid out on a table. Fortunately, there was a cloth covering it.

Dazielle glanced over her shoulder, shook her head, and waved me over. "Cassiel has finished her examination of Ian's body."

"What did you find?" I said.

Cassiel's cold blue gaze ran over me. "There's residual magic, suggesting it was used to incapacitate the victim before he died."

"Is there enough to get a magic signature?" I asked.

Cassiel shook her head. "It's only a partial. We can't track the magic source back to anyone. The victim had a head injury, which he may have gotten when he hit the ground. There's also evidence of the fight he'd had earlier in the night, some bruising on his knuckles and torso. It's hard to determine, but some of the bruises could have been inflicted when he was attacked the second time. He was repeatedly run over by a bike. At least a dozen times."

I glanced back at the covered body and swallowed. "What about the time of death?"

"Between two and five AM."

"Have you got an idea of what kind of bike was used?" I said.

"The tire marks would be identifiable. There are clear imprints on his skin."

"So, we find a match for the tires, and we've got the killer."

"It's not that simple. The Tusks all use the same model of bike," Dazielle said.

I groaned. "Which means they use the same tires?"

"Got it in one," Dazielle said.

"What about the Willow Tree Falls gang?" I said. "This tire evidence could discount them all as suspects."

"I've had the angels out looking at the bikes," Dazielle said. "Some of them have the same tires. Not all."

"What about Rhett's bike?" I said.

"His tires are a match," Dazielle said.

That wasn't helpful evidence. I didn't want Rhett being on the suspect list for this murder. He'd never kill a member of his gang.

"Has Ian's family been informed about what happened?" I said.

"He doesn't have much family," Dazielle said. "We're trying to locate a half-brother, Paolo Blaine."

"Okay. I'll tackle Gideon, since he's the prime suspect, see if he lets slip anything useful."

"I wish you luck," Dazielle said. "He was most unpleasant when I spoke to him. He kept telling me to keep my nose out of gang business, it was being handled, and there was nothing we needed to do."

"His idea of handling things will result in more deaths," Cassiel said. "The sooner he's out of our village, the better."

"Hopefully, he'll be behind bars for a long time once we prove he murdered Ian," I said.

"You need to find the evidence before that happens," Dazielle said.

"That's what I plan to do." I was glad to leave the lab and head out of the building with Wiggles. The cool evening air washed away the smell of the chemicals in Cassiel's lab.

As I got to the end of the lane, the rumble of several bikes had me turning.

The Tusks rode past, Gideon in the lead. They were heading in the direction of Cloven Hoof.

I increased my pace. "It looks like the Tusks want an evening of fun."

"Let's go say hello and spoil that, shall we?" Wiggles trotted ahead of me.

I arrived at the club to find all their bikes parked outside. Perfect. I could interrogate them on my home turf.

The club had only been open half an hour, so it was quiet. There were a few regulars sitting at the back in the booths. The Tusks were at the bar.

I walked over and eased myself in between Gideon and an enormous biker who had Death holding a scythe on his leather jacket. "You're back again?"

Gideon glanced at me. "Oh, you. I'd forgotten you were in charge of this place."

"Everyone's welcome here," I said, "as long as you're not going to cause any more trouble."

"The boys may get a bit rowdy. They're bored and need an outlet. It would help if they could leave."

"It's a shame a murder is stopping you from going anywhere." I twirled a straw in my hand. "However, if you'd like to confess, we'd be happy to let them all go free."

He handed over his money to Merrie and dished out a tray of shots. "Nice try. Does that ever work?"

"You'd be surprised. Some people want to do the right thing."

Gideon grunted as he picked up his shot and downed it. "It's not right. The angels have this place locked down tight. I tried to get through the barrier, and they turned me away."

"Those angels are so annoying. They're always trying to stop criminals from getting away with murder."

"You hear that, boys? This witch is still accusing me of murder." Gideon smirked and looked around at his gang.

"Why don't we take this somewhere quiet?" I said.

"You don't have to worry about the boys. They won't come after you, unless I tell them to. And you're not going to do anything to anger me, are you?"

"Nope. I just need to ask you a few questions. You've got to admit things don't look good for you when it comes to Ian's murder."

"You've got nothing on me."

"He was run over by a bike that has the same tire tread as yours."

"So what? There are thousands of people who ride the same style of bike as me. And my gang all use the same brand of tires. If you accuse me of killing Ian, you need to accuse them as well. And probably half your local gang, too."

"So, discount yourself from this investigation. Tell me where you were when Ian was killed. He was murdered between two and five AM."

"I was with the gang. They'll back me up."

"How convenient for you."

"It's convenient, but it's also true."

The guys around me all grumbled an agreement.

"I've heard you're interested in taking over Willow Tree Falls. Did you kill Ian to get rid of the competition?" I asked.

"Ian Blaine had a bad attitude and a worse reputation, but he wasn't a threat to me. I didn't need to kill him because he wasn't standing in my way."

"Why are you interested in such a small place?"

"I never said I was."

"You don't want to get your hands on the magic concentrated here? It would make you a powerful gang leader if you could tap into the stone circle every time you needed a re-charge."

Gideon shrugged a shoulder. "It's of mild interest to me. And I heard rumors that people were unhappy with the way things were being run around here. Apparently, the local gang leader is a soft touch." He smirked at me. "I guess you'd know about that, since you're so close."

"The Willow Tree Falls gang does just fine," I said. "We don't need a change of leadership. And we definitely don't want anyone to muscle in on territory that doesn't belong to them."

"I've got enough ground to keep me busy. If you're looking for the killer, you need to look much closer to home," Gideon said.

"Do you want to give me a name to go along with that accusation?"

"I'd be happy to. Although if I share my information, what will you do for me?"

"Not have you arrested for Ian's murder," I said.

He chuckled. "You could take me in, but I'd be out within twenty-four hours. You see, you need a little thing called evidence to charge someone. And I know you're fishing. You've got nothing on me. You never will."

"How about I don't kick your butts out of this place?"

"I'd like to see you try."

"I'm happy to oblige," I said.

Gideon knocked back a shot. "I'll tell you this for free. Especially if it gets you off my back. I heard Ian wasn't happy with someone in his own gang because they were seeing the same woman."

I shook my head. "The gang is loyal to each other first. A woman wouldn't get in the way."

Gideon leaned back. "I'm telling you what I heard. You should speak to someone called Drake, see what he has to say. You might like to check where he was when Ian was being run over."

"I'll check, but I still think you did it," I said.

He turned away. "You can think what you like. I've got my gang backing me up. They'll alibi me out. You're wasting your time coming after me. Now, we have some serious drinking to do. You should get lost."

I gestured at Wiggles that it was time to leave the bikers to their fun. I'd pushed Gideon far enough.

I'd investigate the possibility that Drake Gilbert had a problem with Ian. But I knew Drake. He was a giant of a guy, scary to look at but a softie on the inside.

Gideon was guilty. I just had no idea how to prove it.

Chapter 8

I jerked upright as something warm and wet smeared across my cheek.

Wiggles jumped back, grabbing one of my pillows as he leapt off the bed. "I thought you should know there's someone outside."

I rubbed wet dog nose off my cheek, yawned, and looked at the time. "You're kidding me. It's not even nine AM. Who'd be crazy enough to..." I groaned. "Is it Aurora?"

"Yup. She's been knocking for a while. We had a chat through the door, and she convinced me to wake you up."

"Does she have food with her?" I grumbled as I rolled out of bed and pulled on my robe.

"I can confirm there's something delicious wafting under the door."

I stumbled out of my bedroom and over to the front door. If there was one thing I could guarantee with my sister, she always arrived bearing delicious treats. And they were always worth getting out of bed for. I pulled open the door.

"Ta-dah! Look at my mouth. It's back to normal."

"Huh! You figured out the spell?" I stepped back and let Aurora into the apartment. Sox and Charlie were right behind her. They spotted Wiggles and charged at him.

"I'm not sure which spell got rid of it. The gross purple was still there this morning when I woke. I tried six different removal spells, one after the other. I definitely got a fade on the second one. Then all of a sudden, it was gone. I'm so happy." Aurora sat on a stool by the kitchen counter and opened the brown bag she carried.

Wiggles was by her side in an instant. "What did you get me?"

She hovered her hand over the bag. "How about a biscuit cinnamon roll with extra sugar sprinkles?"

"I'm sold." Wiggles grabbed the treat and bounded away, while Sox and Charlie tried to take it from him.

I brewed coffee then settled on the stool next to her and helped myself to a biscuit cinnamon roll. "I'm glad you got rid of the purple stain, but you didn't need to wake me so early to let me know."

"I had to share the good news. This is a positive sign. The wedding is going ahead."

"Of course it is. You're not having any doubts, are you?"

"Not about marrying Lex. He's been so sweet since we got together. I plan to spend the rest of my life with him."

"And I'm sure he'd love you even if you had a purple mouth for the rest of that life."

She grinned. "He would. So, how are you getting on with finding out who killed Ian?"

"I'm working on it. The angels questioned both gangs, but unsurprisingly, they're not talking. I got a chance to speak to Gideon last night when he dropped by Cloven Hoof. He reckons he was with his gang, and they all agree with him, which is no help."

"Typical bikers. They always stick up for one another. You think it was him, though?"

"It makes sense. He has a motive, and he'd have had the opportunity, despite having his gang tell me otherwise. Someone will trip up and reveal what he did. In the meantime, I need to have a chat with Drake. Gideon reckons he was seeing the same woman as Ian, and things were tense between them."

"Ooh! A jealous love rival. That's also a good motive," Aurora said. "Who's the popular lady?"

"Gideon wouldn't tell me. I'll track down Drake and ask him myself. He's one of the friendlier members of Rhett's gang, so I don't mind speaking to him."

"It'll be hard to prove who did it. These gang members always cover for each other. It's one of the benefits of being in a gang. Plus, they get to ride those amazing bikes."

"I didn't think you liked the bikes. You told Lex to stay away from them."

"Because he has terrible balance. He'd fall off. I wouldn't mind having a ride on one. Auntie Queenie is always talking about how much fun they are. And there's something to be said for feeling the wind in your hair and having that sense of freedom."

"You should take Lex up on his offer to get you a bike once you're married. You could use it to go away together at weekends."

"I'm not sure I'd suit a full leather outfit. Do you think I could pull it off?"

"Aurora, you'd look great in a trash bag." I narrowed my eyes and stared at her. "Um, you've got a problem."

She swiped her mouth with the back of her hand. "Have I got cinnamon cream smeared down my chin?"

I kept my expression neutral, despite wanting to laugh. "No, but your lips are turning green."

She squeaked, leapt from her stool, and dropped her biscuit. Wiggles raced over and grabbed it.

Aurora ran to the mirror and stared at her reflection. "No! This is terrible. I thought I'd fixed this spell." She pulled at her lips and stuck out her tongue. "Eww! My tongue is turning green, too. And it looks furry."

"Are you sure it wasn't these biscuit cinnamon thingies?" I set down the biscuit I was eating. "Where did you get them from?"

"It's not those. I picked them up from Patti on my way over. I have to get out of here. I need to get to the store and fix this. It's so unfair. I have twenty things on my to-do list today. None of them include reversing the color of my mouth. Come on, Sox and Charlie. We're leaving." She waved goodbye as she raced out the door, the cats bounding after her.

Wiggles trotted over, chewing on what was left of Aurora's biscuit. "She didn't hang around for long."

"Nope. And she left all this delicious food behind. Let's finish it then go find Drake."

An hour later, I was showered, dressed, and full of delicious breakfast foods, and on my way to hunt down a biker.

I didn't have to look for long. There were half a dozen Willow Tree Falls bikes parked outside Aidan and Maddie's repair truck.

I walked over and discovered Drake leaning on the side of the truck, drinking coffee. He was a big guy with muscles and a shaggy dark beard.

"Hey, Drake. You got a minute?" I asked.

"Sure. I'm just waiting for my bike to be looked at. What's up?"

"I heard a rumor you and Ian were seeing the same girl," I said. "Who would that be?"

He straightened slowly, and his expression tightened. "Why do you wanna know about that?"

"Because Ian was killed, and I'm looking into the reasons why that happened."

"And?"

"And if you were dating the same woman, maybe things got difficult between you. Who is she?"

"I don't know who you're talking about. You've got me mixed up with someone else." He turned away.

I caught hold of his arm. "I'll find out, eventually. Then I can ask her myself, if you like. Find out which one of you she preferred."

"Don't do that. She's got a temper." Drake sighed. "I've got nothing to hide. I had no problem with Ian."

"And you didn't mind he was interested in the same woman as you?"

"We had an... understanding."

"What was that?"

"One you don't need to know about. I had nothing to do with what happened to Ian. Sure, we bugged each other, and he was always hitting on the same women as me, but we're in the gang. Our first priority was to each other."

"What if you learned Ian was going behind your back? He could have been seeing this woman and not telling you. Things could have gotten serious between them, and he wanted to cut you out of the arrangement. You'd have hated that."

"He'd have told me. And I knew all about it."

"And that got you angry?"

"Nope. I was cool. Now, I need to check on my bike."

"Your bike will be fine for another five minutes." My gaze ran over Drake. He was very calm. I couldn't see him as a killer. Although he could hug you to death with those enormous arms. "Two more questions. Where were you between two and five AM?"

"That was when Ian was killed?" Drake asked.

I nodded. "Can anyone testify to your whereabouts?"

Drake stuffed his hands in his jeans pockets and looked away. "I was probably asleep."

"Were you sleeping alone?"

"Yeah. I sometimes do. We went to Rhett's apartment after the race and had a few drinks."

"What time did you leave?"

"I don't remember."

"Try."

"I... let me think." He blew out a breath. "You're making me twitchy. It wasn't me. Tempest, you know me. I'm always getting my beard tugged about being too soft on people."

He had me there. I liked Drake, but without an alibi, I couldn't discount him. "If you're not involved, who had it in for Ian?"

Relief crossed his face. "Other than Gideon Blazeheart, you mean? He's the guy you should be going after."

"I'm looking hard at him. But he has his gang backing him up and giving him an alibi for the time of the murder. It's making it tricky to pin anything on him. You think the Tusks are definitely behind Ian's murder?"

Drake ran his fingers through his beard. "I reckon so. Although you should have a chat with his half-brother."

"The angels are looking for him. Paolo, isn't it?"

"That's right. They didn't get along."

"What was the problem between them?"

"Paolo didn't like Ian being in the gang. It messed up the family's reputation or some trash like that. The last time they met, it got physical. Paolo threatened him. He told Ian to stay out of the family business and that he was an embarrassment. Ian was angry about that for ages. He kept saying he'd get back at him."

"Do you know where I can find Paolo?"

"I can't help you. The guy's not from around here."

I stored that information. It was another name to go on the list if Gideon was innocent, which I was certain he wasn't.

"What's going on?" Rhett marched over. "Is everything good, Drake?"

Drake rubbed the back of his neck. "Err, sure. Tempest was just..." He gestured at me.

I appreciated Drake not revealing what we were talking about. But I was a big girl, and I knew Rhett would hate what I was doing. "I was asking about his alibi for Ian's murder."

A brief flash of surprise crossed Rhett's face. "I'll vouch for him. Drake was at my apartment when Ian was killed."

I frowned at Rhett. "He was there the whole time? He just told me he was sleeping alone."

"We'd all had a lot to drink. It's easy to lose track of time when you're enjoying yourself." Rhett slung an arm around Drake's shoulders. "He couldn't have killed Ian."

"Rhett, you can get in trouble for giving a false alibi for someone," I said.

"There's nothing false about this alibi. None of my guys are involved in what happened to Ian. Why are you hassling Drake, anyway?"

"Because they were dating the same woman. Maybe he was jealous. Drake wanted this woman, but she rejected him and picked Ian instead."

Drake shook his head. "No way. Moon wouldn't do that."

"Moon?" I tilted my head. "There's only one Moon I know around here. You're talking about Moon Fairfax? She started the race."

Drake grimaced. "I don't want her involved, but it's no secret. I've been seeing her for a while. She'll only get stressed out if you question her."

"Thanks for telling me who your mystery woman is. And don't worry. I won't stress her out. But it's important I have the facts, so we get the right person." Drake needed to be careful not to get his heart broken. The guy I'd seen Moon with at Cloven Hoof on the night of the race hadn't been Ian or Drake. She was a popular lady.

"Why aren't you hassling Gideon?" Rhett said. "He's your killer."

"I'm talking to everyone who may have had a problem with Ian," I said. "It doesn't help me go any faster when you make up alibis for people."

We glared at each other for several tense seconds.

"I'll catch up with you in a few minutes, Drake. Go see how your bike's doing." Rhett strode over to me. "Can I have a word?"

"I thought we were already having words. Some of them not all that truthful."

He caught hold of my arm and walked me away from the truck. "Stay out of this. My gang isn't involved. And quit hassling Drake."

"Ian and Drake were fighting over the same woman. That gives Drake a motive."

"Even if they were both dating Moon, and I'm not saying they were, they'd have come to some deal."

"Yeah, Drake mentioned an arrangement. Maybe it was an arrangement he wasn't happy about. He kept his mouth shut for the good of the gang but was seething about having to share his girlfriend. That's got to sting."

"Tempest, please, I'm handling this."

"No, you're not. You're lying to me about suspects and alibis."

"And what are you going to do about it?"

"I could have the angels arrest you."

He snorted a derisive laugh. "You wouldn't do that. Focus on Gideon. The sooner you find something that shows he's guilty, the sooner you can lock him up, and we can get the Tusks out of the village. Don't you want that?"

"What I want is to get to the truth. Sometimes, that can be uncomfortable. You need to be prepared for that."

He dropped his hold on my arm and stepped back. His eyes were cold. "I'm not prepared for the fact that my girlfriend is hassling members of my gang."

"Get used to it. If any of them know something, I will find it out."

He shook his head, scowled at me, and then walked back to Drake.

Maddie was standing at the bottom of the ramp, a concerned expression on her face. She raised a hand at Rhett and Drake and then walked over to me. "Hey, is everything okay?"

"No. The bikers are digging in their heels over this murder investigation."

She flipped an oily rag over her shoulder. "You have my sympathy. It used to drive me nuts. My dad was just the same. He had this annoying saying: *Bikers before broads*. It sucked. His family, his girlfriends, even me were in second place to the gang. If they needed something, he was there for them."

"Sometimes, these gangs are a pain in the behind."

"They definitely are," she said. "But it's the biker code. It's ingrained in their DNA when they join. They'll do anything to protect a member of the gang."

"Even lying and making up alibis to protect a killer?" I said, my gaze on the truck.

"Most likely. Don't be too angry with your guy. He's looking out for people he cares about. And, if it's any comfort, I've been around Gideon Blazeheart plenty of times. He's a bad guy. Most of the bikers are rough around the edges but have hearts of gold when you get to know them. Not Gideon. He's always late paying, he always finds a way to haggle down the price with Aidan, and he insists his bike gets looked at before anyone else. I keep telling Aidan to stop dealing with him, but Gideon's got influence. If he puts the word out that Aidan's work isn't up to standard, it'll be bad for business. We're stuck with him."

I focused on Maddie. She was making a lot of sense and helping me to calm down. "Do you think Gideon is guilty of killing Ian?"

She shrugged. "I don't know much about it. But if I had to pick out of Gideon or Drake, it would be easy. Gideon Blazeheart isn't a nice guy."

"Thanks, Maddie. And thanks for the pep talk about Rhett. I knew what I was getting into when I started dating a biker. It's never been a problem before."

She patted my arm. "No worries. Being a woman in the male-dominated world of bikes, leathers, and testosterone fueled banter, you get used to their quirks. You'll figure things out. I'd better go. I've got a ton of work to get through." She waved goodbye and headed back to the bikes.

Wiggles wandered over from behind the truck. "What do you want to do now?"

"Kick Rhett for being so stubborn," I said.

"You could do that. I heard you arguing. That's why I hid. I get all sweaty and itchy when Mom and Dad fight."

"He doesn't understand that he's getting in the way."

"Yeah, but it is kinda cool the way he looks out for his gang."

"By cool, do you mean annoying?" I walked away from the truck with him.

"That too. But at least he's loyal."

"He should be loyal to me. I'm trying to find a murderer."

"How about we talk to Moon?" Wiggles said. "She could clear Drake's name so you can focus on Gideon. That will make Rhett happy."

"Nothing will do that." I looked back at the truck. Rhett was standing beside it, watching me. "It's a good idea, though. Let's go see what Moon Fairfax has to tell us about the fun she's been having with the bikers."

Chapter 9

I discovered Moon in the Ancient Imp. She wasn't working, but she was at the bar, dressed in a tight black and red leather corset and a butt skimming leather skirt. Her boots were black leather and stopped at her knees. Red curls hung down to her waist.

A guy was whispering in her ear and making her laugh as we approached.

"Moon, have you got a minute?" I settled on the bar stool next to her.

She lifted one manicured finger and leaned into the guy who was still whispering sweet nothings.

I gestured at Petra Duke behind the bar for a drink.

She strolled over and smiled at me. "Hi, Tempest. What can I get you?"

I glanced at Moon, who was still ignoring me. "I'm tempted to say something very strong but give me anything soft."

She poured a lemon and ginger fizz and placed it on the bar. "Bad day?"

"Busy day. Did you hear what happened to Ian?"

Petra pursed her lips and nodded. "I did. I have to say I'm not surprised. I've had to throw him out so many times I've lost count. He had a bad temper. Who did he finally push too far?"

"That's what I'm trying to find out."

Petra glanced at Moon, and her eyes widened. "Do you think..." She nodded at Moon.

I shrugged and sipped my drink.

She lifted her chin, and a knowing glint entered her eyes. "You're investigating for the angels?"

"Yep."

"Say no more." Petra looked down at Wiggles. "I've got leftover chips in the back if you're hungry."

Wiggles raced around the bar and vanished.

Moon swiveled in her seat. "What were you saying about Ian?" Her large green eyes narrowed a fraction as they settled on me. "Oh, Tempest."

"Yep, it's me. I was talking to Petra about Ian's murder."

Moon tossed her hair over one shoulder. "It's a shame he's dead. He was cute."

"Cute enough for you to date?" I said.

She twirled her finger around the top of her glass. "I don't remember dating him, as such."

Petra returned from her mission to feed Wiggles and jammed her hands on her hips. "Moon, you've been in here with Ian several times in the last two months. You were dating."

"Oh, they weren't dates. We just hung out together. Like I said, he was cute."

The guy who'd been whispering in Moon's ear mumbled some excuse, grabbed his drink, and scurried away. He must have sensed the rising tension.

Instantly, he was replaced by another guy with an eager look on his face. "Can I buy you a drink, Moon?"

She giggled and ran a hand down his chest. "You're adorable. But I'm fine. Maybe later. I'm having some girl time."

The guy's chest deflated, and he sloped away.

"How well did you know Ian?" I asked Moon.

"I guess we were friends. We didn't share secrets or anything like that. I wasn't planning to marry the guy."

"Do you have secrets that need hiding?" I said.

Petra smirked. "She's probably hiding the number of guys she goes on dates with every week."

"Don't you have glasses to clean?" Moon's top lip curled up.

Petra rolled her eyes and stomped away.

Moon turned back to me. "Why are you asking me about Ian?"

"Because you were involved with him. And you don't seem all that sad he's gone."

"I'm sad. But I rarely frown. I don't want to get wrinkles." She tilted her head. "You must frown a lot."

"All the time when I'm dealing with idiots."

She clicked her tongue. "I went out with Ian on a few dates. He was sweet. That's it."

"Were you exclusive with him?"

She gazed at the bottles behind the bar. "I'm young. I'm not ready to settle down."

"So you were dating Ian and other guys at the same time?"

"When I find the perfect guy, I'll be loyal to him."

"Which doesn't answer the question. Were you loyal to Ian?"

Her bosom heaved in her tight leather corset. "Maybe there were other guys. It's not a crime to play the field."

"And how serious were things with Drake?"

"Oh! You know about him?"

"I do. Did you have a preference between Ian and Drake?"

"They both had their charms. Drake's a cutie pie. He's adorable."

"What did Ian think about you seeing other people?"

"He was too busy with the gang and his dumb bike to notice. My perfect guy will be devoted to me. I'll be his only interest. I deserve to be adored."

"That sounds creepy and intense. Surely you want a guy with his own interests, or he'll get under your feet."

"No, that's what I want. Ian was never my forever guy. Rhett only had to snap his fingers, and Ian would come running. It showed he had no backbone."

"Did you argue over his commitment to the gang?"

"I told him I didn't like it, but he'd never leave that gang." Her gaze flicked over me. "You must find it just as frustrating since you're dating Rhett."

Our recent clash over his dedication to the gang was on my mind, but I wasn't sharing that with

Moon. "Where were you when Ian died? He was killed between two and five AM after the bike race."

She shifted in her seat. "I don't remember."

"Were you with someone else?"

She laid a hand on my arm and leaned closer. "I know I shouldn't, but have you seen some of the Tusks gang members? They're delicious. I just about fainted with lust when I saw them riding through the village. And I know one or two of them. I go to a lot of bike rallies, and they're often there."

"Is that the guy I saw you with in Cloven Hoof? You're dating someone from the Tusks? Ian would have hated that. I imagine Drake wouldn't have been happy, either."

"Again, dating is such a strong word. Neither Ian nor Drake had a clue what I was doing most of the time."

"What's the name of the guy you're seeing who rides with the Tusks?"

"Does it matter?"

"It does if you want me to stop hassling you. If I'm hanging around, it'll stop guys buying you drinks." I glanced at another sucker hovering close by.

Moon made a sound of disgust in the back of her throat. "It's Slater Creed. He's Gideon's number two. I knew he'd be coming to the village to take part in the races. We decided to meet up. He has muscles to die for. We were together that night."

"He'll confirm that?"

"Don't go bothering him. I'd never kill anyone. Ian could be annoying, but he was generous with his money. I used to guilt him into buying me things because he wasn't always around. He got me this." She jangled the silver bracelet around her wrist.

"You were using Ian for his money?"

She tipped back her head. "There's nothing wrong with expecting gifts from the men you're dating. It's good manners to treat your woman well. It doesn't happen often enough these days. I'm not a fan of this equality nonsense. I want a man to provide for me."

"So you can sit at home and be a lady of leisure?"

"It takes time to look this good. Anyway, how is this relevant to what happened to Ian?"

"You could have been taking advantage of him. Did Ian figure that out and you argued?"

"I wasn't using him. He gave me gifts because he cared about me and wanted to make sure I was looked after."

I sipped my drink. I doubted whether Moon would want to get her manicure messed up by taking down Ian on the back of a huge, dirty great bike. "If you had nothing to do with what happened to Ian, who do you think killed him?"

She tossed her hair again. "Everyone's saying it was Gideon, but I don't think it was him. I know they fought, but Gideon always gets into rumbles with other people. He may be gruff, but he doesn't hold a grudge."

"You seem to know him well. Let me guess. You're dating him, too?"

"Only once. Or twice. Don't be so judgmental, Tempest. I may want a guy to keep me, but I can still take my time finding the right one."

More like the richest one. And I was judging her. I couldn't help it.

Moon tapped her nails on the bar. "Ian complained about his half-brother."

"I've heard other people mention him. Why didn't they like each other?"

"Paolo's a snob. He has something against the gang. Ian never talked much about his family, but his parents are dead. They left Paolo their money and the family home. They cut Ian off because he was in Rhett's gang. It was so unfair. If they'd given all the money to Ian, we could have married, and I'd have had my own home."

"That's the perfect reason to marry a guy," I said. "Have you ever met Paolo?"

"No. Ian spoke to him a few months ago. I don't know what about, and I wasn't that interested in the conversation. They weren't close."

Another guy was skulking toward Moon, a hopeful look on his face. It was time to leave before I lectured him on appropriate women to date. If he wanted to try his luck, who was I to convince him otherwise?

"Thanks for the information," I said.

"Hey, you don't think I'm involved with what happened to Ian, do you? I am sad he's dead."

"You play the grieving girlfriend to perfection." I left the pub with Wiggles, Moon's protests ringing in my ears.

"What do you think about Moon?" Wiggles said.

"She's on the suspect list for now. Moon clearly likes to play the field, which is fine, so long as everyone involved knows the score. She was dating a rival gang member, though. If Ian found out, he'd have been raging mad. Maybe he threatened to expose her dirty little secret, so she killed him."

"I don't think it was her."

"You've been bewitched by Moon, too?"

"No, but she always wears those tight leather outfits. How could she get a leg over a bike in a skirt that tight?"

"You were checking out her legs?"

Wiggles flipped his ears up. "I'm a hot-blooded alpha dog. We may be a different species, but even I appreciate a fine set of legs."

I wrinkled my nose. "It's an interesting point. We need to check out her alibi, which means another trip to see Gideon's gang. That'll be fun."

"Hey, Tempest, wait up."

I turned to see Petra striding toward us. "Hi. Everything okay?"

"Despite Little Miss Leather's dismissal back there, I heard most of your conversation," Petra said. "She's trouble when it comes to guys."

"What kind of trouble does she cause?"

"She goes on a date with a different guy all the time. I'm a modern woman and am all for having fun, but she takes it to the extreme. She brings them to the pub or makes them take her to Tilly's restaurant and buys the most expensive things on the menu. She loves guys spending cash on her."

"Moon did mention her interest in wealthy guys," I said. "What did you think of her relationship with Ian?"

"She was using him, just like she uses all her dates. He wasn't her usual type, but it was more of a lust thing between those two."

"And their relationship wasn't exclusive?"

"Moon doesn't do exclusive. She picks her targets based on what she can get out of them. And she loved it when they fought over her. Sometimes, she'd even arrange to meet two guys at the same time and then act like it was a misunderstanding. Then she'd stand back and watch them fight."

"She's a charmer."

"Yeah. I'd fire her, but she does bring in the crowds when she works the bar. I guess that means I'm using her to make money, just like she does with her guy friends."

I chuckled. "Just don't ever be exclusive with Moon. She'll only break your heart."

"There's not a chance of that. Do you think she had something to do with Ian's murder?" Petra's eyes gleamed with interest.

"I'm checking out her alibi, but I don't think so."

"I hope you catch whoever did it. I'd better go. I need to get back to the bar." Petra lifted a hand, turned, and hurried away.

"Do you still like Moon's legs now you know what a man-eater she is?" I said to Wiggles.

"I can still admire beauty, even if there's a twisted, cold, money grubbing heart that goes along with it."

"That's such a boy comment. Shall we go see the Tusks? Get it over with."

"We could do with some feathered friends for backup. I mean, I could take them down with one paw tied behind my back, but I've had a big meal and I'm feeling sluggish."

"And you don't think I can handle some angry bikers?"

"Sure you can, but these bikers won't put up with being prodded for much longer. We can use the angels as fodder while we make an escape if things turn bad."

I shook my head and laughed. "Good thinking. Let's go grab ourselves some angels."

Chapter 10

"No, I can't spare any angels. This audit is important." Dazielle pushed past me, a pile of files in her hands.

I followed her around the office as she barked orders at other angels. "I need resources. I can't go up against a group of bikers on my own."

She slid me a glare. "We're all busy. This audit has to be perfect."

"You can spare me someone for an hour." I'd given Dazielle an update on the progress made with the investigation. She'd been unimpressed.

"Can't you speak to Slater on his own? Confirm Moon's alibi that way?" She set down the files and yanked open a drawer.

"The Tusks are sticking together. They know things don't look good for them. And maybe Moon was dating more than one of them. I need to tackle the group head-on so I can discount her as a suspect."

Dazielle gave a dramatic sigh. Her gaze went around the office. "Take Dominic. He's been getting under my feet all day. I gave him the task of ensuring the cold cases were properly filed. Now they're a mess. Take him off my hands. Dominic, get over here."

He hurried over, an anxious look on his face. "I'm sorry about those files, Dazielle. I—"

"Let's not discuss that ever again. You're with Tempest for the rest of the day. She's following up some alibis on Ian Blaine's murder. Provide her with all the support she needs."

His face lit up, and he smiled at me. "Great. I thought you were going to punish me. I love working with Tempest."

"I'm looking for muscle more than anything else. I need back-up when I speak to the Tusks," I said. "They can get mean when I ask questions."

He fluttered out his wings, and his chest expanded. "You can rely on me to keep the peace. I'll make sure the Tusks don't cause you any trouble."

"Then let's go." We left Angel Force and strolled through the village.

"Where will we find the bikers?" Dominic asked.

"We'll start at the mobile repair truck. That's where they seem to like hanging out at the moment. I guess it's neutral territory."

"Who do you need to speak to?"

"I'm checking Moon Fairfax's alibi. She was dating Ian, but she was also dating a guy called Slater who's in the Tusks. And she's been on a couple of dates with Gideon. And also Drake."

"Wow! Moon Fairfax is... well, she's stunning to look at, but she terrifies me."

"You're scared of a woman?" Wiggles said. "What kind of angel are you?"

Dominic blushed. "I can handle a woman. It's just all that leather. And she has this way of looking into your eyes. It gets me flustered, and I forget my own name."

"Moon does have an uncanny ability to make guys fall under her spell," I said. "Could she be part siren?"

"She could be. She always gets me hot under the collar. I avoid her when I can," Dominic said.

"I reckon you could pull off the all-in-one leather catsuit look," Wiggles said to me. "Moon often wears those. That could be the trick to getting everyone panting after her. Hey, Dominic, would you like to see Tempest dressed in leather? She could crack her whip at you if you're a bad boy."

Dominic gulped. "Oh, you'd look great in anything, Tempest. You'd look stunning in a leather catsuit. Do you really have a whip?"

"You're never gonna see me in a leather catsuit. Or any kind of catsuit. And that's a no to the whip." I glared at Wiggles. "We're here to discount a murder suspect. Or to keep Moon on the suspect list. She was using Ian, along with all the guys she's been dating. There's a jealousy motive here."

"You haven't discounted Gideon, though?" Dominic said.

"He's still top of the list. But while his gang's protecting him, there's not much we can do. Unless he decides to confess, we have to keep digging until we find something that proves he's the killer."

"I'm happy to help. Whatever you need, just say. And I'm glad you got me out of Angel Force. Dazielle's been giving me daggers ever since I messed up the cold case files. I didn't mean to do anything wrong, but they seemed so sad, sitting in their beige files with no one paying them attention."

I slid him a glance. "Dominic, what did you do to those files?"

"I... updated them."

"Updated them how?"

"I got a bunch of brightly colored files and matched them in color order. I put gold stickers on them, too. Some are now a pretty pastel pink, some are yellow, and I found a lovely dark purple folder set. I thought Dazielle would be pleased. It shows we're paying attention to our cold files. We still care about them."

I bit my bottom lip. "Maybe you should go back to filing them in alphabetical order. That way, they're easier to look through. If you have thirty pastel pink files out of order and you need a particular case file, it'll make extra work for you."

"Yes, I realized that after Dazielle yelled at me for ten minutes. I wasn't doing it to cause a problem, but those case files make me sad. The crimes have never been solved, and all that's left behind is a pile of notes and a mystery."

"You should give the cold files to Tempest," Wiggles said.

I shook my head. "No, thanks. We've got enough on our plate dealing with a current murder. And there's Aurora's wedding to focus on after this is out of the way."

"I'm looking forward to that," Dominic said.

"Are you bringing anyone with you?"

"No, I don't have a date. But Aurora and Lex have invited everyone from Angel Force, so I'll have plenty of people to hang around with."

"Tempest will save you a dance." Wiggles trotted ahead of us. "She loves to dance."

He was being a brat today. "I don't like to dance."

"Oh! I'd love to dance with you," Dominic said. "I'm a great dancer. I know all the good moves."

I sighed. "We can have one dance. Just one, though."

He grinned. "Great. Now I'm really excited about the wedding."

We arrived outside the mobile repair truck to find a dozen bikes parked outside. They all belonged to the Tusks.

Gideon was sitting astride one of the bikes, talking to a couple of his guys. He glanced up as I approached and waved them away. "What are you doing here, Tempest?"

"I'm looking for Slater. Which one is he?"

Gideon eyeballed Dominic before focusing on me. "Now, what do you want with one of my guys? You're not hounding him as well as me, are you?"

"I haven't been hounding you. I've left you alone."

"For now." Gideon sat up straight and folded his arms over his broad chest. "Well, what do you want with Slater?"

"Amazingly enough, we have other suspects in Ian's murder. Slater was jinxed as an alibi for one of those suspects. I need to confirm if that's true."

Gideon glanced at the group of guys close by, listening to the conversation. "Was he now? Slater, get over here."

A huge guy with a mess of dark curls and a strong jaw covered in stubble strode over. "What's up, boss?"

"This witch says someone's been gossiping about you."

"I never said that. Are you Slater Creed?" I asked.

The guy glanced at Gideon, as if seeking permission to speak.

Gideon nodded. "Go ahead."

"That's me," Slater said.

"I'm interested in what you were doing around the time of Ian Blaine's murder," I said to him.

He shrugged. "I don't recall."

"That's a shame. It means you can't provide an alibi for someone who's a suspect in the investigation."

"Who are you talking about?" Slater said.

I turned away. "It's not important. If you can't remember where you were that night, I'll keep her on the suspect list. Maybe I should bring her in for formal questioning, especially if she lied about her alibi. And she has a good motive for murder. Dominic, why don't you—"

"Wait!" Slater strode closer. "Do you mean Moon?"

"Maybe I do. Are you two friendly?" I said.

Slater glanced at Gideon. "I was with her. We got together after the race. I hung out with the guys for a bit then snuck off to see her."

"You've been dating Moon Fairfax?" Gideon scowled at Slater.

"It's nothing serious, boss. I don't want to tread on your toes. I'll back off, but she said she was single."

Gideon waved a hand in the air. "She's not important to me. But you need to watch her. She's only interested in guys for two things: a roll in the sack and their money. When she gets what she wants, she moves on."

"Did you know she was also dating Ian Blaine?" I asked Slater.

Gideon raised his hand. "Don't answer any more questions, Slater. You've given Moon her alibi, which discounts her from this investigation."

"You're not helping yourself," I said to Gideon. "If I'm discounting other suspects, it still leaves you in the frame."

"Which is impossible, since I have all these guys backing me up. You're not getting me for this," Gideon said.

"Do you want me to go get Moon?" Dominic whispered in my ear.

I shook my head. "No, we're good."

"You've got nothing on Moon," Slater said. "She didn't kill Ian."

"Slater's right. If Moon wanted anyone dead, she'd bat those killer lashes and ask someone like me to do her dirty work," Gideon said.

"And did she ask you to kill Ian for her?" I said.

"Not that I recall." Gideon waved away Slater, and he was quick to hurry off.

"Hey, wait. I could have more questions for him."

"No, you don't." Gideon leaned forward on his bike and beckoned me closer. "I've been thinking some more about who wanted Ian dead."

I didn't move. "It sounds like you're thinking about him a lot. Have you got a guilty conscience?"

"Nothing like that. But I don't like my name dragged through the mud. I could share my thoughts with you. It seems you've gotten your panties in a twist over who's involved. I hate to see a pretty witch struggle."

"Nothing's in a twist. But what will that information cost me?"

Gideon looked at his gang. "You leave me and the boys alone."

"That's not happening. But if you give me a solid lead, I'll follow that for a while. Would that make you happy?"

"It wouldn't make me angry. Although I'm getting used to having you around. You'd be a good fit for this gang."

"No, I wouldn't. I'm listening. Who have you got in mind?" I said.

Gideon looked at the repair truck. "What do you know about Aidan Quinn?"

"I know you all worship the ground he walks on because he makes your bikes hum like contented panthers. What else should I know?"

"I'm not one for gossip, but Aidan wasn't happy with Ian. He refused to work on Ian's bike this time around."

"Why would he do that?"

"The last time Aidan overhauled Ian's bike, they argued. Ian accused him of ripping him off."

"Would Aidan do that?"

Gideon sat back. "No, Aidan's a good guy. He's the go-to guy when we have problems with our bikes. But Ian always thought he was right and never backed down. I'm sure it was just a misunderstanding between those two, but these things can turn nasty. And Aidan's a big guy. Plus, he's handy with his fists. He has to be to survive in our world."

"You're suggesting Aidan killed Ian over an argument about his bike?"

"Maybe Ian confronted Aidan and things turned sour. Aidan has a reputation to maintain, and Ian had a big mouth. He wouldn't have wanted Ian spreading lies about him ripping off his customers." Gideon's gaze moved over my head and he frowned before a lecherous smile crossed his face. "Well, now. Who's this hot little piece of pie coming my way?"

I turned on my heel and spotted Aurora racing over, Sox and Charlie running along beside her. Her hair was a shocking shade of pink. It was so pink it almost matched her flushed cheeks.

"Tempest, help me!" She grabbed my arm and pulled on a lock of her hair. "Look what's happened."

"Why did you do that to your hair? I mean, it looks fun, but do you want pink hair for your wedding?" I asked.

"Aren't you going to introduce us?" Gideon slid off his bike and strolled over, a cocky smile on his face.

"No, I'm not. Aurora, not now. I'm in the middle of an investigation," I said.

"It has to be now! I don't know what happened. My new conditioner did this." Aurora gasped in a breath. "I'm hideous."

"Cutie, that would be impossible, no matter the color of your hair." Gideon held out a hand. "Come sit with me on my bike. I'd love to get to know you better."

I pushed away his hand. "Ignore him. Aurora, your hair just reacted to chemicals in the conditioner. Go rinse it out."

"No! This was magic. The color started at the roots of my hair and spread down. There was nothing I could do to stop it. And I've already washed my hair three times. It's not budging. Someone is playing tricks on me."

"Aurora. That's a pretty name," Gideon said. "How do you know Tempest?"

She glanced at me, and I shook my head. I didn't want Gideon getting anywhere near her.

"We're sisters," Aurora said.

"You're kidding. But Tempest is so..." Gideon waved a hand at me.

"Watch what you say, Gideon," I said.

He flashed me a sharp smile. "You look so different, that's all. You're both cute in your own way."

"We have the same smile," Aurora said. "And I'm usually blonde, not nightmare pink."

"The pink suits you." One of the other bikers strode over and grinned at Aurora. "I always think pink hair on girls is sweet."

I groaned. Not another amorous biker cracking on to my sister. "Aurora, go back to your store. I'll catch up with you later."

"But... but my hair! This is an emergency."

"You shouldn't neglect your family," Gideon said. He shook his head and raised his eyebrows at me.

"You can stop stirring things up. Aurora, now's not a good time to be worrying about your hair."

"How about I take you for a ride on my bike?" the other guy said. "You'll forget all about your hair. I'll soon have you laughing."

Aurora blinked up at him. "I'm not sure. Which bike is yours?"

He pointed over his shoulder. "The one with the naked woman painted on the side. She's almost as hot as you."

Aurora stared at the huge chrome and black bike. "That looks like a powerful ride."

"It is. It's great fun. And you'll be safe. I can lend you a helmet. It would hide your hair." He reached forward and tugged a strand of her hair.

Aurora's cheeks grew even pinker. "Oh, no. I don't think—" She squeaked as the biker grabbed her around the waist and carried her away.

Sox and Charlie bounded after her, hissing at the biker.

"Hey, jerk! Put my sister down." I dashed after him, ignoring Gideon's laughter.

The guy lifted Aurora onto his bike. "I'll take you for a ride."

Aurora stared at me, her eyes wide. "I shouldn't. I'm not all that into bikes."

"Let me make you a convert." The guy unhooked a helmet from the back of the bike, passed it to Aurora, then flipped his leg over the seat.

"Aurora, get off there," I said.

"I'm trying, but I'm wedged in." She wriggled in the seat.

I stumbled forward as a flash of Frank's energy shot up my spine. I turned away and took a deep breath, almost bumping into Gideon, who'd come to join in the fun.

He grabbed my shoulder and tilted my chin. "What's with your eyes? They've turned red."

Dominic hurried over. "Tempest, are you okay?"

I shook Gideon off, my teeth grinding as I tried to keep control of Frank. "Not now. Both of you need to back off."

"Is that your demon making an appearance?" Gideon's eyes sparked with interest.

Dominic pushed him back. "You heard Tempest. Give her room."

The biker who'd sat Aurora on his bike revved the engine.

My head shot up, and Frank's energy blasted through me. "Get off the bike!"

"Are you jealous your sister's getting the attention?" Gideon said.

"It's not that," Dominic said. "You should back away, Gideon. And tell the rest of the gang to do the same."

Gideon bared his teeth. "You don't give me orders, angel."

The color on Aurora's face faded as she stared at me. "Frank, is that you?"

Dominic jumped in front of me and spread out his wings, blocking my view of Aurora. "Take deep breaths. You can get control of this. Ignore the bikers. Ignore your sister. Just look at me."

"Get out of my way." My hands fisted, and I lunged at Dominic.

He dodged away but whacked me in the face with a wing. "Calm down, Tempest. Get control of Frank." He ducked as I tried to grab him.

"Boys, we need help over here," Gideon said, his tone serious. Within a few seconds, he was surrounded by the rest of his gang.

I growled at them, sparks of dark magic snaking out of my fingertips and fizzling on the ground. "You can't stop me."

Dominic glanced at Gideon. "Aurora must leave. Tempest is angry. Or rather, her demon is angry. And he's always interested in Aurora. Not in a friendly way."

Gideon's mouth twisted to the side before he nodded. "Deano, get Aurora out of here. As quick as you can."

"No! She stays here. She's mine." My body shook as I tried to regain control of Frank. He'd sprung up out of nowhere. I'd had no idea he was about to strike.

A bike roared, tires spun, and Deano and Aurora shot off.

I lunged after them. Dominic's wings slapped me in the face. I staggered back and hit the dirt. I flipped up, shot a blast of magic into his chest, and sent him flying into a tree.

Three Tusk bikers jumped me. One blasted me with a hot spell, taking my legs out from under me. Another jumped on my back and shot a stinging spell in my face.

Frank's power poured through me. I flung out my arms, sending the bikers flying. I rolled over and jumped to my feet.

Gideon was in my face, green magic sparking from his fingertips. "Calm down, witch, demon, whatever you are. You can't beat us all."

I roared and fired a ball of flames at him.

I was jumped on again by more bikers, who pinned me to the ground.

"Don't hurt her." Dominic appeared in my sight line, one of his wings bent. "She doesn't mean to do this. Her demon's in control."

"Then that demon needs to be destroyed," Gideon said.

"It's not that simple," Dominic said. "They're... connected. Normally, Tempest can contain him."

"It doesn't look like he's contained now," Gideon said. "Boys, take her out."

"No!" Dominic leapt on the bikers and yanked them off my back.

I was suddenly free. I rolled away, sparks of dark, toxic magic dripping from my pores. The desire to kill was overwhelming as I spun around to face the bikers.

A line of eleven angry, magic wielding bikers stood in front of me. Dominic hovered over them, his wings spread and a huge ball of white light balancing on one palm.

"I'll kill you all," I said.

"No, you won't." Wiggles slammed into me. He was joined by Sox and Charlie. As he sank his teeth into my leg, the cats covered my face in a flurry of claws and fangs, so I couldn't see. All I could taste was hot cat belly and dusty fur.

I was whacked in the chest and back with blasts of tingly magic from the bikers as I fought to get the furballs off me.

"Keep going, Wiggles! It's working," Dominic yelled.

Pain shot up my leg and radiated through my body, but Frank didn't care I was being blasted on all sides. He wanted to kill. And he wanted Aurora.

Sox hissed in my ear and bit down hard on my shoulder.

I staggered over something and fell. A heavy weight landed on my chest as the blasts of magic from the bikers pounded into me. I fired out a spell and grunted in satisfaction as someone yelped.

The pain in my leg eased a fraction. Sox and Charlie dropped off my face, and Wiggles appeared.

"Tempest! Get control, or the bikers will kill you." Smoke billowed from his mouth. "You want to protect Aurora. Fight Frank. Don't let him beat you."

I roared out a protest, my throat burning and my limbs shaking.

"Kill your sister." Frank's voice boomed inside me. "Destroy the bikers, slaughter the hellhound, and give me what I deserve."

"No!" For a few seconds, I had control. "Wiggles, bite me again."

"You sure?"

"Yes! Do it."

Sox leapt on my face and hissed tuna scented magic up my nose.

I yelped as teeth dug into my thigh. That was good. The pain was keeping me centered.

"Dominic! Hit me with everything you've got." I couldn't stop Frank from blasting spells in all directions. And from the sound of things, he was hitting his targets.

Wings swept over my head, and I was engulfed in a torrent of chilled magic. It swept through me like a cold wave, slamming into Frank's heat.

I lost count of all the spells and magic hitting me, but suddenly I was back. Frank was under control.

"Wiggles, that's enough." A fiery ache throbbed through my chewed on leg.

Wiggles nudged Sox and Charlie away from my face and tugged my sleeve to help me sit up.

I waved a shaky, sweaty palm at the bikers who were still standing. There were only four on their feet. The rest were flat on their backs. "I'm good. Frank's gone."

Dominic stood to one side, his wings down as he gasped in air.

"Dominic, you doing okay?" I asked.

He raised a hand but didn't speak.

"What the heck was that about?" Gideon kept a healthy distance as he stared at me. His wounded gang of bikers flanked him, wary looks on their faces. "Do you often try to kill your sister?"

I was on my feet and limping in the direction Aurora and Deano had fled. "Only about once a month. Come on, furballs. Let's go get Aurora."

Chapter 11

I caught up with Aurora five miles along the lane, heading toward the barrier. I rubbed my eyes, not believing what I was seeing. Aurora was on the front of the bike! She was riding it, while Deano clung to the back.

"Hey! Wait up," I called, my throat scratchy from all the yelling.

She glanced over her shoulder and slowed the bike. "Are you back in control of Frank?"

"Just about."

She wheeled the bike around and rumbled it toward me.

As soon as she stopped, Deano jumped off and stood in front of the bike, a sharp expression on his face. "No dodgy business, witch. I don't know what was going on back there, but I didn't like it. Neither did Aurora. She said something about a stinkin' demon. We don't want one of those here."

"I'm not planning on doing anything. Aurora, are you okay?" I said.

"Yes. Tempest is fine, Deano." Aurora kicked down the bike stand and slid off. She placed a hand on his arm. "Thanks for saving me. You're a hero."

She kissed him on the cheek before walking over to me.

Deano's face grew pink, but he kept glaring at me.

Sox and Charlie leaped into Aurora's arms and settled their front paws over her shoulders, contentedly purring.

She kissed their heads, a wary look in her eyes as she got near me.

"I'm sorry. I didn't think that would happen," I said.

"Neither did I. How are you doing?" Her gaze was full of concern.

"Fine. Better. Not worrying about Frank. I feel terrible. I didn't realize he was paying attention. But the second those bikers got interested in you, he reared up and took over. I couldn't stop him. Nothing I did made a difference."

"It must have been all the testosterone flying around," she said. "Those bikers ooze manliness. It's intoxicating."

"If you like that sort of thing." I inspected the painful bite on my calf.

Aurora placed Sox and Charlie on the ground. "It has an appeal. But I'm happy with Lex."

"Good. Listen, Aurora, I messed up."

"No, you didn't. I'm fine. There's no harm done. Although you look beat up. Let me help with that." She cast out a flood of pale yellow magic.

It clouded around me, the scent of peaches and lemon filling my nose. I breathed it in deep. Aurora's healing magic always smelled amazing. The throbbing ache in my leg faded, and the shuddering that had slid into my bones subsided. I felt almost normal.

"There would have been harm done if Dominic and the Tusks hadn't stopped me." I glanced at Deano, who was still glaring at me. "As much as I hate to say this, I owe Gideon thanks. He took charge."

Aurora looked back at Deano. "We're good here. You can go if you like."

He hopped on the bike, roared it to life, and idled it closer to her. "You sure, Aurora?"

"I'm just perfect. And thanks again for the ride." She beamed at him.

"Anytime you want another one, just come find me." Deano shot me a glower before riding off.

"You have a new admirer," I said.

"It must be the hair." She sighed. "What am I going to do with it?"

"You almost got attacked by Frank, and you're worried about your hair?"

"I'm worried about my wedding and not looking like an enormous meringue topped with pink icing. Everyone will laugh at me."

Only my wonderful, ditzy sister would so quickly forget about a near miss with a killer demon. I guess you got used to something when you were around it all the time.

"No, they won't. Not if the Tusks behavior is anything to go by. The pink is popular."

Wiggles nudged me with his head. "How's the leg doing?"

I petted him. "All good. I needed your fangs to jolt the sense back into me."

"I'm always available if anyone needs to be bitten. Just say the word." His gaze shifted past me, and his red eyes glowed. "We've got company."

I turned and looked at the forest we were next to. Someone was stamping around in the woods, cursing and muttering.

"Is that Fallon?" Aurora said.

"I think so." I walked over and peered through the trees. "Hey, Fallon, what are you doing?"

"I'm the protector of the forest, idiot. I'm supposed to be in here." She didn't even look over her shoulder as she finished securing an enormous shimmering web over a thick tree branch. She blasted it with a spell and stepped back, rubbing her hands together. "That should stop the intruders."

"Have you had problems with people coming into the woods?" I asked. Fallon was ultra-protective of the forest. She took her role as Forest Guardian seriously.

"I'll kill those bikers if they keep messing around in here," Fallon said. "They have no respect for its power. They trample around, breaking branches, lighting fires, and acting like frat boys on spring break. I'll show them who's in charge."

"You're talking about the Tusks," I said.

"The Tusks." Fallon smirked. "More like the Wonky Horns. I've seen more impressive bikers riding their trikes at the kindergarten. They need to learn some manners. I'm planning on excavating half a dozen new pits, especially for them. I've been sharpening spikes to put in the bottom. Anyone who rides around in my forest won't be on two wheels for long."

"Is there anyone in particular causing you problems?" We joined Fallon and walked alongside her as she dragged more netting into place.

Sox and Charlie chased after the net and tried to bite it.

"The big one, with the long dark hair and those evil eyes. He keeps coming in here," Fallon said.

"You're talking about Gideon Blazeheart?" I said. "The leader of the Tusks."

"That's him. He likes throwing his weight around. He told me I was a jumped up imp with an attitude. An imp! I fired flaming arrows at him until he left."

"When was the last time you saw him in the forest?" I said.

Fallon grunted as she slung down the netting. "It was in the early hours of the morning, after the race had taken place."

"Was he near the site where Ian Blaine's body was found?"

"Yes! And that's another thing I'm angry about. If you have to murder someone, don't do it in my forest. There are plenty of other places to dump a body. The swamp will do in a pinch, although that's technically my territory, too, although I rarely go there. Any of the commercial dumpsters would do, or—"

"Fallon, are you sure that's when you saw Gideon?" I said.

"Of course I'm sure. I'm always keeping watch over the forest. Apart from when I'm having a sleep, eating, or taking a ride on Wiggles. And of course, when I'm setting these traps. The new traps have been occupying my time. But I need visitors to know they're not welcome."

"Can you remember what time you saw Gideon?" I asked.

"Not for certain. It was still dark. Maybe around three AM. Why?"

"Gideon's the prime suspect in Ian's murder," I said. "The problem is, he's got his gang covering for him."

"And he told you he was with them, didn't he?" Aurora said. "You've just found out he wasn't being truthful."

"I always knew he was lying," I said. "But with his gang protecting him, it was hard to make anything stick. Now, I have a witness to show he was in the woods at the right time."

"Are you going to help me with this magic web or stand around gossiping?" Fallon pointed at the net on the ground. "I only have short arms. I could do with a hand getting this up."

"I'll help." Aurora grabbed the netting. "Where do you want it?"

"Up on that third large tree branch." Fallon pointed over our heads. "It needs to be slung over the top and secured, then I can blast it with magic. Anyone who walks into that will regret it."

Aurora scrambled up the tree trunk and tied the netting, while Sox and Charlie did everything they could to yank it down.

I stood to the side. I finally had something on Gideon. I always knew he was hiding the truth. Now I'd gotten him.

Aurora slid down the tree trunk and plucked a couple of leaves out of her hair. She sighed as she stared at a pink lock of hair. "I should get going. I need to sort this out."

"You should," Fallon said. "You gave me a fright when I saw you. Did you do that deliberately?"

"No! This wasn't deliberate."

"Is that the color theme for your wedding?" Fallon said. "You're going for bright pink? The guests don't have to wear pink, do they? I'm not coming if that's the case. I only wear forest colors."

"Definitely not. Fallon, you wear whatever you like," Aurora said. "Tempest, will you come to the store with me? I've got dozens of spells to try and want to make sure I haven't missed anything that could reverse this nightmare."

"Oh, sure! You two leave me to do the heavy lifting when it comes to dealing with these annoying bikers," Fallon said.

"You're doing a great job," I said. "They won't dare set foot in the forest now. I'll warn them all to stay away."

We left Fallon to her muttering and cursing and walked back to the village and into Aurora's store.

Wiggles, Sox, and Charlie raced in ahead of us and vanished out the back, no doubt looking for snacks.

Aurora placed the open sign on the door and then grabbed spell books and potions off the shelves. "You look through the pile on the left, and I'll work my way through these books."

"If we can't fix it, the color is growing on me the more I see it." I flicked open the first book and scanned down the contents list.

Aurora slumped against the counter. "No it's not. This is another black mark against the wedding." She twisted a piece of hair around her finger. "It's a sign."

I glanced up from the book. "A sign about what?"

She was quiet for a few seconds. "I'm thinking... the wedding shouldn't go ahead."

I stared at her. "Aurora, you love Lex. You've always wanted to get married. Now, you've found the right guy. You should stick with it."

"As much as I love Lex, how many portents should I ignore? First, the message about the wedding being canceled, then my mouth changed color, and I'm not convinced it won't come back if I'm not careful. Now, my pink hair! That's three things in a row. Three signs that this wedding is jinxed."

"Or it's three signs you're stressed and making mistakes because of it."

She pursed her lips. "I didn't send that message to the wedding planner, who I've fired by the way. Neither did Lex."

"No, you didn't. But maybe your harassed former wedding planner mixed up the messages. It could have been a simple error on her part."

"There's nothing simple about that error. It would have been devastating if I hadn't caught it in time. And I definitely didn't turn my mouth a strange color."

"That was odd. But whoever sent the cake could have put a spell in it that backfired. It could have been meant to enhance your beauty, or give you plumper lips, or… I don't know, make sure you were radiant on your wedding day. They could have sent it with good intentions, but it went wrong."

"Why didn't they sign the card? Why not reveal who sent me that cake? They didn't sign it because they didn't want me to find out their name. They knew I'd kill them if I did."

I chuckled. "Aurora, we've been over this. You'd never kill anyone."

"Jinxing my wedding is a big deal. No one ruins my big day and gets away with it. And how do you explain this pink nightmare on my head?"

I studied the shockingly pink locks. "Were you doing anything to your hair when it changed color?"

"I've told you I got a new conditioner. After I'd applied it and left it on for the recommended five minutes, I rinsed it out. Then my hair changed color."

"You didn't use anything else? Nothing that could have altered the natural color?"

Her gaze went to the door that led to her apartment. "I tried a treatment last night. But it was fine when I washed it out."

"Does that treatment have magic in it?"

"Only a tiny amount. And I've been using it for weeks. I wanted to make sure my hair was extra glossy."

"So you've used magic on your hair for weeks, and it suddenly changes color. Hmmm, I wonder why. Your hair can only handle so much. It protested by turning pink."

Aurora flipped through several pages of the spell book she was looking at. "I... well, I suppose it's vaguely possible. I only wanted to look my best. Maybe I used too much magic in the last application of hair tonic. I wasn't happy with the result."

"How much extra magic are we talking?"

"I doubled the dose. But it's a simple spell. It shouldn't do this." Aurora pointed at her hair.

"A simple spell that's built up over a few weeks. Aurora, you're stressing yourself out and making mistakes with magic. Lay off the spells. Lex is already head over heels in love with you. That won't change if your hair isn't extra glossy."

She closed the spell book and sighed. "This is all me, isn't it? I'm worrying about nothing."

"Well, you should worry about fixing that hideous pink hair. But yes, you're worrying when you don't need to. And re-hire Marisa. She was doing a great job of sorting the wedding. That is when you let her get involved."

"But she tried to cancel my wedding!"

"Talk to her. Maybe she's been stressed, too. After all, you've put her under a lot of pressure."

Aurora was quiet again. "Marisa wasn't terrible at her job. I miss not having someone to contact every hour to see how things are going. And I know you hate talking about the wedding."

"That's the kind of thing I mean. Don't keep checking in all the time. It's bad for you. It makes you worry. Let Marisa put the finishing touches to your wedding, and then you can enjoy it. After all, isn't the day about you and Lex publicly declaring your love for each other in front of people you care about? It's not about the perfect flowers or the perfect food. It's about you two. That's all that matters."

She grinned. "I didn't know you were such a romantic."

"I'm not. I'm trying to get you to see sense. Now, let's deal with this hair and your stress levels. Go check the ingredients of that magic hair tonic you used. We'll reverse the spell and then stick to the products you usually use. Also, hire back Marisa, try to relax, and look forward to your wedding. Aurora, this will all be fine."

She hugged me. "I knew there was a reason you were my favorite sister."

"When I'm not trying to kill you."

"That was Frank's doing." She stepped back. "Let's have tea and brownies and talk about something other than the wedding. How are things going with Rhett?"

My mouth twisted to the side. That was a subject I wasn't comfortable discussing. "I wish I could stop, but I need to get to Cloven Hoof. And I have to figure out a way to deal with Gideon and get him to confess to Ian's murder."

"Oh, I suppose that is important. Make sure you thank him and his gang for keeping me safe from Frank."

"Yeah, that's something I'm looking forward to doing." I headed to the door with Wiggles.

"I'll be in touch and let you know how my hair goes," Aurora said.

"I can't wait." We said our goodbyes, and I headed out of the store.

"Have we got time to stop at Mystic Mushroom? I'm craving a large triple cheese meat extravaganza," Wiggles said.

"We can order in. I need to get to work. I've been neglecting Cloven Hoof in favor of bikers, bad hair, and murder."

"Merrie will have things running smoothly."

"Even so, I need to show my face. First thing tomorrow, we'll find Gideon and get a confession out of him."

"He's in big trouble, lying about his alibi."

"He is. And now we can take him down and get him and the Tusks out of Willow Tree Falls for good."

Chapter 12

"I'll take a dozen caramel and pecan muffins," I said to Patti over the counter at Sprinkles the next morning.

"Sure thing. You're up early." She grabbed a box and placed the muffins inside.

"I've got some apologies to make."

"Oh! Who are you apologizing to?"

"I may have accidentally blasted Dominic off his feet. I blame Frank."

"Ah, I wondered if your demon was being tricky." Patti placed the box of muffins on the counter.

"What makes you say that?" I handed over some money.

"Your eyes are red."

I frowned and scrubbed my eyes. "He's not all that excited about Aurora's upcoming wedding."

"He's the only one who isn't. I can't wait. I got a new outfit and am getting my hair done. Although I saw your sister with pink hair yesterday. Is she trying out a new look for her special day?"

"Something like that." I grabbed the box of muffins. "She'll be back to blonde by the big day.

Thanks for these." I headed to the door and walked outside.

Wiggles was drooling against the window. "Some of those had better be for me. Dominic doesn't need all those muffins to show him you're sorry."

"He may share one with you. And he does deserve them. He was trying to keep everyone safe, and I hurt him with magic."

We walked into Angel Force and headed past the reception and into the main office.

I stopped and looked around. Everything was neat. Not just normal neat. It was like someone had gone around with a ruler and straightened everything. All the angels worked quietly at their desks with their heads down. No one was talking.

"Where are all the cookies?" Wiggles returned from the coffee table, which was usually strewn with food. "Don't tell me everyone's on a diet."

One of the angels looked up from her desk and pressed a finger to her lips.

"What's going on?" I said.

She pointed over her shoulder. "The auditor is here."

Dazielle's office door opened. A woman I'd never seen before breezed out. She was dressed in a fitted cream suit and had long silky blonde hair. I could tell she was an angel from the enormous wings, but she had a sharp look about her.

Dazielle spotted me. She froze for a second before gesturing at me to leave.

The woman she was with turned and stared at her. "What are you doing?"

"Oh, nothing. Shall I show you the archive room?" Dazielle shot me a look of desperation.

"Not yet. I want to speak to some angels on duty." The woman looked at me and tilted her head. "Who is that? She's not an angel."

"No, but she's not important. She's not part of my team." Dazielle hurried along beside the woman as she strode over to me.

Not important? I'd be sure to remind Dazielle of that the next time there was a murder she needed help with.

The sharp looking angel peered down her nose at me. "And you are?"

I shrugged. "Not important enough to be bothered with, apparently."

Dazielle sighed. "This is Tempest Crypt."

"Why are your eyes red, Miss. Crypt?" the woman said.

"I'm trying out a new look. Who are you?"

"Tempest, this is Corinne. She's auditing our work," Dazielle said.

"Is it usual to have visitors loitering around the work area?" Corinne wrote down a note on the clipboard she carried.

Dazielle peered over Corinne's shoulder to see what she'd written. "No! It's most unusual. Visitors wait in the reception area, then we take them to the interview rooms. Tempest shouldn't be here."

"Your surname is Crypt," Corinne said. "Are you connected to the witches who look after the demon prison?"

"That's right. My family has been caretaking the demons for centuries."

Her chin lifted a fraction. "I was led to believe there was an uneasy relationship between the angels and the witches in this village. Yet here you are, walking around the office as if you own the place. Why is that?"

"Tempest must be making a delivery." Dazielle gestured at the box in my hand. "You can leave now."

"What is that?" Corinne pointed at Wiggles as he squeezed out from under a desk. He was chewing on something.

"His name is Wiggles. He's my hellhound."

Wiggles mooched over. He swallowed his mouthful of stolen food. "Hey. Who's this?"

"Dazielle, there's a clear no pets at work rule in the handbook." Corinne scribbled on her clipboard.

"I'm not a pet," Wiggles said. "Well, I'm sort of Tempest's pet, but we're more partners."

Corinne pressed a hand against her nose. "You smell disgusting."

"Please, just go." Dazielle flapped her wings at me.

"Wait! She's not even wearing a visitor's badge." Corinne pointed at me. "Everyone in this area must be identified." She made another note on the clipboard.

"Of course. Tempest, leave the parcel and go. Immediately," Dazielle said.

I tightened my grip on the box and scowled at her. "I can see my services aren't needed."

Dazielle opened her mouth as if to protest then glanced at Corinne. "Yes, come back another time."

"Or not at all," I muttered under my breath as I stalked away.

"Corinne was horrible," Wiggles said. "And what's wrong with Dazielle?"

"She's more interested in making sure her paperwork is up to date than solving this murder." I'd reached the door of Angel Force when someone called out my name. I turned to see Dominic hurrying after me.

"Sorry about that," he said. "Dazielle's been snapping at everyone since Corinne arrived. They don't have a great history."

"Tell Dazielle she'll have to make it up to me if she wants me to keep working on this case."

"Oh! Don't give up. I'm sure she's sorry." He shrugged. "You know how proud she is of this place. She always wants things to be perfect. We have a lot of rules to follow."

"If she puts it in writing, I'll consider staying on the case," I said.

"Um, I'm not sure—"

"I'm joking. Relax. How are you doing after yesterday? I'm sorry about blasting you off your feet."

He flared out his wings, sending tiny white feathers everywhere. "It's fine. Angels are made of sturdy stuff. Although Frank's energy does have a nasty tingle to it. I didn't feel myself for the rest of the day. How's everything with Aurora?"

"Amazingly, she was fine. She has this way of disarming people by being horribly sweet to them. By the time I caught up with her, she had the biker wrapped around her little finger."

"And things are good between you two? You gave everyone a scare when Frank emerged so suddenly."

"He surprised me as well, but everything's good. Here, I got you these muffins to say sorry for whacking you with magic."

Dominic peeked inside the box and smiled. "That's nice of you, Tempest. You always say your sister is the sweet one, but I know the truth."

"You know, Dominic, nice people share their food," Wiggles said. "How about you dish out the muffins while we're here to show what a great angel you are?"

Dominic glanced over his shoulder. "I can't be long. Corinne is threatening to talk to all of us. I'm terrified of what she'll ask me." He took out a muffin and threw it for Wiggles.

Wiggles caught it in the air and sat there chewing contentedly.

"Would you like a muffin, Tempest?" Dominic held out the box.

"Not right now. I've got an update about Ian Blaine's murder. After I caught up with Aurora, we met Fallon. She revealed that Gideon lied about his alibi. She saw him in the forest around the time Ian was killed."

"Which proves he got his gang to cover for him," Dominic said.

"It does. We have a witness to show he was in the forest."

"This has made my day so much better. Muffins from my favorite witch, and our prime suspect's alibi has been blown apart. Shall we bring him in for questioning? It would impress Corinne if I helped solve this murder while she was here. It might even make Dazielle smile."

"That's an excellent idea. Let's go find ourselves a bad guy and cheer up Dazielle."

"Are you really telling me none of you have seen Gideon today?" I stood outside the mobile repair truck. Gideon's gang members were there, but he was conveniently missing.

They shrugged, looked around, and did everything they could not to meet my gaze.

"One of you must know where he is," Dominic said. "This is important."

"He mentioned something about going to the stone circle," one of the biker's said.

"Nah, he was checking out the thermal spa," another one said.

"The last time I saw him, he was heading into the village," another guy called out.

There were several laughs from the group.

"So, he could be anywhere," I said. "Are you covering for him?"

"Why would we do that?" Slater strode over, his arms crossed over his chest. "What do you want him for, anyway?"

"I'm checking the details of his alibi for Ian's murder," I said. "Would your leader ever lie to the angels to cover up something illegal?"

There were several more quiet chuckles.

"He's an upstanding member of the community," Slater said. "He wouldn't lie to law enforcement. We'll let him know you dropped by. He'll be happy to chat with you when he's got the time."

We were getting exactly nowhere by talking to the Tusks. "Tell him I need to speak to him as soon as possible."

"Yeah, you'll be top of his list," Slater said.

I shot him an evil glare before walking away with Wiggles and Dominic.

"You know what we need," Wiggles said.

"More pizza?" I said.

"Pizza? Really? That sounds fun," Dominic said. "Do you always have pizza when you're investigating?"

"Always. It's the best brain food," Wiggles said.

"A large slice of gooey pizza each is what we need. It'll put me in a better mood after wasting our time with the Tusks," I said.

We headed to Mystic Mushroom and grabbed three large slices of pizza to go. We walked through the village, keeping an eye out for Gideon as we ate.

"This is great. Dazielle never lets me eat in public. She says the uniform stains easily."

"White generally does," I said.

"You need regular injections of fuel to solve crime," Wiggles said. "We stop for food every couple of hours. It's why we're so good at doing this."

I finished my pizza and wiped my hands clean with a paper napkin. Now that I was fortified with junk food, I was up for a challenge. "I'm overdue a visit to see Rhett. He may know where Gideon is. I expect he's keeping a close eye on his rival."

"You're not going to fight again, are you? It stresses me out when you two fight," Wiggles said.

"You're having problems with Rhett?" A hopeful gleam entered Dominic's eyes.

"No, we're good. And I'll keep things civil, so long as he does." I'd been keeping away from Rhett. Things had been tense ever since we'd argued about me siding with the angels. We'd sort this out. It was a small bump in the road. All relationships had them.

As we approached his apartment, there was a crash of something metallic hitting the ground.

"You did this. I know you did."

"That's Rhett." I increased my pace, and we dashed around the side of the building.

"I wouldn't get my hands dirty killing that loser."

"And that's Gideon," Wiggles said.

I stopped by the side of the building and peered around the corner. Rhett and Gideon stood toe to toe. Not far away, smashed on the ground, was one of Rhett's metal sculptures.

"Everyone saw you fighting. You didn't like the guy," Rhett said.

"I don't like a lot of people, you included, but you're still breathing, for now," Gideon said. "And I know you covered for that member of your gang. Why would you do that if he wasn't guilty?"

I inhaled sharply. So, Rhett had lied to me. He'd given Drake a false alibi for Ian's murder.

"Should we go break things up?" Wiggles whispered.

"Let's wait a minute," I said.

"I covered for Drake because I know him. He wouldn't kill over Moon Fairfax. They weren't serious. And he doesn't need to be hassled by the angels. They have to focus on bringing you down."

"You mean your girlfriend wants to bring me down," Gideon said. "Aren't you embarrassed that she's in the pocket of the angels? If she was my woman, I wouldn't allow it."

Rhett growled. "Tempest is free to do what she likes."

"It bothers you. I can tell it does."

"My relationship with Tempest is none of your business."

I clenched my fists and nodded. Gideon needed to keep his nose out of my personal life.

"What are you doing hanging around with her, anyway? All that creepy demon business freaks me out. You can't seriously be into her and her demon. I've seen that thing in action. She needs putting down," Gideon said.

"Watch your mouth," Rhett said. "And my relationship with Tempest has nothing to do with you."

"It does now. You're both accusing me of things I haven't done, and you're hassling my gang. We should be allowed to leave this uptight little place, yet you've got angels parked by the barrier. And I know you've got members of your gang tailing me. You're wasting your time. I won't make a mistake."

"I thought you wanted to take over this place. You want this territory. It's never going to happen. You're going away for a long time," Rhett said.

Gideon snarled and shoved Rhett away. His fist shot out, and he blasted a jagged ball of magic at Rhett.

Rhett deflected it and shot back his own spell.

"Okay, I've heard enough." I raced around the corner of the building with Wiggles and Dominic.

Gideon slammed another spell at Rhett.

He dodged it and shot out a swirling blue ball of magic.

"That's enough!" I slammed a knock back spell into Gideon.

He staggered away. Dominic enveloped him in his huge wings and clamped him to his chest, while Wiggles bit Gideon's leg.

"Get off me, you feathered freak." Gideon growled and twisted in Dominic's iron tight grip.

I glared at Rhett. "You've been busy. Doing some investigating of your own?"

His fierce gaze shifted from Gideon to me. "What are you doing here?"

"I came to see if you knew where Gideon was." I looked over at Dominic. "Are you okay to take him to the station? I'll be there soon. I have a few things to say to Rhett."

"Of course. I'll take him in right away." Dominic marched away with a protesting Gideon.

Wiggles clung onto Gideon's leg until they reached the end of the lane then let go and ambled back to me.

I looked back at Rhett, a heavy feeling in my heart. I'd never caught him in a lie. We didn't lie to each other.

"It looks like you've got something on your mind," he said.

I blew out a breath. "I do. Rhett, we need to talk."

Chapter 13

"What do you want, Tempest?" Rhett glared at me. "I'm busy looking after my gang."

"I want you to admit you lied to me," I said. "You gave Drake a false alibi."

He shrugged one shoulder and looked over my head. "That's not your business."

"It is. He's a suspect in a murder investigation. And he has no alibi. That bumps Drake to the top of the list of suspects."

"No, it doesn't. You know who killed Ian. I don't know why you're wasting your time."

"Gideon's not going anywhere. And as you've just seen, he's being taken in for formal questioning."

"So, why bother hounding Drake?"

"Right now, I'm more interested in why you lied to me."

He looked away and scrubbed the stubble on his chin. "Don't take it personally."

"I am. We're always honest with each other. If one of us is having a bad day, or things aren't going so well, we talk it through. We figure things out together."

He lifted his chin and crossed his arms over his chest. "This is different. Drake didn't kill Ian. They had their differences, but Ian rubbed a lot of people the wrong way. Drake knew what he was like. He kept out of his way most of the time."

"Maybe things changed once Moon got between them," I said.

"They wouldn't kill over a girl. The gang always comes first."

As I was finding out. "You realize you could get in trouble for lying? And Drake won't fare any better letting you cover for him."

"You're going to tell the angels what I did?" His scowl deepened. "I thought you were on our side."

"This isn't about sides. It's about doing the right thing. You complicated things by lying for Drake."

"He didn't ask me to lie. But the gang is my family. I'd do anything to keep them safe. You're the same with your family. I know you'd kill for them."

A shiver of unease ran through me. "Is that what happened with Ian? Did he betray the gang, so you had to do something to protect them?"

"You're unbelievable! Now you're pointing the finger at me?" Rhett shook his head. "I thought better of you, Tempest."

"And I thought I was dating someone who wasn't a liar."

There was a tense silence for several long, uncomfortable seconds as we glared at each other, neither one willing to back down. There was no way I was budging. I was right about this.

"Gideon did this," Rhett said. "Stop wasting time and charge him with murder."

"He won't be charged with anything until we have evidence or a confession. It's up to me and the angels to decide if he's actually guilty."

He snorted a derisive laugh. "I can practically see the halo glowing over your head. Why don't you sign up for Angel Force and be done with it?"

"Maybe I will. It would be better than hanging around with someone I can't trust. At least the angels are honest with me."

He tipped back his head and blew out a long breath. "I have to protect the gang. I didn't want you getting distracted because Drake doesn't have an alibi for the time of Ian's murder. I know what you're like with these mysteries. You see a lead and you pursue it to the end."

"Which makes me good at my job. You're acting like there's something wrong with that."

"There is when you're hassling my gang." He reached for my hand, but I stepped back and shook my head. I was gutted he'd lied to me, and I was angry, too.

Rhett sighed. "Tempest, you know Drake. He's one of the good guys in the gang. He wouldn't do this. I don't know how many ways I can tell you."

"You're still missing the point." I did know Drake and had the exact same opinion of him, but my thoughts were clouded by Rhett's deceit. I understood his reason behind the lie, but that didn't make it sting any less.

"I shouldn't have covered for him. That was wrong. But my first instinct was to look out for him. He's not as tough as the others. And yeah, he did like

Moon. He probably still does. He's always been an idiot around women. They take advantage of that."

"You can tell me he's innocent as many times as you like, but I still need to question him," I said. "Without an alibi, he has to remain a suspect."

His scowl returned. "You're making a mistake."

"I'm not the only one making mistakes around here. See you around, Rhett. Let's go, Wiggles." I turned and walked away.

"That wasn't at all awkward," Wiggles said.

"Tell me about it." My stomach and thoughts churned.

Wiggles glanced behind him. "Rhett's watching us. He looks angry."

"Ignore him."

"And maybe a bit guilty."

"Good. Rhett lied. And we don't like liars." I kicked a pebble along the road.

"Do you really think Drake was involved with Ian's murder?"

"No, Gideon did it. But Rhett's being stubborn. He has to learn when to bend. If it's always the gang first, second, and third, then we have a big problem."

"He is the head of the Willow Tree Falls gang. They're his family."

"And I'm his girlfriend."

"Who's also a bit stubborn."

"If you want to side with Rhett, why not go join his dumb gang?"

"That's a great idea. I do have the collar for it. I'm liking these studs."

We walked along in silence, not going anywhere in particular, but I needed to blow off steam and calm down.

I let out a big sigh. "Let's do something positive. Our prime suspect is being settled in at Angel Force, probably with a cup of coffee and a cookie."

"Then we should hurry. I don't want to miss out on cookies." Wiggles trotted in front of me.

I had to focus on the investigation, not my issues with Rhett. It was time to talk to Gideon and sort this mess out.

I headed back to Angel Force and approached the reception desk. Cassiel was standing there, looking at some papers.

"Hey, is it safe to come back in?"

She arched an eyebrow. "This is the safest place in the village."

"I mean, has the nasty auditor gone?"

"Oh, yes. She left ten minutes ago. Dazielle is decompressing in her office. She doesn't want to be disturbed."

"Good. I'm not here to see her. I want in on the interview with Gideon Blazeheart."

She lifted her head slowly. "What are you talking about?"

It was good to see Cassiel was in her usual sunny mood. "We brought Gideon in for questioning over Ian's murder. Dominic was just ahead of me. They should be here by now." I glanced over my shoulder, but there was no sign of Dominic coming through the doors.

"I've been on this desk the last half an hour. Dominic hasn't come in with anyone."

"He wouldn't have made a detour." Unease curled up my spine. "Is there a back way in?"

"Yes, but we all come through this way. Wait! Where are you going?" Cassiel grabbed the back of my jacket to stop me from getting through the main door.

"To see where Dominic is."

"Sign in and take a visitor's badge." Cassiel pointed at the sign-in book.

"No way! I never do that."

"You do since the audit. Dazielle is reading through the dozens of comments Corinne made about the slack attitude in this station. We have to follow the rules."

"But Dominic is on his own with Gideon. He'll need back up if he's questioning him alone."

"Sign the book, take the badge, and you can go through and see Dominic."

Two minutes later, I was hurrying through the office. There was no sign of Dominic. I checked all the interview rooms and the cells.

"What's he playing at?" Wiggles said.

"I don't like this." The initial unease I'd felt only grew.

"Tempest! Get out here." Cassiel gestured me back into the reception.

"Is it Dominic?" I raced after her.

"No, but I think those creatures belong to your sister. They're being a nuisance." She pointed at Sox and Charlie. They were outside, their mouths full of large, white feathers.

"Huh! What have they been up to now?" Wiggles trotted over to the door.

I pushed it open and bent down. I extracted a feather from Charlie's mouth. "This is an angel wing feather."

The cats bounced around Wiggles, their tails up, seeming delighted with their find.

"Err, Tempest, some of these feathers have blood on them," Wiggles said.

"Blood!" I grabbed a wing feather and inspected it. "Sox, Charlie, take us to where you found these feathers."

They lowered their ears a fraction, looked at each other, touched noses, and then raced off.

I jogged along behind them with Wiggles. Angels were notorious for shedding small feathers, but what Sox and Charlie had collected were fully formed angel wing feathers. And they didn't like to lose those.

The cats raced into the forest, bounding along the path in front of me.

As I followed them, more white feathers drifted around. "Dominic, are you in here?"

"You think Gideon did something to Dominic?" Wiggles said.

"Unfortunately, I do. Dominic's missing, Gideon's a scumbag, and there are angel feathers everywhere. Dominic! Are you okay? Call out if you can hear me."

There was no reply, which only intensified my worry.

The cats sped deeper into the forest, and I was soon pushing branches out of my face as we headed off the main path. They stopped at the base of a tree and shimmied up it, climbing up like small koalas on a sugar high.

"Don't fall!" Wiggles paced anxiously at the bottom of the tree.

I looked up to where the cats were heading. My eyes widened, and my mouth dropped open. Dominic was strung up between two trees. His head rested on his chest, his arms stretched out and tied with rope, and his once beautiful wings had been partially plucked.

"Dominic! I'll kill Gideon for doing this to you." I inspected the rope holding him up. "Wiggles, grab as many fern branches and leaves as you can. Pile them underneath Dominic. He'll need a soft landing when he falls."

We raced around for ten minutes, shoving leaves under Dominic and laying down large fir tree branches.

"Okay, here goes nothing." I blasted the first rope with a small ball of flames. It burnt through in a few seconds. Dominic swung from the single remaining piece of rope.

I dashed around, burned through the rope, and blasted him with a slowdown spell. Even with the use of my magic, Dominic crashed to the ground. Feathers flew everywhere, and a cloud of gritty dust filled the air.

I raced over and turned him onto his back. I checked his pulse and let out a sigh. "He's alive." But his wings were bent out of shape, he had a large lump on the side of his head, and fresh bruising on his face.

"He doesn't look so good," Wiggles said. "Can angels die?"

"This one won't. I'm transporting him to the hospital. You hunt around here with Sox and Charlie, see if there's any sign of Gideon. Let me know if you see anything."

"Don't worry. We'll track him down. As soon as I stop Sox and Charlie playing with these feathers."

I nodded at him, performed a translocation spell, and arrived inside the small village hospital.

"I need some help!" I crouched by Dominic as a nurse dashed over.

"What happened? Oh! That's Dominic." The nurse ran her hands over him, and a glow of green magic flowed from her palms. "He's in bad shape. Did you do this to him?"

"No! I found him like this."

A doctor hurried over, and I helped them get Dominic onto a gurney.

They whisked him into a room, and the door was shut in my face.

I paced the corridor, anger throbbing through my veins as I waited for news. Dominic was a friend, and Gideon had hurt him.

I should have known better. Gideon was a dangerous warlock, and he was getting desperate. He was wanted for murder and now for trying to kill an angel. I'd do whatever I had to, to take him down.

No one hurt my friends and got away with it.

Chapter 14

I'd been at the hospital for over an hour when Dazielle strode in.

She marched over to me, her wings fluttering around her. "What have you done to my angel?"

"You need to ask Gideon Blazeheart that question," I said.

She pursed her lips. "How's Dominic?"

"He hasn't woken yet. The doctor is still treating him. He's got injuries to his wings. He lost a lot of feathers. I'm not sure he'll be able to fly for a while."

Dazielle's frown deepened. "Tell me what happened."

I let out a sigh and sank into a chair. "We were looking for Gideon. We found out he'd lied about his alibi for the night of Ian's murder. He said he was with the gang, but Fallon saw him in the forest, close to where Ian's body was found."

Dazielle sat in a seat next to me. "So, you found Gideon. What happened next?"

I decided to leave out the bit about Rhett lying to me. Dazielle wouldn't take it well. "Dominic was bringing Gideon in for questioning."

"On his own? Where were you?"

"I, um, I had a bit of business to deal with. I was less than ten minutes behind him. I figured he'd be okay."

"When handling dangerous criminals, my angels work in pairs," Dazielle said. "You should have been with Dominic. And he shouldn't have taken a potential killer into custody on his own. He knows the rules."

"He's an enormous angel with super strong wings. I figured he could handle one smug biker."

"You figured wrong. Where did you find Dominic?"

"Sox and Charlie alerted me to what happened to him."

"Your sister's cat familiars found him?"

"Yeah. Well, they found his wing feathers. They came to show Wiggles."

Dazielle let out a soft moan. "Feathers lost from his wings." She stroked her own wings and curled them around her torso.

"Yes. They led us to Dominic. He'd been strung up in the forest and left for dead."

She hissed air through her teeth, anger sparking in her blue eyes. "Gideon is in serious trouble. An attack on an angel will bring down the full force of the law on him."

"He'll be in trouble when we find him. But he's on the loose. Have you still got the barrier covered by the angels? We don't want him sneaking out. He could be desperate enough to try."

"I have angels watching to make sure none of the Tusks leave. But I'll double patrols. Give me a minute." She stood and strode to the reception desk and commandeered the snow globe.

Wiggles, Sox, and Charlie raced into the waiting area. They were pursued by an unhappy looking nurse.

I sat forward in my seat. "Hey! Any sign of Gideon?"

Wiggles shook his head. "We looked around for ages. We followed some fresh tracks for a while, but they faded on the lane out of the forest, and we lost them."

"These animals can't be in here," the nurse said. "They'll have to wait outside. This is a place of calm and healing. And I know this one." She jabbed a finger at Wiggles. "He's anything but calm."

"Sure, sorry. Just give me a minute," I said.

The nurse pursed her lips and tapped her foot on the ground.

"You'd better wait outside," I said to Wiggles.

"How's Dominic doing?" Wiggles said.

"I don't know. The doctor won't tell me much. I'm hoping, now Dazielle is here, we'll get in to see him."

"Out. Now!" the nurse said.

I lifted a hand. "They're going. I'll catch up with you later," I said to Wiggles.

He nodded and herded Sox and Charlie ahead of him, under the strict gaze of the nurse.

"How's Dominic?" I asked the nurse when she came back from her guard duties.

She pursed her lips again. "He keeps saying your name."

"He's awake?" Dazielle strode over.

"No, but he's mumbling. I've heard him ask for Tempest several times," the nurse said.

"He's not asking for her. I expect he's angry with her for getting him injured," Dazielle said.

"Hey, I didn't know Gideon would do this to him."

"It would be easy to assume Gideon wouldn't go quietly. You were Dominic's back up. I'm disappointed in you."

"Thanks for the guilt trip. But shouldn't you have assigned me more angels since you knew Gideon would be so much trouble? I practically had to beg you to get Dominic."

The nurse cleared her throat. "The patients need calm. Now, do you want to see Dominic, or do I need to ask you both to leave?"

"I'll see him," Dazielle said.

The nurse glanced at me. "It could be beneficial if Tempest was in the room. He may welcome her presence since she's clearly in his thoughts."

"What if she annoys him?" Dazielle said.

"I won't! I want to make sure he's doing okay. If he doesn't want me around, I'll leave."

"Very well." Dazielle scowled at me.

We walked along a cream corridor and into the last room on the right. There was one bed in the room. Dominic lay on it, his eyes closed and his hands folded over his chest.

The nurse led us to the bed and stood by the end. "All the signs are encouraging that he'll soon wake up. We've applied healing spells, and his injuries are much improved. He just isn't ready to wake."

"What about his wing feathers?" I stared at the sad looking, half-plucked wings. Dominic was so proud of his wings.

"Those will take longer to heal and repair. Magic can only do so much. He won't be able to fly for a few months."

"He can't click his fingers and regenerate," Dazielle said. "Angels aren't held together by bits of magic and charms."

"You're saying witches are?"

The nurse cleared her throat again. "Dominic needs peace while he recuperates. I trust both of you understand what that means?"

"You won't get any problems from me," I said. "The angels are another matter. They never do what they're told."

The nurse raised her eyebrows. "Ten minutes, then you both need to leave." She turned and left the room.

Dazielle sat in a chair beside the bed and leaned over Dominic. "Dominic, can you hear me?"

I studied a burn mark on the side of his neck. "It looks like Gideon pressed something hot to his skin."

"Hmmm, and there are more burn marks on his arms." Dazielle lifted one of Dominic's muscular arms and turned it over.

"At least we can get Gideon for attempted murder, even if we can't get a confession out of him about Ian," I said.

"We need to get Dominic awake, so he can tell us exactly what happened." She held out a hand. "Give me your magic."

I stepped away from the bed. "Err, why do you want that?"

She waggled her fingers at me. "I can transfer my energy into Dominic. Given the severity of his injuries, a magical boost would be appreciated to go alongside that. It'll ensure he recovers faster. He could even wake up."

"Huh! You can give another angel your power?"

Her eyes narrowed. "Yes, but keep that knowledge to yourself. We only share our energies with each other. And it's not right that Dominic's in pain. He's not the best angel in the world, but he always turns up on time for work and has a smile on his face. Everyone likes him. They wouldn't want to see him in this condition." She wiggled her fingers at me again.

I shrugged and grabbed hold of her hand. "I'm happy to give him a magic boost."

"You add healing spells, while I transfer my energy." Dazielle placed her free hand over Dominic's forehead and closed her eyes.

I rested my hand on his bare arm and conjured a strong healing spell. I tensed as a cool blast of power slid up my arm. It tingled below the surface of my skin before fading and spreading through me like a calming wave. I concentrated on the healing magic, pulsing it into Dominic.

We stayed like that for several minutes, casting magic and flooding Dominic with angel energy.

He groaned and his eyes fluttered open.

"He's coming around," I whispered.

"Dominic! It's Dazielle. You're in the hospital."

He turned his head slowly. He looked first at Dazielle then me. "Ugh! What happened?"

"Gideon Blazeheart happened. Don't you remember?" Dazielle removed her hand from his forehead and gestured at me to stop the healing magic.

"Um... I remember being with Tempest. Rhett and Gideon were fighting. We had to stop them when things got physical." Dominic's face wrinkled. "Then Tempest said to take Gideon to Angel Force."

I nodded. "That's right. I stayed behind to talk to Rhett, and you went off with Gideon. What happened after that?"

Dominic stared at the ceiling. "Gideon kept telling me he didn't do it. He got angry. I... I told him to calm down, but he punched a spell in my face and ran off. I chased him into the forest. Hmmm, it gets blurry after that. Something hit my head. I fought back. I didn't make it easy on him."

"Of course you didn't," Dazielle said.

"Then something hot pressed against my skin. I fell down. My energy faded."

"It sounds like angel kryptonite," I said. "Is there such a thing?"

Dazielle's eyes narrowed, but she didn't say anything.

"Could you help me to sit up?" Dominic said. "And I could do with some water."

We both helped him to get upright, and Dazielle handed him a glass of water.

He took a long drink. "Thanks. It's coming back to me. I didn't see clearly, but Gideon had something on a gold chain. It looked like an amulet. There was a large piece of amber in it. Gideon kept touching me with it, and I couldn't fight back. He kept yelling about being set up. I must have passed out. How did you find me?"

"I had help from Sox and Charlie. They found your feathers and led me to you. Gideon tied you up in the forest and left you."

Dominic slowly extended one wing. His mouth drooped as he looked at the mess made of his wings. "They don't look too good."

"The injuries are healing. When you come back to work, you can stick to desk duties until you're ready to fly again," Dazielle said.

"Desk duties?" Dominic stroked a hand along his ruined wing. "I'm not a real angel without my wings."

"You are! You're my favorite angel," I said.

His face brightened. "And you rescued me! I knew you'd help me."

"You wouldn't have needed help if you'd followed protocol," Dazielle said. "Gideon is dangerous. You shouldn't have been on your own with him. You should have called for backup."

"I thought I was helping," Dominic said. "I figured the quicker we got him back to Angel Force and questioned him, the better. I'm sorry. I really messed up."

Dazielle sniffed. "You did your best. That's all I can ask you to do. Next time, make sure you have backup. Don't follow Tempest's instructions. She's not always right."

"I am most of the time," I muttered. "Sorry, Dominic. I didn't know Gideon would react like that. I figured you'd be able to handle him."

"I would have, if it wasn't for that amulet."

"Tell me more about the amulet." I looked at Dazielle and raised my eyebrows. "There's really a stone that can take an angel's power?"

"No, not permanently," Dazielle said.

"It could be amber infused with a suppressing sigil," Dominic said. "I've only ever read about those kind of amulets. They're rare, but they exist."

"Gideon is running around the village with something that can zap your energy." I blew out a breath.

"Which makes him extra dangerous. It's important we bring him down quickly." Dazielle pushed back her seat and stood. "I need to warn the angels to be on their guard. I'll be back soon, Dominic." She patted his arm and left the room.

I settled in the seat she'd vacated. "I feel really bad about what happened to you."

"It's not your fault. As Dazielle said, I should have known better. She always tells me I'm too trusting. I figured Gideon would come quietly. After all, if he's innocent, he'd want to clear his name by answering our questions."

"You really are a good angel," I said. "And it's not a bad thing, thinking the best of people. I usually think the worst, but then I spend most of my time around demons and people hiding their crimes. It makes you jaded after a while."

"You're not jaded. You're great. I'm already feeling much better now you're here. I wanted to make sure you were okay. Things seemed tense between you and Rhett when I left with Gideon."

I looked away and wrinkled my nose. "You could say that."

"Did he admit he'd covered for Drake?"

"We both heard what he said. He did it because he was looking out for his gang. Which I'm not saying was the right thing to do, but I understand it. But you never know how someone will react when they're pushed too far. Rhett got this wrong."

Dominic straightened the sheet covering his legs. "And how about Rhett? What are you going to do about him?"

"Do you mean, you want to charge him because he lied about Drake's alibi?"

"Oh, no, I wasn't thinking that." Dominic's face flushed bright pink. "Although that is a crime. I understand why he did it, though. I... I was actually thinking about your relationship with him."

"My... relationship? You've lost me."

He looked at me from under his thick, dark lashes. "Rhett lied to you. Do you want to be with someone who doesn't tell the truth?"

I pressed my lips together. Was Dominic hitting on me? I opened my mouth, but nothing came out.

His gaze shifted away. "You should be with someone you trust. Someone who will always do the right thing."

My heart sank. I'd been wondering the exact same thing about Rhett, but when Dominic actually said it, it hit home like an uncomfortable boot in the butt. "We should focus on the murder."

"Oh! Of course. I... I just want you to know that you have other options. You know, if you're not happy with Rhett."

I bit my bottom lip to suppress a smile. "What options are we talking about?"

He shifted on the bed and looked down at his hands. "I don't know. I mean, I'm single, and we get along well. I make you laugh. We could go on a date if Rhett's not around anymore."

I couldn't help but chuckle. I didn't mean it unkindly, but it was so odd, the idea of dating Dominic.

I took hold of his hand and gave it a friendly squeeze. "Dominic, you're such a decent angel. I almost get you killed and you want to go on a date with me."

"What can I say? I like a bad girl. I mean, not that you're bad. You're very nice. I think you're lovely. I'd really like to take you out. Could you ever be interested in an angel with damaged wings?"

I stood and kissed his cheek. "You're far too good for me. You don't want me messing up your life. Not only do I have to live with a demon all the time, but I'm always chasing after them and coming home stinking of demon goo. You're better off finding a nice angel to date. Someone whose life is less complicated."

"I don't mind complicated. I enjoy it when we work together. You always get me to see things differently. I like that."

"You'd hate the stress, the odd hours I work, the fact Wiggles would always be around stealing your food, and the annoying demon inside me who pops out when I don't want him to."

His smile drooped. "It was just an idea."

"It's a great idea. But let's stay friends. That works best for me, and it'll work so much better for you."

The door to the room opened. Dazielle walked in with an enormous blue iced cake in her hands, covered in silver stars. "This arrived from everyone at Angel Force." She set the cake down in front of Dominic, along with a knife and two plates.

His face transformed, and a smile lit him up. "Cake! I love cake. After I've eaten this, I'll be ready to leave."

"Not so fast," Dazielle said. "I've spoken to the doctor. He wants you in here for twenty-four hours. I've told him you're awake, and he's coming to do some tests."

"Tests! There's no need for tests. You can tell the doctor I feel better now I've had visitors and cake. Sit down, and we'll enjoy this together."

"I'd love a piece of cake, but Tempest needs to leave." Dazielle sliced into the blue icing.

"I do? Where am I going?"

"To fix your mess. Gideon Blazeheart is still out there. He's our killer. You need to find him before he strikes again."

"Isn't that your job? Don't you head up Angel Force?" I looked longingly at the cake. A huge slice of iced, gooey deliciousness would be perfect.

"I'm looking after one of my wounded angels. An angel who got injured working with you." Dazielle sat in the seat and passed Dominic a slice of cake.

"We can give Tempest a piece of cake to go," Dominic said.

"No! She's too busy to eat cake," Dazielle said. "And we have work to talk about. I'll speak to you soon, Tempest."

I eyed the cake jealously before heading to the door. "I'll go find the killer, while you enjoy the cake. I hope it doesn't choke you." I stomped out of the room and left the hospital.

Wiggles, Sox, and Charlie were sitting outside, waiting for me.

"What's the news on Dominic?" Wiggles walked along beside me with his furry friends.

"He's on the mend. He's eating cake with Dazielle."

Wiggles stopped and looked back at the hospital. "And he didn't share?"

"Dazielle wouldn't let him. She's blaming me for Dominic's injuries." I shrugged. "He's an enormous angel with wings that could break me in half. I didn't think he needed backup. I sometimes forget that Dominic is a big softie."

"No cake?" Wiggles' tail dropped. "I was in the mood for cake."

"Well, get in the mood to catch a killer. We're finding Gideon and bringing him in."

Chapter 15

"He has to be somewhere. The village isn't that big. Where's that snake hiding?" I stomped along with Wiggles beside me. We'd been looking all afternoon for Gideon, and he'd vanished.

"You don't think he slipped through the barrier, do you? Those angels do get easily distracted," Wiggles said.

"They'd better not have let him go free. But if he's escaped, why are the Tusks still hanging around? They'd know if he was gone and follow him. No, he's still here. I just know it."

"The Tusks are hiding him," Wiggles said.

"Most likely. But we've already spoken to them five times, and they're staying tight-lipped."

"They're gonna keep their boss hidden when he's wanted for murder."

"And assault on an angel." I slowed as we reached Angel Force and stood outside the main door. I wasn't sure how to break the bad news to Dazielle that Gideon was still on the loose.

"Get out of my way. I need to get inside."

I jumped at the sound of a high-pitched nasal voice and turned. A short, dumpy man with a dark comb over and small dark eyes peered up at me.

"I'm in a hurry. You're blocking my way." He waved a hand at me, as if trying to get rid of an annoying fly.

I pasted on my brightest fake smile. "Maybe I can help you. I work here."

His head pulled back and his chin receded, making him look like a wrinkled tortoise. "No, you don't. You're not an angel."

"I'm freelance. I'm Tempest Crypt. And you are..."

"In a hurry. My idiot half-brother has gotten himself in trouble. I've been sent to fix it."

"Your brother? Who would that be? I've lived here all my life, so I know everyone."

He looked around, a sneer on his face. "How unfortunate for you."

"You don't like Willow Tree Falls?" Wiggles said.

The guy stared at Wiggles, disbelief in his eyes. "You talk?"

"Yep. I also bite if you're rude to Tempest. Why are you here?"

He adjusted his tie and took a step back. "As I said, my useless, layabout half-brother is causing trouble for the family."

"And your brother is?" I asked.

"My half-brother. Ian Blaine. I'm Paolo. I've no idea what he's gotten himself into this time, but Dad insisted I sort things out."

"You're related to Ian?" They looked nothing alike.

"We have the same father. Do you know Ian?"

"Yes!" I glanced at Wiggles, who tilted his head and lifted one paw. "You don't know what happened to him?"

"No. What's he done? Robbed a store? Stolen from a little old lady? How far has he fallen this time? He's always doing something stupid. He has a temper and only a tiny amount of sense. I blame his mother. Our dad left her a long time ago. She never disciplined Ian. He only had to scream and shout and she gave in. Look how that turned out for him. He's running wild with a pack of inbred bikers."

"Careful what you say, short stuff. One of those inbred bikers is my boyfriend," I said.

Paolo's head did that tortoise-like movement again. "You have my sympathy."

This guy was growing on me. "Didn't your dad give you any information about Ian? He's not committed a crime."

"No! He just asked me to deal with things. Has he been injured? He's not coming to stay with me while he recovers."

"You won't have to worry about Ian stomping mud on your carpet. Your brother's dead."

Paolo's eyes widened. A small, pink tongue appeared from between his lips. "I knew this day would come. He was always drawn to trouble. Was it a biking accident?"

"No, someone killed him."

"Oh! Really? Because of his temper? I'll admit there was a time or two when I came close to throttling him."

Wiggles snorted. "You wouldn't have stood a chance against Ian. He'd have squashed you like a bug."

I had to agree. Paolo looked like he was made mainly of blubber. "You realize that what you've said puts you in the frame for his murder? You didn't think much of your brother."

Paolo sputtered out a few words. "Half-brother. I didn't kill him. I mean, we weren't close, but there's no point in lying about that. And we have come to blows in the past. He was a hothead, and he bullied me. I was the younger brother. He should have looked out for me. Instead, he was only interested in hanging out with idiots on motorbikes and showing off to women. It was pathetic."

"And your family found his behavior embarrassing?" I said.

"That's right. After Ian went off the rails, my father disowned him. He said he wanted nothing more to do with him. But Ian kept coming back and asking for help when he got into scrapes. Those problems were usually money related. It made me angry the way Dad would give into him. He only did it to get rid of him and keep him quiet. You see, we have a high standing in the community. My mom comes from a wealthy family. We don't need bad blood causing problems."

"You gotta admit, it's a good motive for murder," Wiggles said. "You got rid of your brother because he was an embarrassing family problem. Did he ask your dad for one too many handouts, so he got you to deal with him?"

"I'm not the killer. And I haven't spoken to Ian for ages. I never wanted anything to do with him. He moved out when he was eighteen and came here. Everyone was glad to see the back of him."

"If you had nothing to do with what happened to your brother, you won't mind giving me your alibi for the time of his murder. He was killed four nights ago."

"That's easy. I was working." A satisfied gleam entered Paolo's eyes. "Yes! I have dozens of people who can tell you where I was."

"In the middle of the night?" Wiggles said. "Ian was killed in the early hours of the morning."

"Oh! Still, I was at a conference, in a hotel seven hundred miles away. If you check with the receptionist at the hotel, she'll confirm I was in my room. Hundreds of people will have seen me there. I didn't like my half-brother, but I wouldn't kill him."

That pretty much ruled out Paolo. If he'd had anything to do with Ian's murder, he'd have claimed they were best buddies, not freely admit to loathing him. Still, it would do no harm to check his alibi.

"How long will you be staying in Willow Tree Falls?" I asked.

"I want to leave as quickly as possible. I'm a busy man."

"You need to stay for a few days. The angels will want a formal statement so they can discount you from the investigation."

"I can't stay long. I work for my father. He's a potion bottles wholesaler. I go to events and secure new customers. He won't be happy if I get stuck here and miss the next conference."

"You'll need to make arrangements for your brother's body," I said. "That can take time."

He scowled at me but nodded. "That's why I'm here. Although I didn't think I'd be collecting a body. I can extend my stay at the unpleasant little hotel along the road. I suppose Ian has things that need to be collected, too. Does he still ride that noisy motorbike?"

"He does. Why don't we go get it now?" I said.

"Oh! I don't know anything about bikes. Isn't that something you can deal with?"

"Nope. And I expect the Willow Tree Falls gang are looking after it. I'm sure you'd like to say hello to his extended family."

Paolo gulped loudly. "Not really. I have nothing in common with those people."

"I insist. You'll want to hear some stories about your brother. After all, you're never going to see him again." I'd just grabbed hold of Paolo's arm when the rumbling sound of motorbikes filled the air. I turned to see the Tusks riding toward us.

"Are those members of the gang Ian was in?" Paolo backed away.

I narrowed my eyes and tightened my grip on his arm. This little snake wasn't going anywhere. "No, they're not Ian's friends."

The Tusks formed a semicircle around us, the air alive with the roar and rumble of eleven bikes.

Slater slid off his bike and strode toward me. "We want a word with you."

"Is there a problem?" I said.

"Yeah, a big one. We don't like how you operate. Leave us alone. And keep those angels off our backs."

"I don't control the angels. Why don't you ask them nicely if they'll leave you alone? Oh, no, they won't do that, because you're hiding a killer."

"What's this about a killer?" Paolo said. "Did one of these men murder Ian?"

"Gideon Blazeheart is the leader of the Tusks," I said to Paolo. "We believe he murdered your brother."

Slater glared down at Paolo. "This is Ian Blaine's brother?" He snorted a laugh.

"What's funny?" Paolo straightened his insubstantial, wobbly frame, and his cheeks flared red.

"Are you planning on taking his place in the gang?" Slater said. "The family of dead gang members get an automatic pass. Rhett would be thrilled to have such an asset join him."

"Is that true?" Paolo's eyes widened, then he shook himself. "I would never lower myself to get involved in a biker gang."

Slater stepped forward and growled at him. "What's wrong with being in a gang?"

"Keep it calm," I said. "Paolo is here to collect Ian's body and deal with his personal effects. Show some respect."

"I will when he does." Slater turned his attention to me. "Back off, Tempest. We're not involved with what happened to Ian."

"If you hand over Gideon and stop covering for him, I'll see what I can do."

He grabbed my shoulders and shook me. "I won't warn you again."

Wiggles growled, and flames flickered from his mouth. "Do you want me to burn him, Tempest?"

"You're good, Wiggles. Slater, don't be an idiot. We're standing outside Angel Force. If you want a fight, you've picked the worst place to start it. There are dozens of angels in there who'd be happy to arrest you. The gang is already in enough trouble."

His gaze flicked to the building. He gave me another shake before stepping back. "Stay out of our way."

I straightened my jacket. "You're hiding a killer. Gideon isn't a good guy. You need someone better leading the Tusks."

There was a loud grumble of disagreement from the other bikers. Several of them slid off their bikes and walked closer.

"Be careful what you say next," Slater said. "We're loyal to Gideon. He always looks after us."

"I, um, should I go get the angels?" Paolo was backing away toward the building.

"Stay where you are, pipsqueak," Slater said. "If you so much as twitch a muscle, one of the guys will take you down."

Paolo whimpered and froze in place.

"So, Tempest, you gonna say sorry for disrespecting Gideon?" Slater said.

"Nope. Killers don't deserve respect."

Slater's hands clenched, and magic sparked across his chest. "Make your move, witch."

Aidan and Maddie's repair truck appeared at the end of the lane and raced toward us.

Aidan pulled up and hopped out, concern on his face as he strode over. "Hey, how's everything going, guys? I thought you'd abandoned me when you left the truck in such a hurry. Was it something I said?"

Slater continued to glare at me. "Not now, Aidan. This nosy witch needs to be taught a lesson."

Aidan took his life into his hands as he walked past the bikers and slapped Slater on the shoulder. "Everyone's so tense. I tell you what, I'll give the first five guys who get their bikes on the truck a free magic boost. I'll have the bikes purring like werecats before you know it."

Several of the guys backed away toward their bikes.

"That's right." Aidan winked at me. "And if you hurry, Maddie and I were going to the Ancient Imp for a few drinks. The first round's on me, but only if you beat us there."

The mood changed. Several of the guys looked at Slater as if seeking his approval.

He slid a glance at Aidan. "My bike could do with a magic blast. Something's off with the flow."

"Grab your bike and we'll get to work. Then we'll head to the pub for some drinks." Aidan gestured at the truck. "You go ahead. Leave your bikes here, and we'll catch up with you. And make sure they know the drinks are on me."

Slater rolled his shoulders and nodded. "That's decent of you. Guys, you heard Aidan. Let's roll."

Several of the bikers left their rides by the repair truck then hopped on the back of other bikes before zooming off. Within a minute, there were no mean bikers looking for a fight.

Maddie hurried over. "Are you okay, Tempest? We saw the Tusks heading this way and thought there could be trouble. They always give off an angry vibe when they're looking for a fight, so we followed them. I hope you don't think we were interfering."

"I appreciate you being here. Slater was looking to cause trouble," I said.

"Was it about Gideon?" Aidan said.

"Yep. They don't like me asking questions about their missing leader."

"We heard he'd vanished after he attacked that angel," Maddie said.

"Which needs to change," I said. "Oh, this is Paolo Blaine. He's Ian's brother."

"His half-brother," Paolo said. His forehead was sweaty, and his chin wobbled. "I'm here to deal with Ian's mess."

"Oh! You'll be wanting his bike?" Aidan said. "I got it off Rhett. I've been keeping it in the truck. We weren't sure what to do with it."

Paolo dabbed at his forehead. "I suppose I should take it."

"It's a great bike. A real smooth ride. Ian loved her."

"I'll sell it. It's not something I want," Paolo said. "I don't even know how to ride."

I glanced at Wiggles. If Paolo didn't know how to ride a bike, that ruled him out of being the killer. Everyone thought it was so easy to sling your leg over a powerful bike and zoom away, but it took skill and practice.

Aidan rubbed the back of his neck. "It would break my heart to sell her. She's a thing of beauty. Ian spent a lot of money fixing her up. Don't you even want to come take a look?"

"Absolutely not. I want nothing to do with it," Paolo said. "If you're so interested in it, make me an offer. You can buy it off me."

"It's not a bad idea." Aidan glanced at Maddie. "Get Ian's bike off the truck. Let Paolo see it."

"I'm on it, boss." Maddie walked away with Paolo beside her.

"Thanks for the save," I said to Aidan.

"No problem. I've been around bikers long enough to know they tend to act before they think. It's the pack mentality. The Tusks are wound up over what happened to Ian and all the questions they're being asked. And they hate the fact they can't leave. That's one of the things they value, their freedom and being able to be on the road at a moment's notice."

"If we can find Gideon, they can all leave," I said. "They'd be helping themselves if they told me where he was."

"I wish I could help with that, but he's always been sneaky."

I recalled what Gideon had told me about Aidan having an argument with Ian. It was a long shot, but since he was here, there was no harm in asking him about it. "How well did you know Ian?"

"We were good friends when we were younger, but as he got involved in the gang, we drifted apart.

We both shared a love of bikes, though, and used to meet at the races."

"You never had any problems with him?"

His forehead wrinkled. "Nothing serious. Why do you ask?"

"Someone mentioned you'd had a disagreement with Ian not long before he was killed."

"Did they? Who was that?"

Maddie walked over. "I've left Paolo looking at the bike. Shall I get started on the magic boosts for the bikes?"

"Yeah, that'll be great, Maddie," Aidan said. He looked back at me. "I think I know what you mean. Ian wasn't happy about the cost of a repair job. He challenged me over it. But those bikes aren't cheap to fix."

Maddie turned back. "And Ian's was especially expensive because he needed imported parts, so we had to ship them from across the pond. They were super expensive and hard to fit, so the labor costs were always high."

"I get why you're asking me about Ian, but I like all the bikers, even the ones who aren't fast at paying their bills. You need to focus on Gideon for this," Aidan said. "It has to be him. They had that fight the night of the race, and Gideon is proud of his reputation. He hates anyone who makes him look bad."

"You don't think Aidan had anything to do with Ian's murder, do you?" Maddie said.

I studied Aidan's expression. He looked a bit cautious, but he wasn't nervous. "No. I was just tidying up a loose end."

"Aidan couldn't have done it. We sleep in the truck when we're on the road. We've got a space at the back we use as a chill out place. We were both there. I'm a light sleeper, so I always hear if Aidan leaves."

He shrugged and nodded. "I was asleep when Ian was killed. I worked all day on the bikes and was exhausted. I stayed up for the race, had a quick drink, and then crashed."

"Okay, I needed to check. You're right. We have our prime suspect. I just need to find him," I said.

"I understand," Aidan said. "If I get a hint of where Gideon is, I'll let you know. The Tusks have a bad reputation. I was worried something like this would happen. Gideon uses force to get what he wants. And he always pushes too far."

"If you keep doing that, something's bound to go wrong. It's just a shame it happened here," Maddie said. "I like this place."

Aidan nodded. "We need to get to work on the bikes, or the bar will be dry, and I'll have a huge bill to pay." He lifted a hand before walking off with Maddie.

I watched as they headed to the truck and talked to Paolo.

"What do we do now?" Wiggles said.

"We figure out how to hunt down a sneaky, murderous biker who doesn't want to be charged with murder and assault," I said.

"So, just another typical evening of fun."

"Yep. Let's go find our killer."

Chapter 16

I stood with my hands on my hips outside Cloven Hoof. I'd spent hours with Wiggles still searching for the elusive Gideon. We'd come up empty-handed again, and my patience was running out.

"My stomach's growling," Wiggles said. "We need dinner."

I sighed as I scanned the lane. The sun had long since dipped below the trees, and the doors of the club were open. I turned just as the main doors slammed against the wall, narrowly avoiding getting my nose crunched.

Suki stood in front of me, breathing heavily. "Tempest! I got a message from Fallon. There's something in the woods."

"What are we talking? An out-of-control werewolf? A vampire gone rogue? Has a demon gotten out of the prison and is ripping up the forest?"

"No! But it's urgent. She found a bike."

"Err, a bike?"

"A burned out motorbike. She's furious and is planning on hunting down the Tusks and giving them a piece of her mind."

"Did she say what kind of bike it was?" My thoughts went to the murder weapon that killed Ian.

"No! But it's a big one."

"Where's the bike?"

"Fallon gave me the directions. I can take you there," Suki said.

"Then let's go," I said.

"That's not all. Fallon mentioned a trail. It took me a while to understand her, because she was cursing and growling and listing off all the people she planned to kill."

I had to jog to keep up with Suki as she power walked through the village. "A trail? Someone is using the woods as their hideout?"

"Someone like Gideon?" Wiggles said.

"That's what we wondered. Everyone's talking about him hiding after attacking Dominic. No one's happy about it. We all want him found."

"Gideon must be getting help if he's hiding in the woods. I bet his bikers have been bringing him food," I said.

"No one sneaks about in that forest without Fallon noticing," Suki said. "I've trained her well as a Forest Guardian."

"She does make an enthusiastic Forest Guardian," Wiggles said. "And while she's so busy setting new traps to deter the bikers, she hasn't been hassling me to go for rides."

"You like giving her rides," I said.

"I don't hate it as much as I used to," he said. "And she did spend all that money on getting me a special saddle. It wouldn't be right not to wear it now and again."

"This way." Suki left the lane and headed onto a main forest trail. "We need to be careful. Fallon's set dozens of traps since the Tusks arrived. She doesn't trust them."

"She mentioned they'd been causing trouble."

"Some people have no respect for ancient places." Suki stroked a hand across the bark of a tree. As a giant wood nymph, she had a natural affinity for all things forest related.

"Wait! Don't move, or you'll die!"

We froze to the spot as Fallon's loud voice rang out over our heads.

I risked a glance into the trees. Fallon was perched on a wide tree branch, a rope tied around her waist.

"What are you doing?" I said.

"Saving your lives. If you take another step, you'll set off the fire balls," Fallon said.

"Are fire balls in the forest a good idea?" Suki said. "You know the rules. No flames in a wooded area unless there's a direct threat to life."

"This is an emergency. I've got a killer living in my woods. I'll use whatever means necessary to slay him." Fallon launched off the branch and swung to the ground using the rope. She landed in a huge pile of leaves and rolled over, leaping to her feet. She gave a flourish as she bowed, then untied the rope around her waist. "What took you so long?"

"We came as soon as we could," Suki said.

"What did you find?" I said.

"Two things I'm deeply unhappy about. This way." Fallon stamped through the forest, heading off the path and into the wild undergrowth.

"I'll go first," Suki said. "I can usually spot one of Fallon's traps."

"If any bikers dare step foot in my forest now, they'll regret it," Fallon said.

"How do the traps know when a biker is around?" Wiggles said.

"Well, technically, the traps will splat anyone. It's the price you pay for getting rid of trouble."

"Fallon, you know people like to walk in the forest. That's not a crime." Suki glanced at me and shook her head.

"We're Forest Guardians. We always put the forest first. The greenery has had a shock having a body dumped here. Now, I find more mistreatment. The forest needs to rest. It can only do that when there aren't individuals stamping around and causing damage."

"Suki mentioned a trail," I said, hoping to nudge Fallon back on course.

"We'll get to that soon. The bike is over here." Fallon disappeared from view, and we all hurried to keep up with her.

Wiggles ran ahead of me and joined Fallon by a large black lump on the ground.

I stopped by the charred looking metal.

"I couldn't believe it when I discovered this sacrilege," Fallon said. "It's a disgrace."

"How did someone get the bike in the forest?" Suki said. "Shouldn't your traps have stopped them?"

Fallon sniffed. "As you know, this forest is large. I do my best, but now and again, evil slips through."

I walked around the bike with Wiggles. "This could be the murder weapon. Gideon used this bike to kill Ian and burnt it to destroy any evidence."

"Is it the type of bike the Tusks ride?" Suki said.

"I'm no bike expert, but it could be," I said.

"This is easy to solve. I can tell you exactly how to find your killer," Fallon said. "You look for the biker who's missing his ride. I could have solved this mystery in an hour."

"None of them are missing a bike," I said. "At least, not that I've noticed. It's hard to tell, though. They're always leaving their bikes at the repair truck. It's possible a bike is missing. But that doesn't mean whoever's bike is gone is the killer. It could have been stolen. And since Gideon's the boss, he could have ordered someone to hand over their bike. If that's the case, no one in his gang will reveal that nugget of information."

"I need to have this mess gone," Fallon said. "The forest is unhappy. The willows by the swamp were being particularly weepy this evening."

"Have you told the angels about this?" I asked Fallon.

"No! What good will they do?"

"Send them a message. They'll need to see this before it's moved."

Fallon huffed out a breath. "They'll only trample where they're not supposed to and shed feathers everywhere."

"Fallon, the angels have to be informed," Suki said. "Send them a message on the snow globe. It won't take long. And the sooner they're here, the sooner the bike can be removed."

Fallon gave a dramatic sigh before stomping off.

I knelt by the bike and ran my hand over it, using a reveal spell to see if I could get useful information off the charred mess. I passed my hand over it several times, but nothing was showing up.

"No good?" Suki peered over my shoulder.

I sat back on my heels. "No. Someone did a good job of destroying the evidence. I reckon I should be able to wheel the bike out of here if I'm careful. We might find something on it if we look hard enough."

Fallon returned. "The message has been sent. The angels are on their way."

"While I'm here, did you see what happened to Dominic when Gideon attacked him?" I said to her. "He's still in the hospital. Gideon really messed him up."

"Oh, no. I must have been napping. I only realized something was going on when I spoke to Suki."

"Are you sure you can manage this forest on your own?" Suki said.

Fallon glowered at her. "I need my regulation naptimes. Otherwise, the whole thing falls apart. I'm handling things just fine."

"I could always help out on my days off," Suki said. "I love spending time here. I miss it."

"No! This forest is mine. I work better alone," Fallon said. "Enough staring at this piece of junk. I've got more to show you. Follow me." She turned and clumped away through the forest.

We hurried along after her for another ten minutes.

"This is it," Fallon said. "Someone's been living in this cave."

I walked up to the cave entrance and peered inside. There was a small pile of clothes, some tins of food against one of the cave walls, and a pile of blankets on the floor.

Wiggles walked in and sniffed around. He spent a long time inspecting the tins of food.

"Can you smell Gideon in here?" I said.

"It doesn't smell male," he said. "But someone's been here, and recently."

"If this is Gideon's hideout, he's sunk low if he's been forced to live in a cave. He'll hate this," I said.

"Gideon reeks of alpha male, all peppery and sweaty," Wiggles said. "And I'm not picking up any of that. It smells like a female has been living here. There are traces of magic, too. Someone with power has been hiding out in this cave."

"Why would they do that? If they're that powerful, there's no reason for them to hide." I walked in and inspected the blankets before shaking them out. There was nothing in them to give me a clue as to who was living here. A quick inspection of the clothes confirmed what Wiggles said. They were definitely clothes worn by a woman.

"You haven't seen a mysterious woman walking around in the woods?" I said to Fallon.

"No. I only realized this cave was being used when I discovered the bike," Fallon said. "I looked around and discovered a track leading to this cave."

"So, whoever's hiding out in this cave knew about the burned-out bike," I said. "Could they have dumped the bike and set fire to it?"

"If that's true, then we have a new mystery suspect. There aren't any female bikers in the Tusks," Wiggles said. "Only rough, smelly men who don't give good belly rubs or hand out treats."

"Fallon, can you keep an eye on this cave? I need to know who's staying here," I said.

"Of course. I had plans to set a few traps around it to catch them."

"Don't use anything lethal. Whoever's using this place could have seen who destroyed the bike. They may know who killed Ian. They could be too scared to come forward. Everyone knows the Tusks' reputation, and most people have heard of Gideon Blazeheart. She could be scared to report what she saw for fear the Tusks will come after her."

A high-pitched, terrified scream echoed through the trees. It was followed by a loud, nasally whinny of fear that had us all jumping and turning around.

Fallon leapt in the air and thrust her fist upward. "A trap has caught an intruder."

"Maybe it's the woman who's been hiding in this cave," I said. "Show us the trap."

Fallon raced through the trees. "It sounded like my spring netting was triggered. Whenever someone stands on it, it wraps around them and flings them into the trees. Most people break a bone or two. It's amazing."

"Not for the person who gets the broken bone," Suki muttered.

"They take their chances when they come into my home," Fallon said. "Hurry! I can't wait to see who's been caught."

"Did I imagine it, or did a horse make a noise when the trap went off?" Wiggles said to me.

"Yeah. There was a strange sound accompanying the scream," I said.

I was out of breath by the time we reached the clearing.

Fallon had raced ahead of us and was standing in the middle of the clearing, scratching her chin. She glanced at me. "Um, don't be angry. I may have captured your sister and her giant toad-pony."

My mouth dropped open as I stared at what was inside Fallon's trap. "Aurora! What are you doing up there?"

She was squirming inside the net, half-laying on the back of a large pale green horse. "Tempest! Get me down from here. One second, I was walking along with Diamond Buttercup, and the next, we were flung in the air. I thought we were going to die!"

"You set off Fallon's trap." I gestured at Fallon to release the trap.

"Do you see how effective this is, Suki?" Fallon said. "I caught a witch and a giant toad-pony."

"You're very clever. Now, let's get them out." Fallon bustled Suki away to deal with the ropes and magic holding Aurora and the horse above our heads.

"What are you doing with that horse?" I asked.

"We were following you," Aurora said. "Tilly saw you heading this way into the forest with Suki. I need your help." She shrieked as the netting around her loosened and clutched the horse's neck.

The horse whinnied and turned its head.

Only then did I spot the enormous horn jutting out of its forehead. "What the... Aurora, is that a unicorn?"

"This is what I need your help with." She squeaked as the net plummeted a few feet toward the ground.

"Sorry! That was my fault," Suki said. "Give us another minute. We've got this. You'll soon be down, Aurora."

I stared in disbelief as Aurora clung to the greeny-yellow unicorn as she was lowered to the ground.

The unicorn staggered to his feet and shook out a huge mane of gray-yellow hair before stamping his hoofs.

"Good boy. You're all right. That was a surprise adventure for us." Aurora stroked the unicorn's nose several times. She turned to me. "You have to help me with Diamond Buttercup."

I walked over and stared at the unicorn. "Unicorns are never this color. Is he sick?"

Wiggles trotted over and sniffed the unicorn. "This is one funky looking beast."

Diamond Buttercup tossed his head at Wiggles.

"I know!" Aurora said. "I collected him this afternoon so I could practise riding him. This was supposed to be a surprise for Lex. The plan was, I'd ride to my wedding on a beautiful, sparkling white unicorn. I'd made the arrangements, and Diamond Buttercup was happy to spend a few days with me before the wedding, so we could get used to each other. I collected him, brought him back to the store, and he changed color." She clutched my hand. "You have to fix this for me. Otherwise, my wedding will be blighted. I can't ride to my ceremony on a baby sick yellow unicorn."

"Aurora, I know this unicorn is important to you, but there's still a killer on the loose."

"But... But there's no way I can ride this to my wedding."

Diamond Buttercup tossed his mane and whinnied.

Aurora patted his nose. "I didn't mean any offense, but you can see this color doesn't suit you."

The unicorn stamped his hoofs.

"He's magnificent." Fallon walked over. "Look at that muscle tone and the luscious mane. If I had a saddle, I'd ride him all day."

"You only ride me," Wiggles said. "I'm much better than a unicorn."

Diamond Buttercup lowered his head and pointed his enormous horn at Wiggles.

"Have you tried a spell to remove the magic that altered his color?" I said to Aurora.

"Of course. I've tried dozens of spells. Poor Diamond Buttercup got so dizzy, at one point, he fell over."

"Aside from the color, he sure is a beautiful animal." Suki walked over and gently stroked the unicorn. "You're lucky to have one agree to be a part of your wedding."

"I was. But after this tragedy, the unicorns won't want anything to do with me," Aurora said. "They'll think this was my fault."

"Did you put that special conditioner on his mane?" I said. "That's what caused your pink hair."

Aurora grimaced. "Don't mention the hair. I'm still working on that. And I did nothing to his mane. He was perfect."

I approached Diamond Buttercup. He gave me a thorough nuzzling with his velvet soft nose before allowing me to touch him.

Strong magic prickled across my skin as I ran my hands over the unicorn's flanks.

"Do you know what spell was used?" Aurora said. "I can't figure it out. I tried reversal spells, color changing spells, and isolation spells. Nothing worked. You've got to do something, Tempest. Fix this for me, or I won't be able to show my face at my wedding."

Fallon shuffled closer. "I'll take him off your hands if you don't want him. Suki, lift me up so I can get on the unicorn's back. With your permission, of course, Mr. Unicorn."

"Hey, stop that. You only ride me." Wiggles stamped his paws. "He's way too big for you."

"I can handle this magnificent beast," Fallon said. "Suki, lift me up, now."

"We should leave the unicorn alone," I said. "Let's lay off the magic spells and not ride him about like he's a toy. It must be stressful changing color and having spells blasted at you."

Diamond Buttercup tipped his head in agreement.

"What am I supposed to do? What if he's stuck this color?" Aurora said.

"You could always change the color theme of your wedding so everything fits." I eyed her hair.

"Yes, go for bubble gum pink and..." Suki waved a hand at Diamond Buttercup.

"Baby sick green," Fallon said.

Aurora's lips pressed together, and a line appeared between her eyebrows. "I'll be a laughingstock. Everyone will talk about my wedding for the wrong reasons."

"Okay, Suki, you and Aurora take away the unicorn. The stress won't be helping the magic vibes, and we don't want him running off. See if you can figure out what triggered the color change." I lifted a hand as Aurora was about to protest. "And since you've been doing loads of spells, your magic needs to re-charge. Go to the stone circle. Soak up the good vibes then try again."

"What are you going to do?" Aurora said. "I need your help."

"I am helping. But I've got a murder to deal with. Don't tell me your wedding is more important than that."

"And we've just found the murder weapon," Wiggles said. "We've almost got this solved."

Aurora jutted out her bottom lip. "You must come see how I'm getting on as soon as you're done. It's not right that you're more interested in death and destruction than seeing your sister's wedding go off without a hitch."

I raised my eyebrows. "I'll let that slide since you're stressed. Suki, help Aurora with Diamond

Buttercup. Take a time out at the stone circle to see if that helps. We'll deal with the bike and the cave."

Aurora grumbled for several seconds. "Fine. Come on, Suki." She led Diamond Buttercup away with Suki.

"I've never seen such an incredible animal." Fallon watched the unicorn trot away, her dark eyes gleaming with interest. "Such a dignified air, considering how terrible he looks."

Wiggles head-butted her in the back. "I'm your ride."

"Of course you are, my little pony. But if I could get my hands on that unicorn and convince him to stay in the forest, imagine the fun I could have."

"You have fun with me."

"Let's not get jealous over the baby sick tinted unicorn. We've got a bike to deal with," I said.

We returned to the burnt out bike and found Dazielle and Cassiel on the scene.

Dazielle glared at Fallon. "You said the forest was in grave peril. How is one burnt bike a peril?"

I nudged Fallon to the side before she started hurling insults and threatening murder. "This could be the bike that killed Ian. We didn't want to move it until you'd taken a look."

Dazielle scowled at Fallon. "I thought a horde of trolls were attacking. You could have said that when you contacted Angel Force."

"I did! I just didn't use those exact words."

"Let's take a look." Dazielle and Cassiel walked around the bike several times.

"Did you mention the cave?" I said to Fallon.

"Of course. It falls under the grave peril category."

"What cave?" Dazielle said.

"We've found someone hiding in a cave. We thought it was Gideon, but now we're not so sure," I said.

"Show it to me."

I did as instructed, letting Fallon lead us through the wild undergrowth back to the cave.

Dazielle and Cassiel poked around for a few minutes.

"This has nothing to do with Gideon. Have you had someone staying here, Fallon?" Dazielle said.

"Nope. And when I find out who's been using this cave without permission, I'm taking them out."

Cassiel shook her head. "Don't do that, or I'll arrest you."

I jammed my hand over Fallon's mouth. "What do you want to do with the bike?"

"Get it over to the repair truck. I know Aidan Quinn. He's helped us with cases involving vehicles. He could find something useful on it," Dazielle said.

"Will do," I said. "How's Dominic doing?"

"He should be out of the hospital tomorrow. He's remarkably cheerful for somebody who almost died," Dazielle said. "The steady supply of cake is helping with his mood."

"I'm glad he's on the mend," I said.

Dazielle looked around before nodding. "I need to get back to Angel Force. Tempest, take charge of the bike. Let me know if Aidan finds anything useful. Let's go, Cassiel."

Dazielle and Cassiel launched into the air and disappeared.

"They don't seem concerned, considering this is a crucial piece of evidence in a murder investigation," Fallon said.

"Dazielle has audit paperwork on her mind. Let's go move the bike," I said.

After much tugging and heaving, I got the bike upright. I pushed it slowly out of the forest and headed back to the village with Wiggles to find Aidan's repair truck.

I puffed out a breath as I reached the truck and settled the bike on the ground. These things were heavy.

Maddie appeared at the top of the ramp. "What have you got there, Tempest?"

"I found it in the forest. Can you take a look at it?"

Her gaze ran over the bike. "Who would do that? There's no way I can repair it. Even we're not that good. It's just scrap."

"It doesn't need repairing. This bike could be involved in Ian's murder."

Her eyes widened, and she looked at the bike again. "Oh! Of course. I didn't think." She hurried over and looked at the bike for a minute.

"Do you recognize it? Could it belong to someone in the Tusks?"

She pursed her lips and used a screwdriver to lift a few pieces of damaged metal. "No, it's not a Tusk bike. Besides, none of them would do this to their ride. The bikes are basically their children. Help me lift it up. I'll take a look on the other side."

I assisted Maddie in moving the bike. She laid it down and spent several minutes peering at various bits of metal and shaking her head.

Aidan walked out of the repair truck, a long piece of exhaust in one hand and a vial of glowing green liquid in the other. "Hey, Tempest. What have you brought Maddie?"

"Something that could be connected to Ian's murder," I said. "I found it in the forest. Dazielle wants you to look it over and see if you can find out who it belongs to."

"Sure. I've worked with Dazielle before. We could run it through an—"

"Ouch!" Maddie held her hand against her chest and grimaced. "Sorry, the screwdriver slipped. It stuck straight in my finger."

"Are you okay?" Aidan said.

"It's not deep. I just need to clean the wound. I'll be right back." Maddie hurried away, holding her hand.

"That's one of the downsides of working on bikes. You end up getting covered in scars." Aidan held out a hand to show dozens of small scars and healed injuries. "Still, I can't complain. I get to do what I love every day." He set down the pipe and vial and walked over to the bike. He paced slowly around it several times.

"Maddie didn't think it belonged to anyone from the Tusks," I said.

"No, this isn't a Tusk bike. You see the curve of the handles? The Tusks have custom-made handles that are unique to their bikes. They put in their order through me, and I send them to a guy who specializes in metalwork. The design on these handles is all wrong. No one in the Tusks would ride this bike."

"So, someone snuck a bike into the village specifically to kill Ian?"

He lifted one shoulder. "I guess they could have done. And they did a great job of getting rid of identifying marks. There's nothing that special about this bike. There are thousands out there that look just like this one."

"Can you see if there's magic residue left behind?"

"Sure. I'll run a few tests and put it through a diagnostic program. But the fire that melted this metal was superhot. Leave it with me. I'll see if I can get anything useful." Aidan lifted his gaze from the bike. "Still no luck finding Gideon?"

"No, and I've looked everywhere. You're close to the bikers. They haven't let slip anything about him?"

"I'd tell the angels if they did. And, just to warn you, the Tusks are getting increasingly restless about being trapped."

"If they gave up their leader, they could leave," I said. "They're only making it difficult for themselves by hiding him."

"That's bikers for you. They never do things the easy way," Aidan said.

I glanced up, and my stomach clenched. Rhett was in the distance, heading toward the repair truck.

I backed up a couple of steps. I wasn't ready to deal with him. "Let me know about the bike. Come on, Wiggles. Let's go."

"No problem. See you later," Aidan said.

I hurried away from the truck, my shoulders hunched and my head down.

"You're avoiding Rhett?" Wiggles said.

"For now. I'm waiting for him to apologize."

"You're as stubborn as he is."

"You could be right. But he's in the wrong this time." I blew out a breath and glanced over my shoulder at Rhett. He stood by the repair truck. His gaze was on me, his arms crossed over his chest. That was something I had no idea how to deal with.

"Are we going to spend the night looking for Gideon? If we are, I'll need snacks, and lots of them," Wiggles said.

"No, I'm admitting defeat for the night. We need an evening at Cloven Hoof, a long line of lemon drops to down, and for this mystery to be over."

Chapter 17

It was late the next morning as I pulled on my boots and jacket. "Let's take a trip to the cemetery. I'm overdue a visit to see the family."

"That suits me," Wiggles said. "If Granny Dottie's on patrol, she always has treats."

We headed out of the apartment and down the stairs, walking out into a pleasant, sunny day.

I already felt better after having taken the night off and spending it in Cloven Hoof. But it was back to business. There had to be a solution to finding the missing Gideon.

We walked through the village, and I spotted Aidan and Maddie's repair truck. I lifted a hand as Aidan came out.

He returned my greeting and walked down to meet me. "How's it going?"

"Great. Have you had any luck with the bike?"

"Yes! I was going to get in touch with you. There's something there. It was hidden under the destruction caused by the fire. It's residual magic. I'm still working through it. It'll take me some time to get a clear read, but I'll drop by the club later and tell you what I've discovered."

"Anything could be useful," I said. "Thanks, Aidan. I appreciate the help."

"Any time." He gestured to three bikes sitting beside the truck. "I need to get on. We've got a ton of work to get through. Business is booming since the Tusks got trapped in the village."

"I guess some good has come out of this."

Aidan winced. "I'm not profiteering, but I won't turn away business."

"Of course not. I didn't mean it like that. Every cloud has a silver lining."

"Yeah. That's it. I'll see you later." Aidan dashed away.

"That sounds promising," Wiggles said as we walked away from the truck. "Finally, a clue."

"Let's hope it leads us straight to Gideon," I said.

We walked through the village and out to the cemetery. I opened the large, black gates and entered the peace of the graveyard. We headed straight to the family crypt. If Granny Dottie or Auntie Queenie were on duty, they always used the crypt as their base, so they could sit and gossip while keeping an eye on the demons.

As expected, the crypt door was open.

"Is anybody there?" I said.

"Only the ghosts and the wispy wraiths of your ancestors. Is that you, Tempest?" Granny Dottie's voice filtered out from the crypt. "Get in here, girl. I've almost forgotten what you look like."

I grinned as I walked into the cool interior of the crypt. "I've not been missing that long."

Granny Dottie sat in a fold out chair. She had a mug of coffee beside her and a plate of sandwiches and cherry scones on her lap.

Her gaze ran over me. "I heard from Aurora that you've been working on the Ian Blaine case. What a terrible business. I was never certain about Ian, though. He always had a sharp look about him and a bad mouth."

"We're working on it, but it's not going so well."

Granny Dottie petted Wiggles on the head and fed him a scone. "Aurora mentioned Gideon Blazeheart is involved."

"He's our prime suspect. I don't suppose you've seen signs of someone hiding in the cemetery? Gideon is missing."

"As if he'd dare come in here uninvited. We'd soon root him out."

"I tell you, that demon's looking to escape. If I have to bash him... Oh! Tempest! It's great to see you." Auntie Queenie hurried over and hugged me.

"You, too. Are you having problems with a demon?"

She wiped demon goo off her hands. "He's a new resident. He keeps protesting his innocence, but we all know what he did. Every chance he gets, he causes problems. We'll have to send him to isolation if he keeps making trouble. He's irritating the others, and when they're angry, they get rowdy, and that leads to more work for us." Once her hands were clean, she grabbed a scone and ate a big piece. "Delicious. That's just what I needed."

"Grab a seat. Tempest was telling me about this investigation she's working on," Granny Dottie said.

"Oh, the murder." Auntie Queenie pulled out her own fold out chair and settled in it. "It's a bad business. How's the sleuthing going?"

"Slowly. Our main suspect is hiding, and the Tusks are covering for him. But we'll find him, eventually."

"It was definitely Gideon Blazeheart?" Granny Dottie said.

"Everything points to him as the killer."

She pursed her lips. "He's a wild one, but he's a good gang leader. He stirs up trouble now and again, but he's been leading that gang for years. He wouldn't be in charge for that long if he didn't know how to do things properly."

"Something must have gone wrong with his particular style of scaring people," I said. "Everyone saw he hated Ian. He didn't want to lose face in front of his gang. He needed to show everyone why he was in charge."

"If you say so. You're the expert," Granny Dottie said.

I tilted my head as I considered her words. Had I been too quick to jump to conclusions when it came to Gideon? It was so obviously him. Maybe it was too obviously him. I shook my head and grabbed a scone. "Any other problems with the demons?"

"They're fine. Nothing we can't handle," Auntie Queenie said. "But I've been meaning to talk to you about a foxy warlock with an attitude."

"Which foxy warlock are we talking about?"

"I've seen Rhett stamping around the village and scowling at everyone. He's usually a charming young man. There's not trouble between you two, is there?"

I heaved a sigh and pulled off a piece of my scone. "There could be."

"Don't tell me you and Rhett have split up," Granny Dottie said. "You make a great couple. What's the trouble?"

"He lied to me. He gave one of the suspects in the investigation a fake alibi."

They both shook their heads and tutted.

"That's not a small lie," Granny Dottie said.

"I sort of get why he did it. And I know the guy he covered for. I can't imagine him killing anyone, but that's not the issue."

"The issue is, Rhett lied to you," Granny Dottie said. "I understand why you're disappointed in him. What are you going to do about it?"

"So far, I've done a great job of avoiding Rhett. I don't know how to handle it. I care about him, but should I stay with someone if I don't trust them?"

Auntie Queenie finished her scone and patted my knee. "It couldn't have been easy for him. He understands you always want to do the right thing and put troublemakers away. But Rhett's loyal to his gang."

"Which means he chose his gang over me," I said. "That bothers me."

"That's the life of a gang member," Auntie Queenie said. "The gang is their family. I should know. I rode with one long enough."

"I think you're good together," Granny Dottie said.

"You are. But I must admit, I prefer having a nice, quiet man as my husband," Auntie Queenie said.

"Your Uncle Kenny is perfect for me. I liked the wild ones when I was younger, but you need someone who'll stick by you, no matter what."

"If Tempest married someone like Kenny, she'd eat him alive," Granny Dottie said.

"I wouldn't. Uncle Kenny is great," I said. "Everyone loves him."

"He's a kind-hearted, loving man. He puts up with my quirks, rarely complains, and is an absolute genius in the bedroom," Auntie Queenie said.

I stuck my fingers in my ears. "I didn't hear that last bit." I lowered my hands. "Maybe a break from Rhett wouldn't be a bad thing. I could take more shifts in the cemetery or get more freelance demon hunting work from the angels. I've not been out of the village for a while. That could be the reason Frank's causing me problems."

"Aurora mentioned you'd had a couple of close calls with him," Granny Dottie said.

"I should get away for a few weeks. Frank's long overdue a vacation. He needs to blow off steam. He's always calmer and easier to handle when he's been allowed to cut loose."

"It's a great idea. We could all go together," Auntie Queenie said.

"If we did that, it would leave Cora handling most of the shifts here. She's got enough on her plate," Granny Dottie said.

"Mom's having problems?"

Auntie Queenie glanced at Granny Dottie. "It's nothing for you to worry about. Things are tricky between your parents right now."

"They are? When I spoke to Mom, she said everything was good between them."

"And it is, on the whole. They're working on things and trying hard, but much like the problems you're having with Rhett, it takes time to rebuild trust. Your dad was missing for years, and he got up to all sorts when he was away from Willow Tree Falls," Auntie Queenie said.

"Not least of which included having a child with another woman," Granny Dottie said. "I keep asking him about Zandra, but he doesn't say much."

Worry fluttered through me. I felt like I was overreacting about Rhett when I considered what my mom and dad were going through.

"They'll sort things out, though, won't they?" I asked.

"They both want to. They're committed to it. And they're generally happy. I'm sure they'll get there in the end," Granny Dottie said. "Don't worry. Focus on your own relationship."

"And catching that killer," Auntie Queenie said.

"Yes. Get Gideon, then fix things with Rhett. Then we can enjoy your sister's wedding."

I finished my scone. They were right. A person could only handle so many stressful things at one time. I'd read somewhere that weddings and relationship issues were two of the most stressful things to deal with.

"About the wedding. Has Aurora told you about the strange things going on?"

"She has," Auntie Queenie said. "She came by yesterday to discuss the unicorn problem.

He's a handsome creature, even though he's an unfortunate color."

"Did you figure out what happened to him?" I said.

"We undid the spell, but it was complicated. We had to combine our powers. Whoever cast that spell has strong magic coursing through them," Auntie Queenie said.

"It wasn't a stable spell," Granny Dottie said. "That got me worried. The magic felt raw and unfocused. And there were a number of partial spells mixed together to create a toxic mess that was difficult to unpick. We were working on it for hours. We can usually figure out a spell in a few minutes."

"You don't think someone's targeting Aurora and Lex's wedding, do you?"

"Why else would they do all these things to her?" Auntie Queenie said. "And I'm concerned because it's focused on Aurora. Lex hasn't been bothered."

I slumped against the wall of the crypt. "I figured it was Aurora messing up because she's been so stressed about the wedding. She admitted she could have changed her hair color. And I assumed the cake was sent by someone who meant well but got the spell wrong. She's really in danger?"

"We're keeping an eye on Aurora to make sure no one comes after her," Granny Dottie said.

I felt terrible. I'd dismissed her concerns as nothing more than a stressed out Bridezilla.

"We've got her back. You concentrate on this murder. Everything will be right on the wedding day," Auntie Queenie said.

"Hello! Is anyone in there?"

"Aurora! Speak of the devil. Well, the angel in her case," Granny Dottie said. "In here. We're all in here. Come in."

Sox and Charlie bounded in through the crypt doorway. They squeaked with delight and raced over to Wiggles, rubbing around him and purring.

He licked both their heads. "What are you two doing here?"

Aurora ran in. She was breathless and sweaty.

"Whatever's the matter, child?" Granny Dottie leapt up and ran over to her.

She gasped out a breath. "It's Lex. He's missing."

I joined Granny Dottie. "What do you mean, missing?"

"I mean, he's gone. I've looked everywhere for him. We were supposed to have breakfast, but he didn't show up. I sent him a message to see what he was doing, but he didn't reply. He never ignores my messages. So, I shut the store and walked to the castle. And... and... it was a mess. There were signs of a fight. Things had been knocked over."

"Who would want to fight Lex?" I said. "Everyone likes him."

Auntie Queenie hurried over and wrapped an arm around Aurora's shoulders. "I'm sure this is a misunderstanding. You didn't get your days muddled up about meeting?"

"No! I was looking forward to our breakfast. I made special muffins. Lex was coming to the store because there were a few wedding things to check through."

"I bet that's it," Granny Dottie said. "Lex is off buying things for the wedding. He was in a hurry when he left and knocked something over on his way out."

Aurora shook her head and swiped a tear off her cheek. "It's not that. The wedding is in three days. There's nothing left to buy. He's missing. What if something bad happened to him?"

There was a rumble under our feet and the sound of cracking rock outside the crypt.

"Oh! Not now. Just when we don't need the demons playing up." Auntie Queenie was already grabbing a large polished stick propped against the wall of the crypt. "I'm sorry, Aurora. I have to see to the demons. We can't have them getting out."

"Of course," Aurora said. "But what am I going to do about Lex?"

Granny Dottie grabbed her own demon whacking stick. "You're worrying about nothing. But take Tempest with you to the castle. She can look around and make sure nothing is out of place. You never know. By the time you get back there, Lex could be home with an enormous wedding gift for you."

I shook my head. "I wish I could help, but I have to work on the murder investigation."

Aurora grabbed my shoulders and shook me. "Lex is missing! We're supposed to get married in three days. He could have been kidnapped. Or worse, he could have changed his mind and fled the castle because he doesn't want to marry me anymore. He's seen my stupid pink hair and doesn't want me."

There was more rumbling under our feet, and a low, angry growl filled the air.

Granny Dottie headed to the entrance of the crypt with Auntie Queenie. "Lex would never leave you. Tempest, go with your sister and see what's happening. I need to help Queenie with these demons." She hurried out of the crypt.

"Tempest, please, you have to help me," Aurora said. "I can't lose Lex."

I had to focus on finding Gideon and solving this murder, but Aurora needed me. I couldn't turn away from her, not when she had tears dripping off the end of her nose and a wobbly chin.

"Of course I will. Let's go to the castle and figure this out."

Chapter 18

I stood in the middle of Lex's study and looked around. A bad feeling ate away at my stomach as I took in the knocked over furniture, burn marks on the walls from where spells had been fired, and a few dots of blood on the wooden floorboards.

"I'm doomed." Aurora was slumped on a chair in the corner. "I should have canceled this wedding as soon as things started going wrong. They were signs that it was never supposed to happen."

"No. They were signs that someone has been messing with you."

"You really think someone is behind the problems with the wedding?" Aurora raised her head.

"I didn't believe it at first, but looking at this, Lex didn't do this himself." I inspected the blood on the floor. There were only a few dots scattered around, the kind that would be left behind if you had an unexpected nose bleed.

Wiggles was sniffing around the room with Sox and Charlie. They all mooched out into the hallway.

"Hey! There's more blood out here," Wiggles called.

I grabbed Aurora, and we followed along behind him. I put an arm around her shoulders. She was shaking and kept dabbing at her nose with a hanky.

"We'll find Lex," I said.

She nodded. "We will. And whoever has done this to him will pay."

I opened the back door out into the yard for Wiggles and the cats.

Wiggles stood outside, sniffing the air.

"Is there more blood out here?" I said.

"There could be. But there's something else. I'm smelling Gideon."

"Gideon took Lex!" Aurora's head shot up. "Find him, Wiggles. No one takes my man and gets away with it."

"It's definitely him," Wiggles said. "I'd recognize that alpha male pong anywhere. This way."

"Could you smell Gideon inside the castle?" I asked as we raced along behind Wiggles, Sox, and Charlie.

"No. I only got his scent when we came outside. It's like he's been lurking around the building."

"He must have been inside to grab Lex," Aurora said. "Could Gideon have kidnapped Lex? He may be holding him to ransom because he knows how wealthy he is. Or he wants to get his hands on some wishes. Lex will never give in if that's the case."

"It doesn't make any sense for Gideon to take Lex," I said. "All he wants to do is get out of Willow Tree Falls. By kidnapping someone, he's only making things worse for himself, and things are already dire for him."

"Which means he's got nothing to lose. He decided, since he was stuck here, to make the most of it and get some money." Aurora scowled, and flashes of pink magic flowed from her hands. "When I catch him, I'll make him sorry."

We headed into part of the enormous estate Lex owned. There were three wildflower meadows, an orchard, and a huge lake. It would take hours to explore it all.

"The smell is strongest over by those barns," Wiggles said.

We headed toward three wooden barns that stood behind the castle.

"What does Lex use these for?" I asked.

"Storing equipment. Nothing exciting." Aurora dashed ahead of me.

I caught hold of her arm. "Stay calm. I know you want to find Lex, but Gideon's a bad guy. If he's got Lex trapped somewhere, he won't go down without a fight."

"Which is what I'll give him," Aurora said. "I'm not scared of Gideon Blazeheart."

We all slowed as we neared the barns. Wiggles went ahead, sniffing furiously for any signs of Gideon, alongside Sox and Charlie. He stopped outside the third barn and looked back at me. He nodded.

I pressed a finger to my lips and gave Aurora a warning look.

She frowned but then nodded.

I crept toward the barn and put my ear against the door. There were shuffling sounds on the other side. Someone was in there.

I flicked my wrist and conjured a fireball. With my free hand, I caught hold of the handle of the barn door. I looked over at Aurora one more time and nodded.

Her own pale pink magic swirled around her, angry looking jagged sparks flickering through it. I'd never seen my sister so mad.

Wiggles, Sox, and Charlie crouched, ready to spring into action.

I sucked in a breath and yanked open the door.

Gideon's head whipped up as the door opened. He was sitting on an overturned box, his leather jacket slung to one side, and his bike parked beside him.

He jumped up and stumbled back. "How did you find me?"

Aurora rushed toward him, a blaze of sparkling magic and pink-haired fury. "Where's Lex? What have you done with him?"

Gideon's gaze slid to me. "What are you talking about?"

"You guys guard the door," I said to Wiggles, Sox, and Charlie. "We'll deal with Gideon."

Wiggles nodded and positioned himself in front of the door, his teeth bared and his hackles raised. The cats puffed out their fur and narrowed their eyes.

I stalked toward Gideon, who was looking at my sister with alarm in his eyes as her magic shimmered around her. "We know what you did. You left behind way too much evidence. We need Lex back."

"And if you've hurt him, I'll kill you," Aurora said.

Gideon licked his lips. "You witches are crazy."

Aurora's hand shot out. She blasted a stream of jagged pink magic straight into Gideon's chest. He yelped and lifted off his feet, slamming back against the side of the barn.

"If you've hurt my husband to be, I'll spend the rest of my life making you pay. That's if I don't kill you, first. Give me back my fiancé."

Gideon struggled against Aurora's magic. "What the heck? I don't know anything about your fiancé. I don't even know who he is."

"Lex Fontaine! The man you took from the castle." Aurora thrust both hands forward, and more magic slammed into Gideon.

I was impressed. Aurora had seriously witchy skills when she was angry.

I touched her shoulder. "We need to keep him alive until we find out where Lex is and get a confession for Ian's murder and the attack on Dominic."

Gideon glowered at me. "You're still going on about that. Haven't you found out who really killed Ian?"

"We know who did it. It was you," I said. "You wouldn't be hiding if you were innocent."

"You've got it wrong." He twisted in Aurora's magic, a spell sparking on his fingers.

I held up the fireball in my palm. "Think very carefully before you fire magic at my little sister. Between us, we'll take you down."

"And it'll be self-defense if you die," Aurora said. "We'd get away with killing you. No one likes you, and everyone trusts us. We'd probably get medals for getting rid of such a meanie."

I leaned closer to her. "Ease up on the killing threats. You're even scaring me."

"I'll do it," she said. "Gideon's a bad man. He won't stop my wedding from going ahead."

He held up his hands, the magic he was conjuring dying. "I know nothing about your dumb wedding. Let me go."

"Why are you hiding in here?" I said.

He scowled and struggled some more before sighing. "Alright, I'll tell you. I was staying here until the heat died down. You and the angels were looking at me for Ian's murder. If I stuck around, you wouldn't look anywhere else. So, I decided to help you."

I gestured at Aurora to draw back the strength of her spell.

Her mouth twisted to the side, but she lowered her hands. She kept magic on the tips of her fingers as she glared at Gideon.

Gideon rolled his shoulders and adjusted his crumpled T-shirt.

"You know I've been looking at other suspects," I said. "But there's a good reason you're the prime suspect. And we've found your murder weapon."

"Yeah! Where did I hide it?"

"Why don't you tell me?"

"Witch, you're pushing your luck."

Aurora shot a knock back spell at Gideon, making him yelp and duck. "You're the one pushing your luck! Where's my fiancé, you creep?"

"Calm her down." Gideon wheezed as he got to his feet. "I know nothing about this guy, or the murder weapon, or the murder."

"We found the bike. You set it on fire, but you didn't do a good enough job. It's only a matter of time before we get evidence off it," I said.

He frowned, and his forehead wrinkled. "I'd never burn a bike. You respect your ride. You don't damage it. Besides, my bike's right here. I don't ride anything else."

"We only have your word for that," Aurora said, "which is meaningless. And I don't care about what happened to Ian. Sorry, Tempest, but this is about my wedding. Where's Lex?"

"If you mean the guy in the castle, I stayed away from him."

"That's not true," I said. "Wiggles picked up your scent outside the castle door."

Gideon lifted one shoulder. "I may have had a look around but only when he wasn't at home. The guy was in and out all the time, so it was easy enough to poke about."

"Someone will have seen you," Aurora said. "Lex has staff. They'd have stopped you."

"I saw a few people inside, but I kept a low profile. I didn't want anyone to know I was here. I figured I'd spend a few days in this barn until Tempest figured out who killed Ian. Then I'd be able to leave Willow Tree Falls without any hassle."

"You're not going anywhere. Not after what you did to Dominic," I said.

Gideon bared his teeth at me. "That was your fault. He should never have tried to take me in. I don't do well in confined spaces."

"You'll have to get used to small spaces. Trying to kill an angel will mean a long stretch inside."

"I'd never have killed him. I was sending a message. A warning so you'd back off."

"That warning backfired. You badly injured Dominic," I said. "The angels have you on the top of their hit list. As does everyone in Willow Tree Falls. Dominic is a popular guy."

"It's not my fault. He shouldn't have fought back. Dumb angel."

"You're the one who's missing the smarts. I know you lied about your alibi on the night of Ian's murder. You were seen by our Forest Guardian around the time of Ian's death. You were in the forest. You could easily have killed Ian and burned the bike. Your gang covered for you, which means they're in trouble too," I said.

"You leave my gang out of this. They only do what I tell them." Gideon sighed and ran a hand through his long, dark hair. "I had good reason to find myself an alibi. I knew you'd automatically think I was guilty. But I had nothing to gain by killing Ian. The guy was a massive jerk, and he disrespected me, but it wasn't the first time that had happened. People are always trying their luck with me, making out they're something special."

"So you decided to show Ian who's in charge," I said.

"No! When you lead a gang, people are always coming for you. You get used to it. You learn to deal with it, without killing everyone who gets up in your face. If I blew my lid every time someone came for me, I'd have dozens of murders under my belt. I didn't kill Ian."

"The evidence suggests otherwise. And you don't need to convince me. You need to convince the angels. You're under arrest, Gideon."

"You can't take him away," Aurora said. "We still have no idea what he's done with Lex."

Gideon's hands flexed as I approached him.

"Keep calm," I said. "You can't get away."

His eyes narrowed. "Are you accusing me of two murders? You think I bumped off the rich guy in the castle?"

Aurora gasped. She flung herself at Gideon and grabbed the front of his T-shirt. "If you've murdered Lex, I'll hunt you down for the rest of your life. Even when you're dead, I'll hassle your ghost. I'll make sure you're never at peace. I know spells that would turn your hair gray with terror."

I glanced at Aurora. For a white witch with shocking pink hair, she was being particularly terrifying.

Gideon tensed as I got close. "Don't make this any harder on yourself. You heard my sister. She's in the mood for performing nasty magic. Come quietly, confess to your crimes, and tell us what you've done with Lex."

Gideon's shoulders hunched. "You'll charge me with this crime whatever I say." He held out his hands and let me put him in magical restraints. They glowed around his wrists, trapping his hands in front of him and preventing him from doing magic.

"Let's move." I kept a tight hold on Gideon's arm as we left the barn.

Aurora stuck to Gideon like glue as we headed away from the castle. "Where's Lex?"

"I have no idea."

"Why did you take him?"

"I didn't take him."

Aurora grabbed Gideon again and shook him. "Tell me where my fiancé is, you dark-hearted biker thug."

Gideon glanced at me. "And I thought you were the crazy one."

"Aurora doesn't like people messing with her fiancé. It makes her twitchy and mean."

"Just keep her away from me," he said.

I snorted a laugh and shook my head. "Nope. Family first. She needs answers."

"That's right. I'll hassle you until you give me the information I need," Aurora said.

I shrugged as Gideon shot me a look of desperation. "Aurora wants the perfect wedding day. You're stopping that from happening. Never stop a bride from getting what she wants. You're learning that the hard way."

Gideon looked over at the castle. "If I tell you what I saw, will you back off?"

"What? What did you see?" Aurora clutched his arm.

"Ease off of the pinching, and I'll tell you." Gideon tried to shrug Aurora away, but she was going nowhere. "Fine. There was a woman watching the castle. I had to be careful when sneaking in and out of the barn to make sure she didn't see me."

Aurora's eyebrows shot up. "What woman? Who is she?"

"I can't tell you that. The only time I've ever seen her was when I was here. She spent ages watching the castle. Well, I reckon she was actually watching your guy. She'd conceal herself behind a tree and stare at him. When he went out, she'd follow him. This morning, she went inside the castle. She walked up to it like she owned the place, opened the back door, and went in. I didn't see her after that."

The color drained from Aurora's face. "This woman took Lex?"

Sox and Charlie leapt onto her shoulders and curled around her, as if sensing her distress and wanting to provide a fluffy, protective shield.

"She could have done. I didn't see them leave together," Gideon said.

Aurora blinked rapidly. Her bottom lip quivered. "Someone's really taken him?"

"Hold on. Gideon, why should we believe you?" I said.

"What's the point in me lying? If I wanted his money, I'd have robbed the castle. I just want out of Willow Tree Falls. And once I'm gone, I'm never coming back."

"Could it be an old girlfriend?" Aurora said, her expression blank as she looked back at the castle. "A jealous rival?"

"I don't reckon he dated this woman," Gideon said. "She's young. Early twenties, maybe. Lex is an old guy."

Aurora grabbed him again. "He's sophisticated and mature."

Sox and Charlie hissed in Gideon's face.

"Whatever you say. But he wears those weird cravats and suits all the time. Anyone in a suit looks old to me. Maybe they did date. I don't know. And I don't care."

"Describe her to me," Aurora said.

"I didn't pay much attention."

"You saw enough to know her age," I said. "Try again."

Gideon huffed out a breath. "She looked the opposite of you, Aurora. She looks more like Tempest. Pale skin and dark hair. She was dressed in black."

"Lex has never dated anyone like that. He likes blondes." Aurora pressed her hands against her chest. "I feel sick. And faint. I may be sick. I need something to puke in."

Gideon stepped back, disgust on his face.

"Take a few deep breaths," I said to Aurora. "The first thing we need to do is process Gideon. Let's get him to Angel Force and out of our hands. Then we can focus on finding Lex and this mystery woman."

"Yes! We focus on that." Aurora bent forward and sucked in air.

I turned to Gideon. "If you're lying to us, we're both coming for you."

He lifted his bound hands. "I'm done with this place. I didn't kill Ian, and I had nothing to do with this guy going missing."

"Let's find out if any of that's true." I grabbed Gideon's arm and caught hold of Aurora's hand. "Wiggles, grab on to me. I'll transport us to Angel Force."

Wiggles hopped onto my feet. "Hold on, Sox and Charlie. We're going for a ride."

I conjured a transportation spell. It pulsed through my veins in hot, urgent waves, and we all appeared outside Angel Force. We headed inside to find the reception area empty.

Gideon scowled as he looked around. "I shouldn't be here."

"That's for the angels to decide. If we can find any." I headed through to the main office. As I pushed open the door, a wave of panic hit me.

Dazielle shot out of her office. She froze when she saw us before striding over. "You finally found Gideon. Where was he?"

"Hiding out on Lex's estate. He's all yours." I passed Gideon over to Dazielle.

"Well, that's one positive. But we've got another crisis on our hands," Dazielle said.

"Don't tell me you've got a second audit?"

She rolled her eyes. "No more audits. It's Aidan Quinn. He's been attacked and left for dead."

Chapter 19

"Aidan's been injured?" Gideon's face showed genuine concern. "Who did it?"

"We were thinking it might have been you," Dazielle said.

"No way! You're not fitting me up for this, too. I've been with these crazy witches. This has nothing to do with me."

"When did the attack happen?" I said.

"Less than half an hour ago," Dazielle said. "Maddie contacted us in a panic. She'd left the van for fifteen minutes, and when she got back, she found Aidan on the floor of the truck. He was unconscious."

"Then it couldn't have been Gideon. We were with him."

"I told you I was innocent," he said.

"Maybe of this crime," I said. "How's Aidan doing?"

Dazielle gestured two angels over to deal with Gideon. "Not good. I was about to go over there. Whoever attacked him left him for dead."

I turned to my sister. "Aurora, we could do with your healing magic."

"You're the best we've got at restorative magic," Dazielle said. "Your help would be welcome. From the report I've had, Aidan may not make it. The doctor is with him, trying to get him stable before he can be moved."

She bit her lip, her eyes filling with tears. "Of course I'll help." She jabbed a finger against Gideon's chest. "But I want to talk to you again about Lex. I need to make sure you didn't miss anything that'll help me find him."

"Lex? What's happened to Lex?" Dazielle asked.

"He's missing," I said.

"Gideon did something to him?" Dazielle's wings fluttered.

"No!" Gideon snapped.

"Possibly. We're not sure," I said.

"I'm filing a restraining order against you two whilst I'm here. This is harassment," Gideon said. "Will someone put me in a cell, so I can get away from these witches before they accuse me of more crimes?"

"With pleasure." Dazielle handed him over to the angels, who escorted him away. "Come on. Let's move. We need to get to Aidan before it's too late. The truck is parked by Mystic Mushroom."

We all raced out of Angel Force. Dazielle flew ahead of us while we sprinted along the lane. I'd have cast another transportation spell, but that kind of magic sucked the juice out of you, especially when you transported a group.

We arrived at the bike repair truck to discover three angels standing guard.

Maddie was pacing outside, her hands clenched together so hard her knuckles were white.

"Where's Aidan?" I asked.

She looked up, tears in her eyes. "He's in the truck. That's where I found him. There's a doctor looking at him." She pressed a hand to her mouth. "They think he might die."

"Let me see if I can stop that from happening." Aurora pushed up the sleeves of her dress.

Dazielle appeared from inside the truck. "Aurora, you're needed."

Aurora touched Maddie's arm before hurrying into the truck.

"Who did this to him?" I asked Maddie.

"I... I don't know. I didn't see anything. I went to grab some coffee and cookies from Sprinkles. When I got back, Aidan was... he was hurt. The truck was a mess. He's got a horrible injury to his head."

"You didn't see anyone leaving the truck?" I said.

She shook her head. "I was fifteen minutes at most. I... I was wondering, could it have been Gideon? I mean, he's already killed Ian. He's out of control."

"This wasn't Gideon," I said. "He's been arrested and is in custody."

"Oh! Well, that's good. I'm glad he's been found." Maddie stared at the truck. "Could it have been one of his gang?"

"We'll find out who did it," I said. "I know you're close but try not to worry about him. My sister's healing magic is incredible."

"Aidan's always been great to me. He took me on and trained me when no one else would. I owe him a lot."

"He's awake!" Dazielle poked her head out of the truck. "You need to be quick. He's in and out of consciousness."

I patted Maddie on the shoulder, and we hurried into the truck. It looked like a tornado had whipped through the place. There were tools everywhere, bikes knocked over, and trophies scattered around.

A doctor from the hospital was kneeling next to Aidan, along with Aurora. Her hands were moving over his body as a pale yellow glow slid from her skin.

The air buzzed with powerful healing magic, leaving the faint tang of strawberries and cinnamon on my tongue.

Dazielle was crouched by Aidan's head. "Aidan, it's Dazielle from Angel Force. Can you hear me?"

He groaned, and his eyelids fluttered.

"It's important not to stress the patient," the doctor said. "He's weak. Aurora's magic is the only thing keeping him alive."

I looked at Aurora. She was trembling, and there was a sheen of sweat on her forehead. She was pushing everything she had into keeping Aidan's heart beating.

"Aidan, who did this to you?" Dazielle said.

He groaned again, lines of pain etched across his face. "I didn't see..."

"You didn't see who struck you?" Dazielle said.

"No. I mean..." He groaned.

"Was it someone from the Tusks?" Dazielle said. "Did you remember something about Ian's murder and they came to silence you?"

"This could be about the bike found in the forest," I said. "Aidan told me earlier that he'd found something on it. He could have discovered evidence to implicate Gideon. Gideon figured out what was going on and sent his guys to stop that from happening."

"Not... Gideon." Aidan's head slumped to the side.

"That's enough," the doctor said. "Now Aidan's reasonably stable, we have to transport him to the hospital."

"I'll come with you," Aurora said.

"I'd appreciate that. He's responding well to your healing magic." The doctor swiftly packed his equipment. He glanced up at Dazielle. "We'll meet you there." He rested a hand gently on Aidan's shoulder then clasped Aurora's hand, and they vanished.

"Aidan wasn't making much sense," Dazielle said.

"It has to be the Tusks behind this. Aidan has evidence in this truck to show that Gideon killed Ian. The gang will do anything to protect Gideon," I said.

"Whatever evidence Aidan found, we'll have to wait until he's talking to learn about it." Dazielle stared out of the truck. "I need to get to the hospital. I'll catch up with you later." She shot into the air on her huge white wings and swooped away.

Maddie hurried over to me. "How's Aidan doing? I wanted to see him before the doctor took him away."

"He was awake, but he wasn't making much sense. We think he was trying to tell us who attacked him. Aidan said Gideon wasn't involved."

She looked around and swiped a hand across her face. "I should leave. It doesn't feel safe here. First, Ian's killed. Now someone's come after Aidan. What if I'm next?"

"Why would you be next? Did Aidan share what he'd found on the bike with you?"

Maddie paced around the truck, pulling up bikes and securing them with straps before starting on tidying the tools. "No, but what if the Tusks think I know? They could target me."

"The angels will look out for you. They can post someone outside if you're worried."

Wiggles was nosing around in the chaos. He stopped by the fallen racing trophies and awards. "Some of these have been dented."

Maddie hurried over and picked up a couple of trophies. "Aidan was so proud of these. I told him it was embarrassing to keep them on display, but he insisted. He said it was good for business. When people come to the truck and see we're both passionate about bikes, it gives them confidence in our work." She lined up several of the trophies. "I hope he recovers. I can't run this place on my own."

I helped her as she grabbed more trophies and placed them on the shelves.

I picked up an old photograph and a newspaper clipping in a broken frame. "Hey, this is our gang."

She glanced at what I was holding. "That's right."

I peered at the picture. "Ian's in it. He's got the trophy. Did he win this race?"

Maddie continued lining up the awards. "Most likely. I've been in a lot of races. I don't remember all of them."

"You're not in the picture," I said. "Didn't you take part?"

"I forget. I should fix up the truck. Or should I go to the hospital? I don't know what to do." Maddie thrust out her hands. "No, I should leave. Get the truck out of here while it's safe to do so."

I scanned the text of the article I held. Ian Blaine had won the race against popular young racer, Maddie Vixen.

I glanced at her and then kept reading. The race had been close, but on a sharp bend, Maddie had lost control of her bike and been injured.

"I'm surprised you don't remember this race. This article said you got hurt. Did you have to stop racing after that?"

Maddie walked away and grabbed up more tools. She shoved them in a tool box. "You get injured a lot when racing. You get used to it."

I stared at the article. "You were racing against Ian."

"So? Why the questions about that race? It was ages ago."

I set the picture down. "Maddie, was Ian the reason you lost control of your bike during that race?"

"Of course not. We all know the risks when we take part in races. Bikes are dangerous. Sometimes the road conditions aren't in our favor. It was my fault. I wasn't paying attention." She kept her back to me.

"But you had to give up something you loved," Wiggles said. "That would make a person angry."

Maddie turned, and her eyes narrowed a fraction. "I don't see how that's relevant. We should be focused on finding out what happened to Aidan."

"I am." I glanced at Wiggles. "And I think Ian really wanted to win that race. He wasn't going to let anything stand in his way. That included you. What did he do, make sure none of the other riders could see and then ram you off the road?"

She pressed her lips together. "No! That's not what happened."

"Ian needed a win. He wanted to prove himself to the Willow Tree Falls gang. You must have been so angry with him."

"Angry enough to get revenge." Wiggles cocked his head. "You killed Ian?"

"I didn't kill Ian." Maddie started pacing again. "I can't ride a bike anymore because of my injured leg."

"I reckon you could for a short amount of time. You're strong," I said. "You've got a bad limp, and maybe your leg muscles aren't that great, but that doesn't mean you can't ride a bike."

She snorted a laugh. "Tempest, you're not making any sense."

"What happened, Maddie? Did Aidan find evidence on that bike I brought in that implicated you?"

"He wouldn't do that, because I didn't ride it." She slung aside the bundle of cleaning cloths she'd picked up. "I have to go. I can't deal with this."

"You have to deal with it. Maddie, you killed Ian," I said.

"No! And you've got nothing that proves I was involved. I was here on this truck with Aidan when Ian was run over."

"We've only got your word for that. Aidan said he was exhausted that night. He had a drink and basically passed out. It would have been easy for you to sneak off, grab a bike, and hunt down Ian. You were the one who told us you were both on the truck all night."

"Yeah. You seemed keen to make sure we knew that," Wiggles said.

"Aidan backed me up. He wouldn't lie about that," Maddie said.

"He agreed with you, but he wouldn't have known what you were up to when he was sleeping," I said. "Did he question you about your alibi? Or maybe he did hear you go out and was puzzled why you lied to me."

"We were here. Ian's death has nothing to do with me. Now, you need to leave. I'm busy, and I'm worried about Aidan."

"I expect you're worried he's going to recover. You hoped you'd killed him. What did you do, attack him, and then leave the truck in the hope he'd die while you were gone?"

Her face paled. "I'd never hurt Aidan. He's my boss and my friend."

"You'd never want to hurt him, but you panicked and made a mistake. When Aidan's fully conscious, he'll tell us what happened. He'll tell everyone you tried to kill him." I held my breath as I waited for her to make a move.

Maddie's hands clenched into fists. She looked at the article, a scowl on her face.

"He got suspicious of you, didn't he? Aidan started piecing things together. First, the fake alibi and then the discovery of the bike. He found something that connected you to that bike. Did he ask you about it?" I said.

Maddie closed her eyes and ran her hands through her hair several times before fixing her gaze on me. "I didn't want this to happen. I got scared and had to act. Everything was getting out of control."

"Tell me what you did," I said.

She slumped against the side of the truck. "I told Aidan I didn't want to come to Willow Tree Falls, but he insisted. He couldn't do it without me because we'd be busy with both gangs demanding attention. I really like Aidan, but he should have kept his nose out of this. He shouldn't have asked questions."

"He figured out you ran over Ian," I said.

Her top lip curled up. "Ian was a snake. I never trusted him. He was so full of himself, always bragging about how amazing he was as a biker. He wasn't that great. I'd beaten him several times. The day of that race, the race that ended my riding career, there was something different about him. A meanness in his eyes. He even warned me not to take part. He said I'd be sorry if I got in his way. I thought he was showing off to his gang. I was young and too confident for my own good to listen to him. And I was determined to beat him."

"So you raced against Ian. He did something during the race?"

"It was the two of us out in front. I was so sure I'd beat him. And I was edging ahead when the back wheel of my bike slid sideways. I'd handled slides before, so I was recovering, but it did it again. I glanced over my shoulder to see Ian throwing spells at my bike. I sped up and tried to get out of his range, but I couldn't get away. He kept hurling spells, and suddenly, the bike went from under me. It shot off the road, and I was pitched off."

"Did Ian stop to check on you?" I said.

"Of course not. All he cared about was winning. I slammed into a tree and rolled down a slope. It was only after he'd finished the race that he told people I'd lost control. I was in agony. My leg was broken in four places. It was so bad, nothing could fully heal me. I was in hospital for a month. I had dozens of spells tried on me. They all helped, but this leg always hurts. And every time it twinges, it reminds me of what Ian did."

"Maddie, I'm sorry that happened to you. Ian was wrong, but you were wrong to kill him. And you were definitely wrong to attack Aidan."

"I know. The second Aidan confronted me, I freaked out. He's such a straight up and down guy. He wouldn't cover for me. I figured no one would find that bike in the forest. I hid it off the main path, covered it in leaves, and the magic I used should have destroyed it."

"But Aidan found your residual magic on the bike?"

She nodded. "He identified it as mine. We've worked together a long time. We know each other's magic intimately. Aidan asked me about it. I tried to cover and say it was a mistake, but he wasn't buying it."

"After I delivered the bike, you injured your hand when you were looking at it," I said. "Did you do that because you discovered something and needed time to cover your tracks?"

"Yeah, the second I started messing with it, I realized I hadn't done a good enough job. And I knew, when Aidan started poking around, he'd see I'd used the bike. He wasn't angry, but he was disappointed. That's what hurt the most. He couldn't believe I'd done such a terrible thing. Then he started asking about the night of the murder and if I'd been in the truck the whole night. He heard me go out. I snuck out one of the spare parts bikes we keep in the back. We have older models in case we need parts we can't get our hands on. Aidan knew what I'd done. I had to silence him."

"Maddie, there are limits to what you should do to win. What Ian did to you showed you that," I said.

She looked around the truck, despair on her face. "I know that now. If I'd just stayed away from Willow Tree Falls, I'd have never seen Ian Blaine again. Seeing his smug face, it brought it all back. He ruined my life that day. I had to do the same to him."

"You really didn't," I said. "Maddie Vixen. You're under arrest for murder."

Chapter 20

I rolled my shoulders and sighed as I stepped out of the interview room. I'd been talking to Maddie alongside Dazielle for the last four hours. She'd confessed to everything. The mystery was solved.

Jophiel walked over. "Um, Tempest, I thought you ought to know your sister's asleep in the reception area."

"What's she doing here? She should be at the hospital with Aidan." I pushed away from the wall and followed Jophiel through the office.

"She turned up an hour ago. Aidan's in a stable condition. It looks like he'll pull through, thanks to your sister. She's been asking to see you."

"Okay, thanks." I headed into the reception area. Aurora was curled up in one of the seats in the corner. Wiggles lay on her feet, gently snoring. Sox was draped around her shoulders, and Charlie lay across her lap.

I walked over and shook her arm. "Hey, what are you doing here?"

She lifted her head slowly, one hand going up to steady Sox. "Lex is still missing. We have to look for him."

The cats hopped off her as she stretched.

"It's getting late, and you've been doing a ton of magic. You should get some rest," I said.

"I have been resting. I didn't mean to doze off, but I sat down, shut my eyes for five minutes, and that was it." Aurora's eyes filled with tears. "Tempest, we have to find Lex."

"I wish I could help, but I'm not finished here."

"You are! You caught the killer. Jophiel told me what's been going on. I can't believe it was Maddie."

"Yeah, we were all surprised."

Wiggles rolled off Aurora's feet. "What's going on?"

"We're done interviewing Maddie, but I want to talk to Gideon," I said.

"Can't you let the angels do that?" Aurora stood and clutched my arm.

I looked back at the office. "He's definitely less spiky now Maddie's been arrested for Ian's murder. I guess they can handle him."

"Then let's go. We have to find this mysterious woman who took my guy." She tugged me to the door. "She must have Lex."

I wasn't so sure this woman even existed, but it made little sense for Gideon to make her up. I left a message with Jophiel so Dazielle knew where I'd gone, and we headed back to the castle, along with Wiggles, Sox, and Charlie.

"How was Aidan when you left the hospital?" I asked.

"It was touch and go for a while. He had a lot of internal injuries, but he's improving."

"Maddie really wanted him dead," I said.

"And she seemed so nice," Aurora said.

"She even gave me that stud collar," Wiggles said. "I'm never wearing that again."

"I'm not saying what she did was right, but Ian ruined her racing career. It's what she lived for. I understand why she held a grudge," I said.

"But to attack her boss, the guy who took her in when she had nothing left, that was wrong," Aurora said.

I slowed as the air was filled with the rumble and purr of motorbikes growing closer. It was the Tusks.

Slater stopped his bike beside me. "Where's Gideon?"

"How should I know?" I said. "He's been hiding from me."

"We all know you found his hiding place. What have you done with him?"

"You said you didn't know where he was hiding. Could you have lied to me?"

Slater scowled. "He's our boss. We always cover for him."

"You won't have to any more. Gideon's in custody. He'll be charged with the attempted murder of an angel. He won't be a free man for a long time."

"You've got nothing on him," Slater said.

"The word of an angel holds a lot of clout. Everyone around here knows Dominic, and everyone likes him. Gideon's not getting away with this. It could be time you found a new leader for the Tusks."

Slater glared at me without saying anything for a few seconds. "Does that mean we're free to go?"

"The restrictions at the barrier have been lifted. No one will stop you if you want to leave Willow Tree Falls. Don't come back."

"Don't worry. We won't be coming back to this place anytime soon. Let's move, guys." Slater raised a hand before riding off. The rest of the gang followed.

"That's one problem solved," I said.

"But we still have Lex to find," Aurora said.

I nodded. It wasn't just Lex on my mind. Seeing all those bikers had me thinking about Rhett and what to do with him. Missing fiancé first, stubborn biker boyfriend second.

We arrived at the castle and did a thorough search, starting at the top and working down. Given the number of rooms and the size of the place, it took about an hour to search everywhere. And there was still no sign of Lex.

"Did Gideon say anything more about the woman watching the castle?" Aurora paced around the library.

"Nothing helpful. She was careful to conceal her appearance. But he figured she was fairly young, so we can rule out old girlfriends with a grudge."

"I can't focus on anything. My mind's all over the place. I have to get Lex back."

I stood in front of Aurora to stop her pacing. "Let's take a break. It's been a stressful day, and it's turning into a stressful night. Go make some tea. We'll drink that as we figure out our next move."

"I don't want tea. I want my fiancé back."

"You need to recharge. You must be exhausted after using so much magic to heal Aidan."

"No, I'm fine."

"Then think of your poor sister. You're not the only one who's tired. We both need a recharge." If I couldn't get Aurora to look after herself, I'd make her think she needed to help me. Aurora loved making people happy.

"Oh! I'm being selfish. You're right. And I feel I've aged ten years," Aurora said. "Not that I begrudge helping Aidan, but I was supposed to look stunning on my wedding day. Now I'll look like some pink-haired haggard old crone, trying to look beautiful on the back of a stunning unicorn."

"I heard Granny Dottie and Auntie Queenie fixed Diamond Buttercup. That's good news. Maybe they'll figure out what to do with your hair next."

"I'm seeing them soon. They've got a few ideas. But I don't care if I have no hair, so long as I find Lex and we can get married."

"Go make the tea. Take a five-minute break, and then we'll get searching again."

"Yes! I'll find some cookies, too. Sugar always helps in times of stress."

"Did someone say cookies?" Wiggles jumped up from his apparently deep slumber. "I'll help you look for those." He trotted after Aurora as she left the room.

I let out a big sigh and walked to the window. I had no clue what was going on with Lex's disappearance. I stared out into the gloom. A huge moon hung low in the sky, illuminating the orchard.

I narrowed my eyes and peered at one of the trees. It looked like it had moved. I continued staring at it. A pale face appeared around the trunk and then ducked back.

Someone was watching the castle! Was it the woman Gideon had seen? Why would Lex's abductor be back? If she wanted Aurora, she'd have one heck of a fight on her hands.

"Sox, Charlie, come with me and guard the side door. Don't let anyone in you don't recognize. And make sure you keep Aurora safe."

The cats were instantly on the alert, their fur crackling with magic as they followed me into the hallway to the side exit.

I crept the door open and snuck out. I didn't use a light to illuminate my way. The moon was doing a good enough job, so I wouldn't alert our peeper.

I entered the orchard, focusing my attention on the tree I'd seen the face poke around.

"I know you're there," I said. "Why are you watching the castle?"

Only the breeze responded as it slid through the leaves.

"If you've taken Lex Fontaine, you're in trouble. And if you've hurt him, you're dead."

There was no response. I inched closer to the tree.

A movement to my left had me turning. Whoever it was, they were on the run. I saw a flash of long, dark hair and gave chase. I conjured a light ball so I could see where I was going. It was definitely a young woman, and she was fast.

"You won't get away. You're only making it worse by running. Don't make me hurt you."

She ignored me and sped up. Magic sparked on her fingers as if she was preparing to attack me. I had to stop her before she got away.

I tossed out three spells, one after the other. A restraint spell, a slowdown spell, and then a warning fireball.

There was a shriek, and the young woman stumbled as my fireball skimmed her head. My restraint magic grabbed her for a few seconds, but she broke through it.

I let out a grunt of surprise. She didn't even have to work hard to destroy my magic. She'd simply flung out her arms, and my spells were gone. This was a powerful witch.

Another fireball was on my palm, just as she flooded the orchard with a bright wave of green magic and I got a good look at my attack. The power of her spell slammed me off my feet, and I hit the dirt.

I lay there a second, too stunned to accept what I'd just seen. It couldn't be. I'd only ever seen pictures of her, but I was certain I was chasing my half-sister, Zandra! But an older version. She should still be a kid, but not now. How had Zandra aged so fast? And what was she doing lurking around Lex's castle?

I leaped up and continued to chase her. "Stop! I don't want to hurt you."

"Liar! You said you'd kill me," she yelled from somewhere in the darkness.

I slowed, trying to get my bearings and locate her as the shock made my head pound. "Zandra, is that you? What happened to you?"

"How... how do you know who I am?"

"Because I've seen pictures of you. Dad showed me." I walked slowly, magic sparking on my fingers. But my desire to kill was no longer there. This was family. I had no idea what she was doing here, or how she was now a teenager, but I didn't want to harm her. "You're bigger than I expected. Older. How old are you?"

I stopped walking as Zandra stepped out from behind a tree. She had her magic primed and ready to go. She looked to be at least eighteen. It wasn't possible.

I let my powers edge back to show her I wasn't a threat. "It is you."

She lifted her chin, her dark eyes fierce. "What if it is? We don't know each other. We're strangers."

"Not out of choice. I only found out about you when I located Dad after he'd been missing."

"Now he's back here, and I hardly see him," she said. "How is that fair?"

"I'm not saying it's fair. And I'm sure he wants to see more of you. He's dealing with a lot, though."

"He's dealing with being back with his real family."

"Zandra! You know what happened to him. He forgot he had a family. We searched for him for years until we figured that out. You can't blame him if he's finding it tough to get the balance right between his lives."

"I do. And I don't just blame him. I blame all of you. He's different. He's found his perfect family, and he wants nothing to do with me. I'm the reject. The embarrassment. The dumb kid he wants nothing to do with."

"You'll never be that. He loves you. He's so proud of you. He wants you to be a part of this family. And you are. I'm happy to have another sister. And I want to get to know you. I want to know all about you. How'd you get so old?"

"You can talk. Is that a gray hair I see?"

"You're eight going on eighteen! Explain that."

She shrugged. "I tried a spell. It worked. I was done being a baby, so found my way to becoming an adult."

"You used magic to grow up?"

"Why not?"

"Because..." she shouldn't be able to handle spells of such power.

"Jealous?"

"Shocked. You have power."

"I do. Maybe more than you."

This was too much to process right away, so I put it on the back burner and focused on something else I had to make sense of. "I need to know why you're here and if you had anything to do with Lex going missing."

"That's right. You only care about your real sister. She's not so amazing now she's been jinxed."

My gut clenched, and my breathing grew shallow. "What have you done? Why are you at the castle?"

Her gaze shifted down. "I wanted to see Dad's real family. I had to know what was keeping him here. What was here that meant he no longer cared about me."

"You've been watching us?"

"Maybe. Not that I'm interested in any of you. I don't want to be a part of this dumb family."

"You should. It's not so bad. And Willow Tree Falls is a great place to live. But if you've been watching us, you know Aurora is about to get married. And you also know Lex is missing."

She glared at me. "Yeah, of course I know that. Aurora seemed so happy about it. And Dad's giving her away."

I closed my eyes for a second. "And you're jealous? You don't want Aurora to be happy?"

"Her life is so perfect. She's always had Dad in her life."

"That's not true. We missed him for a long time. He walked away one day, and we still don't know why." I fixed her with a sharp glare. "Zandra, did you do something to Lex?"

"I wanted your amazing family to see real life isn't so much fun. Bad things happen. Your sister lives a fairy tale. She needs to learn that's a joke."

My fingers flexed, and a pulse of anger hit. "You're the one messing with her wedding plans. And now you've taken Lex."

"Maybe I have her precious fiancé, maybe I haven't."

"This isn't a joke. Aurora loves Lex. If you've hurt him, you're in trouble. If you wanted a way to turn the whole family against you, you've found it. Even Dad won't forgive you."

She lowered her hands, and the magic on her fingers died. "I... I wanted you to see life isn't always easy."

"We know that. We've all had our problems."

Zandra twisted her hair around her hand, looking suddenly young and uncertain. "Dad always said I needed to control my temper. But I got so angry when I saw how great your lives were. Everyone in the village is talking about this wedding and how perfect Aurora and Lex are together."

"You felt left out?" I said.

"Story of my life."

"You'd have been welcome at the wedding. Aurora wanted you there. She asked Dad if you might like to come."

"He mentioned it, but I wouldn't turn up at some stranger's wedding and make nice. It would be weird. Everyone would feel sorry for me. And I'd have needed to explain the age thing. I've lost ten years. Dad's going to freak out."

"That'll take some getting used to. Listen, I get this is tough for you, but taking Lex was the wrong move. You have to let him go."

Her eyes narrowed. It took my breath away how alike we looked when she did that. She really was my sister.

"I don't. I want Aurora to see how difficult reality is," Zandra said.

"If you don't release Lex unharmed right away, I'm telling Dad."

"Oh, mature. Go tell Dad I've been naughty."

I knew she cared about him and wouldn't want him to think badly of her. It was her weak spot.

"I'll do it. He thinks the world of you. You don't want to let him down, even if you don't care about anyone else. He's always been around for you."

Uncertainty flickered across Zandra's face. She looked scared.

Despite being angry at her, I could see how miserable Zandra was. She was acting out because she was unhappy. But that didn't give her the right to ruin Aurora's big day.

"Let Lex go, and I won't say a word to Dad, or anyone else," I said.

"How can I trust you?"

"Because despite you trying to ruin everything, we're family. We all want you in our lives. Don't ruin that chance before we've even gotten to know you. Having another sister would be great. And I can tell you're powerful. You almost knocked me out with that last spell. I bit my tongue when I hit the dirt."

A small smile flickered across her face. "That's something else Dad tells me I need to work on. I didn't get much training when I was younger. And I dropped out of school. I kept getting into fights. I don't mix well."

"If you need pointers on how to control your magic, we can help with that. There are powerful witches in this family."

She tilted her head. "Do you really have to deal with a demon living inside you?"

"Yes. And I can only do that because I have control of my witch powers. At least, most of the time. I have good days and bad days. When I struggle, the family is there to help me. They'll help you, too, if you let them."

She stuffed her hands into her jeans pockets and rubbed the toe of her black boot through the grass. "I guess I wouldn't mind knowing a bit more about how to channel my energy. But that doesn't mean anything. I'm not joining this mythical Crypt witch family. I've got my own family."

"Of course. We take it at your pace. But before we do any of that, let Lex go."

"Tempest, what are you doing out here?" Aurora's voice drifted toward me.

Zandra backed away, panic flaring in her eyes.

"Don't worry. Just go. Do the right thing, Zandra. Send Lex back here," I said.

"Tempest! Your tea is getting cold."

I glanced over my shoulder to make sure Aurora wasn't stumbling into danger. "I'll be right there. Go inside."

When I looked back, Zandra was gone.

Aurora appeared in the distance. "Did you see something out here? What are you doing?"

"It's nothing. I heard a noise. Let's go back in the castle."

Aurora looked around. "A noise? What kind of noise?"

"It was a fox or something. Nothing to worry about."

"Are you sure? Sox and Charlie were being strange when I tried to get out the door. They kept blocking my path. I thought you'd seen someone out here."

"I'm just jumpy." We headed inside the castle and settled on the couch in the library.

"I think we should search the forest." Aurora poured the tea and handed around cookies. "We can get Fallon's help. Lex could be in there. If this woman has taken him, she could be hiding him in a cave."

"That's a possibility." I ate my cookie. My thoughts jogged back to the cave in the forest with the woman's clothes in. That must be where Zandra was hiding.

"Is everything okay?" Aurora said.

"I'm good. Just tying the threads together." I took another cookie.

"What threads?"

"It's nothing to worry about. And I have a good feeling. I reckon Lex will be back soon." I just had to hope Zandra would come through and let him free.

The next half an hour was spent trying to behave normally and not glance out the window all the time for any sign of Lex.

"I'm certain you haven't listened to a thing I've said," Aurora said.

I grinned at her. "What was that?"

She sighed. "If you're too tired to keep looking for Lex, we can take a longer break. But I want to find him tonight."

The front door of the castle slammed open.

Aurora leaped out of her seat. "Lex, is that you?"

"Aurora?" Lex stumbled into the library. He looked disheveled and had a cut on his forehead, but other than that, seemed fine.

I stood back as they hugged and talked over each other.

Aurora was crying and laughing at the same time. "What happened? We've been looking for you for ages."

He blinked several times, a dazed expression on his face. "I have no idea. I don't remember much. I was taking a walk when something hit me on the head. I woke a couple of times, and I was somewhere dark. Then I was transported back here."

"Who took you?" Aurora said.

"I didn't see. It was a young woman, but she never spoke, and she made sure I never saw her face."

"A woman? An old girlfriend?"

"Let's not keep questioning Lex," I said. "He's had a trauma."

"It was unsettling," he said.

"You're back now. And you're safe," I said.

"Yes! It's so good to have you home." Aurora covered Lex's face in kisses.

"Give him room to breathe," I said. "How are you doing, Lex? No serious injuries?"

"Nothing bad, other than the bump on the head."

"Aurora's been worried about you. We all have."

"Thanks, Tempest. I'm glad to be back. Although I'm confused about what happened."

Aurora hugged him tight. "It's over. We can finally get married."

Wiggles nudged me with his head. "Am I missing something?"

I shrugged. "Nothing that matters right now. Everything's back as it should be."

Other than having an unstable half-sister who'd aged ten years to deal with, I couldn't think of a single problem that needed tackling.

Chapter 21

"Aren't some of those for Aidan? He is the patient." Dazielle grabbed the box of assorted cakes I'd picked up from Sprinkles on my way to the hospital.

I yanked it away from her and stepped away from the hospital bed. "Nope. Sorry, Aidan. These are for me. I need to make sure I'm dosed up on all things sugary to keep Frank happy."

"Who's Frank?" Aidan was propped up in the bed. It had been three days since Maddie almost killed him, but he was well on the way to recovery.

"It's a long and boring story." I stuffed a brownie in my mouth. I was feeling mildly sick, but I'd do whatever it took to ensure Aurora had the perfect wedding day. And that meant no demon was allowed to gate crash.

Dazielle's gaze ran over me, her expression critical, before she turned to Aidan. "I heard from the doctor that you should be out tomorrow."

"Yes, that's great news," he said. "Although I'm still getting over the shock it was Maddie who attacked me. I didn't see it coming. She was such a good kid."

"Ian ended her racing career. And he did it deliberately. It must have hit her harder than anyone realized," I said.

"I remember it happening. I was at that race. Maddie was a mess afterward. She sunk into a deep depression. I'd always known she was passionate about bikes, so I figured I'd throw her a bone and see if she wanted a change of job. It turned out she was an amazing mechanic. She literally had the magic touch when it came to fine tuning bikes and diagnosing problems. I'm not sure what I'll do without her. I know she messed up, but I don't hate her for what she did to me. She was scared and angry. She felt trapped."

"It wasn't the wisest thing to do, confronting her with the evidence she killed Ian," Dazielle said.

"I couldn't believe it was her. I figured it was a mistake," he said.

I swiped my hand across the back of my mouth and selected a cherry Bakewell slice from the box. "I don't know Maddie that well, but I liked her. She seemed honest and open."

"She was, which is why I couldn't believe it when I put the pieces together. First, the alibi for the night of Ian's murder. That got me puzzled. It was only when I poked around the bike you brought me that I got worried and asked her about it. How's she doing?"

"Maddie's resigned to what's happening," Dazielle said. "She's been charged with Ian's murder and your attempted murder."

"I don't suppose if I put in a good word it'll help. I don't want her life ruined. She deserves better.

She'd still be racing if it wasn't for Ian. Some people even think he had that coming to him."

"Those people don't include members of law enforcement," Dazielle said. Her hard expression softened a fraction. "Everything will be taken into account at the trial. And if you want to submit a statement supporting Maddie, I'm sure she'd appreciate it. I can't guarantee it'll alter her sentencing, but it's worth a go."

"I'll do that," Aidan said. "I'll give it to you before I leave Willow Tree Falls."

I finished my cake and checked the time. "Sorry, Aidan, I need to get out of here. My sister's getting married in a few hours."

"I hope she has a great day. Wish her well from me."

"I need to go, too," Dazielle said. "I've got work back at Angel Force."

We said goodbye to Aidan and left the hospital.

I collected Wiggles from outside, where he'd been forced to wait, much to his disgust. I threw him half a brownie as a consolation while we walked away from the hospital.

"Since the wedding is going ahead, I trust everything worked out with Lex," Dazielle said.

I shot her a glance. She was digging. "It did. It was nothing. A misunderstanding."

"Aurora almost fainted when she came to Angel Force. She was so panicked. What's going on with Lex?"

"It's sorted." I grabbed a cookie from the box.

Dazielle gripped my arm and plucked the cookie from my hand. "You wouldn't be lying to me, would you, Tempest? There's no threat in the village I need to be concerned about?"

"If it was a serious threat, I'd tell you. We're partners. We work together these days."

"When it suits you."

I grabbed my cookie. "And you. We're as bad as each other." I held out the box of treats, and she took a red velvet cream muffin.

There was no way I was telling Dazielle my half-sister was involved in the chaos surrounding Aurora and Lex's wedding. If she figured out Zandra had kidnapped Lex, she'd hunt her down. She'd consider her a problem. And in a way, she was. But it was a problem I'd handle once I figured out how.

Dazielle ate her muffin as we walked along in a companionable silence.

"Aurora's got the perfect weather for her wedding," Dazielle said. "I'm looking forward to it."

"Surprisingly, so am I. I was worried Frank might cause trouble, but he's gone quiet again. I never understand him."

"That's the point of demons. You're not supposed to understand them. You're supposed to destroy them."

"If only I could this one," I said. "I need to go. I've got to squeeze into my bridesmaid's dress, and Aurora's insisted I have a full makeover."

An amused glint entered Dazielle's blue eyes. "That's something I look forward to seeing."

"Don't you dare laugh at me. I'm doing this for Aurora."

"Enjoy yourself, Tempest. Today is about fun and family and being around those you love. It doesn't always have to be demons and murders."

I looked up at her and grinned. Sometimes, for an angel, she made a lot of sense. "I'll see you at the wedding."

I hurried to Mom's house with Wiggles by my side. Aurora was getting ready there, along with everyone else.

"I'm looking forward to my grooming session," Wiggles said. "Aurora's paid for me to have a nose to tail pamper from Fur Babies. She's even ordered me a bowtie."

"You'll be the handsomest hellhound at the wedding," I said.

His tail flipped up. "That's the plan."

We arrived at Mom's house to discover Diamond Buttercup standing in the front yard. His coat was gleaming white, and there was a faint sparkling shimmer covering him.

He tossed his mane when he saw us and trotted over.

I gave him a bow then patted his nose. "You're looking good. Is everything set for transporting Aurora to the castle?"

He pawed the ground and lifted his head up and down.

"Perfect. Let me know if you need any carrots or anything."

He flipped his head and walked away.

"Are you ready for the wedding chaos to commence?" I looked at the house.

"I can't wait. So long as there are treats available while I'm being groomed, I'm all in," Wiggles said.

So was I. I pushed back my shoulders, and we headed inside the house.

The second I entered, Marisa, the wedding planner, grabbed me. "Where have you been?"

"Hey. I had some work to finish. Is everything going to plan?"

"Come with me. No time to chat." She grabbed a strand of my hair and frowned. "Didn't I tell you to deep condition this?"

"Um, maybe." I was beginning to wish I hadn't suggested Aurora re-hire Marisa. I'd forgotten how intense she was.

She shook her head, her expression suggesting I'd committed a crime worse than murder. "This way. We have a lot of work to do."

The next two hours were a chaotic blur of fabric, make-up, hair styling, and free flowing potent lemon drops, all thanks to Granny Dottie and her mixology skills in the kitchen.

I was primped, dressed in a fitted scarlet off the shoulder floor-length gown, and my hair had never been shinier in its life, as I headed up the stairs and knocked on Aurora's bedroom door.

"Come in," she said.

I pushed open the door and grinned at her. "Wow! You scrub up nicely."

Aurora turned and smiled. There was a shimmer of nerves behind it. She wore a simple cream satin gown that skimmed the floor and had a long train. Her now blonde curls were piled loosely on her head, and several curled around her face. She wore light make-up, and her skin shimmered when she moved.

"Will I do?" she said.

"I was getting used to the pink hair." I walked over and carefully hugged her, making sure not to crumple her dress.

"So was I. Granny Dottie fixed me up and finally got rid of the pink. Once this is all over, I'll experiment with my hair color. Blonde is almost boring." She grinned like an excited schoolchild. "You look really good, Tempest."

"No one will be looking at me when you arrive at the castle dressed like that. Lex will be out of his mind when he sees you. He's one lucky guy."

Aurora turned to the mirror and reached for an amber pendant. "Help me put this on."

"It's pretty. Is it new?" I fastened it around her neck.

"Um, no, it's old. I've been working with the others to make sure I have something super powerful, just in case... well, you know, Frank. This pendant is pulsing with Crypt witch energy."

I rested my hands on her shoulders. "It's all good. I've got him under control. I promise he won't mess this up. If I even get the hint he's making an appearance, I'll vanish."

"I knew you'd fix things. This pendant is just a back-up."

I gave her a quick squeeze. "No last-minute doubts?"

"Not for a second. I've been waiting for this moment all my life. Although..."

"Yes?"

"I'm really glad Lex is back, but it's a mystery about what happened to him. He can't remember much, and he doesn't know anything about the young woman who grabbed him. I'm worried she could still be around. What if she tries something at the wedding?"

That thought had also entered my head. I hadn't seen Zandra since she'd appeared outside the castle, a fiery mess of teenage indignation. "Focus on your wedding. I bet it was a misunderstanding. Maybe it was a kidnap and ransom attempt, but they got cold feet. When they realized we were hunting them, they'd have been terrified."

"Of course. We do make awesome witches," she said.

"You've got Lex back, you look stunning, and you'll have a great day."

"Girls, it's time to go," Mom called up the stairs.

I gripped Aurora's hand and squeezed tight. "I'll look out for any trouble."

Aurora's eyes filled with tears, and she quickly blinked them away. "You're the best sister in the world. I wouldn't be half the witch I am if it wasn't for you."

"Quit it, will you? You're the best sister. You keep me grounded. You stick by me even though I regularly try to kill you."

Aurora shook her head. "It'll never happen. Family first." She leaned closer until her mouth was by my ear. "And Frank, if you're listening, you try anything today, and we will take you down. Even if it takes the rest of our lives. Mess with my wedding, and I'll destroy you." She pulled back and gave me a sunny smile. "Let's grab our bouquets. I'm getting married!"

I shook my head, smiling as I followed Aurora down the stairs, holding her train to make sure she didn't trip. For a magnificent white witch, she had a little darkness in her, too.

"Oh, girls, you look beautiful." Mom walked over and kissed us both.

Dad appeared, a warm smile on his face as he wrapped an arm around Mom's waist. "I couldn't be prouder."

"Let me see! Let me see!" Granny Dottie bustled in with Auntie Queenie. She was resplendent in a startling pink fitted dress with an enormous plume of feathers sticking out of her hair. "Oh! You're so beautiful. Both of you look like angels."

Uncle Kenny mooched in a few seconds later, his tie crooked. "You look great, girls."

"They look better than great," Auntie Queenie said. "They're the most beautiful witches here."

"Stop! Or you'll have me crying," Aurora said.

"There's no time for that," Mom said. "You need to get on Diamond Buttercup, or you'll be late."

There was a bustle of activity as everyone was ushered out the front door, chatting, laughing, and talking at the same time.

Mom caught hold of my hand and held me back. "I wanted to check, is everything okay? How's Frank doing?"

"I'm so full of sugar I've got the jitters," I said. "It's working. Frank's content. And I've promised him a long weekend out of Willow Tree Falls so he can cause chaos. It's enough to placate him."

"You're so good to your sister." Mom gave me a quick hug. "Today will be perfect. Your dad's walking with Aurora to the castle, so we'll go on ahead." She kept hold of my hand as we headed out of the house and joined everyone else.

Aurora was sitting side-saddle on Diamond Buttercup. The unicorn was glowing with magic, and Aurora was laughing and smiling at everyone, waving at the people who'd come out to see her off.

Wiggles trotted over. He was sporting a silky black bowtie and his fur glistened. "Smell me!"

"Why?" I said.

"Abigail did something magic to my fur. Go on. Smell me."

I gave him a tentative sniff. "Whoa! You smell great. Sort of lemony."

"None of the lady dogs will be able to keep their paws off me." He trotted around, his fur gleaming and his claws polished.

"Come on, everyone," Granny Dottie said. "It's time to transport to the castle."

We formed a circle and joined hands. Granny Dottie's magic weaved around us, and within seconds, we were all outside the castle.

"Oh, my! Lex has spared no expense in making this place look stunning. If you didn't know its history, you'd have no idea it was crammed full of ghosts," Granny Dottie said. She grabbed Auntie Queenie, and they bustled away to inspect the enormous arches of fresh flowers and ribbons.

I was taking a look around and saying hi to some of the guests arriving, when I heard a rumble of motorbikes. My stomach tightened, and I turned. Rhett and his gang had arrived.

I had to take a moment to drink him in. He looked gorgeous. Gone was the usual leathers, and instead he was dressed in a smart, black suit, his chin shaved and his hair smooth.

The gang approached the castle and entered.

I caught Rhett's gaze but looked away. That was a problem for another time. My relationship issues wouldn't interfere with Aurora and Lex's special day.

"You two should talk." Granny Dottie appeared by my elbow.

I straightened one of the feathers in her hair. "I think it's gone too far for that. But I'm not thinking about Rhett today. This is all about Aurora and Lex. I'll deal with him in my own time."

"I know how stubborn you can be. Don't leave it too long, or he'll think you've gone off him. Oh, look! They're serving pre-wedding drinks." She hurried after a server who was carrying a silver tray laden with delicious looking fruity cocktails.

Mom walked over and touched my arm. "We need to get inside. Marisa is about to faint if we don't do as we're told. Will you be okay out here on your own?"

"Of course." As the only bridesmaid, it was my job to walk in front of Aurora to help build up the anticipation of her arrival. That meant I was out here alone.

"Good luck!" Mom gave me a quick wave before hurrying everyone else inside.

I spotted Aurora and Dad in the distance, approaching the castle. I couldn't believe it. My little sister was getting married. It felt so grown up.

The back of my neck prickled, and I turned. Zandra stood by the side of the castle.

My gut tightened, and I took a step toward her. If she was here to ruin Aurora and Lex's day, I didn't care if she was my half-sister. I'd have to stop her.

She lifted a hand and shook her head.

I stopped, and our gazes locked. There wasn't anger in her eyes, just sadness.

I let out a sigh. That was another thing to add to my to-do list. Zandra was unhappy. I needed to tackle this with Dad. I didn't know her, but I didn't want her to feel excluded.

Her gaze went to Aurora and Dad. She flinched and then slid away.

I waited a moment then walked over and met Aurora and Dad. "Is everything good?"

"Yes! Everyone in the village was so kind as I rode past." Aurora slid off Diamond Buttercup. "They kept wishing me and Lex well and throwing flowers. I feel like a princess. Thank you for the perfect ride, Diamond Buttercup. There's a special barn around the back where you can relax. There's plenty of food in there. Later, we'll see if Lex would like a ride. He'll be so excited to have you at the wedding."

Diamond Buttercup gently nuzzled Aurora's hand before trotting away.

Dad caught hold of both of our hands, his face shining with pride. "I'm so proud to be back in your lives. I've missed a lot, but I won't miss another second."

"We're glad you're here too, Dad." I glanced over at where Zandra had been standing, but she was gone.

Dad's gaze shifted to the sky. "Should we be worried about that?"

I looked up to see a huge, colorful blur shooting toward us.

"Oh my goodness! Bandit made it!" Aurora squeaked and threw her arms wide.

Bandit swooped her off the ground, and they spun in the air, glitter cascading around us. They'd formed a strong bond ever since Aurora helped her get her memory back.

"That's... Bandit!" Dad shook his head.

"As if she'd miss this. She adores Aurora."

Bandit swooped back to us and placed Aurora down. "Hey, Crypt family. It's great to be back." She scattered sweet smelling glitter in all directions. "What a perfect day. Now, where's the groom? I need to give him the once over to make sure he's right for Aurora."

"It's too late for that." I grabbed her arm. "You go find a seat inside. Lex is great. You'll love him."

"Hmmm. He'd better be perfect, or I'll have words." Bandit kissed Aurora on the cheek. "Have a fab time." She floated into the castle.

Dad blew out a breath. "Okay, are you both ready? Everyone's waiting."

Aurora bit her bottom lip. "I'm ready. How about you, Tempest?"

I brushed glitter off my dress. "I'm always ready. Let's go get you married."

We reached the open castle doors, the entrance sprayed with stunning cream and white flowers.

"This is so exciting," Aurora said. "It's a new chapter in all our lives. Let's hope we're ready."

I looked back at her and winked. "Whatever life throws at us, we'll be ready."

About Author

K.E. O'Connor (Karen) is a cozy mystery author living in the beautiful British countryside. She loves all things mystery, animals, and cake. When she's not writing about mysteries, murder, and treats, she volunteers at a local animal sanctuary, reads a ton of books, binge watches mystery series, and dreams about living somewhere warmer.

To stay in touch with the fun mysteries:

Newsletter:
www.subscribepage.com/cozymysteries

Website:
www.keoconnor.com

Facebook:
www.facebook.com/keoconnorauthor

Also By

Luck of the Witch
Hell of a Witch
Revenge of the Witch
Curse of the Witch
Son of a Witch
Framing of the Witch
Trickery of the Witch
Wishes of the Witch
Harmony of the Witch
Remedy of the Witch
Gift of the Witch
Toil of the Witch
Jinxing of the Witch
Craving of the Witch
Union of the Witch
Chaos of the Witch
Sleighing of the Witch

If you enjoyed

Jinxing of the Witch

turn the page to read an extract from the next Crypt Witch Mystery

CRAVING OF THE WITCH

Amazon US

Amazon UK

Amazon CA

Amazon AU

To learn more about the series, scan your country-specific QR code.

Chapter 1

"Has that cage got a silver coating?" I squinted, a scowl on my face, as an enormous cage was hoisted off the back of a delivery truck at the bottom of the hill leading to the stone circle.

Wiggles' eyes glowed red. "They'd better not be interested in catching a hellhound."

"I don't think they're looking for you. That cage is meant for something huge." My bad mood deepened as the cage was set on wheels and moved away by four burly guys.

"Hey, Tempest. I see you're taking in the show." Tate Rathmore strolled over, his usually cheerful face pensive. He held a pizza box in his hands.

"Hi, Tate. I can't believe this is happening." I gestured at the four trucks and the gaggle of people milling about.

"Is that pizza for us?" Wiggles hopped onto his hind legs and waggled his front paws in the air.

Tate nodded. "It wouldn't be right to ignore my two best customers." He flipped open the lid of the box and pulled out a delicious slice of three cheese and garlic sauce pizza and gave it to Wiggles.

Wiggles made short work of the slice and was begging for a second piece within seconds.

I took my own slice and continued to watch as the crew unloaded the truck. "I'm trying to figure out if our visitors really believe in shifters and magic. From what I've seen of this crew, none of them have any powers, unless they're hiding it."

Tate's expression tightened, making his handsome face look sharp. "I've heard of the guy who's running this show. His name's Kirk Wrangler."

I glanced up at Tate. "That name's familiar."

"It should be. The guy's famous for claiming to have hunted down dozens of supernatural creatures, mainly shifters. It was only a matter of time before he sniffed out this place and came poking around."

My eyebrows lifted at the harshness in Tate's tone. For a werewolf, he was one of the most relaxed guys I'd ever met. "This sounds personal."

Tate lifted one shoulder. "Kirk nearly caught a friend of mine. Hundreds of people turned up to track him down. The guy's a bit of an idiot and went on a rampage one night. He left so much evidence behind, even a nonbeliever would have had a hard time arguing there was no such thing as werewolves. They tracked him for two weeks without letting up. He was so exhausted by the end, he was about ready to throw up his paws and give up. I got him out just before they shot him, but it was a close call. Kirk's ruthless. This is all about making a big name for himself and a heap of cash while he's doing it."

"So this Kirk guy must have magic if he can locate shifters."

"Not that I know of," Tate said. "I've kept an eye on him over the years. He thinks shifters should be locked in zoos, so we can be studied to find a way to eliminate the threat."

"Do you think he wants to wipe out magic?" I already didn't like Kirk for invading our beautiful village, and he'd just plummeted in my estimations if he was eliminating shifters.

"Witches and hellhounds are probably safe." He shot me a smile. "But maybe that's because Kirk doesn't know you exist. I reckon he sees shifters like big game. It's an ego thing about wanting to hunt down something more powerful than he is. It makes me sick. I can't believe the mayor let this guy set up in Willow Tree Falls."

"Mannie always wants to put this place on the map, but even I'm surprised he's letting this happen." I chewed on my slice of pizza as several cars rumbled past, none of their engines sounding happy. Mechanical vehicles never did well in the village because the magic short-circuited them. I'd seen a dozen cars break down.

"I don't like this." Tate crossed his arms over his broad chest and flexed his large biceps.

"You'll be fine. You never cause any problems when you shift."

"That you know of." He winked at me, some of the old Tate charm returning.

"We should monitor the shifters in the village," I said. "We don't want anyone coming to the attention of Kirk, just in case he really is here to find a new trophy for his wall."

Tate shuddered. "I've already put the word out. Most of the shifters know Kirk by his lousy reputation. Some of our older residents aren't that strong, though. They could need extra support to stay hidden. I wish Kirk had never come here. Our old timers just want a quiet life. That's why they moved here."

On the outside, Willow Tree Falls was just another sleepy village, but I'd lived here all my life. Scratch the surface, and there were all kinds of magical deeds going on. It was one of the reasons I loved this place so much.

"There you are!" Dazielle rushed toward me, her large angel wings fluttering around her. "I've just been to Cloven Hoof. I couldn't find you."

"The club doesn't open for hours," I said. "What's up?"

Dazielle stabbed a finger at the truck being unloaded.

"We were wondering why you'd let a shifter hunter set up in the village," I said. "Did you and Mannie get a big payoff to look the other way while he hunts our innocent shifters?"

Dazielle's plump cheeks flushed. "Of course not. I can't be corrupted with a bribe. I wouldn't be heading up Angel Force if I could. But..."

"But what?" I said.

She sighed. "Kirk Wrangler tricked us."

"You can be tricked?" The angel who headed up law enforcement in the village wasn't always top of the class when it came to not being duped. Angels were pretty but often not that smart.

A scowl marred Dazielle's face. "I had several conversations with Mr. Wrangler. He assured me he'd be bringing an entertainment and information show, something fun to entice more tourists. And Mannie always welcomes the opportunity to have tourists visit us."

"More like our mayor welcomes their money," I said. "We have enough tourists. We don't need more."

"But this is out of season. The tourists only visit when the weather is warm. No one wants to look at our stone circle in the middle of winter when it's snowing."

"Good. That means the people who live here get some quiet time."

Dazielle waved a hand in the air. "Mr. Wrangler said he'd bring a show of curiosities. He's a collector of magical artifacts. I was fascinated by the proposal and wanted to see what he'd collected."

"He probably stole those artifacts from our ancestors," I said.

"If I find anything of my ancestors in his possession, I'm taking it back," Tate grumbled.

Dazielle narrowed her eyes at him. "Don't do anything foolish."

"It won't be foolish. It's my right to take back something this moron stole from a shifter."

I looked on with interest as they squared up to each other. I wouldn't mind seeing Tate go up against Dazielle. They were both supernaturally strong and fast.

"Does Kirk have magic of his own?" I asked Dazielle.

She tore her gaze from Tate. "No, we met after I'd arranged his permits. He's not magical."

I groaned. "This just gets worse. You gave him a permit to hunt us?"

"No! I knew nothing about the hunting equipment being unloaded from the trucks. We didn't agree to that. I gave him a permit for a curiosity exhibition, show, and guided walks."

"Guided walks that include silver cages and weapons."

"You've seen weapons?" Dazielle's face paled.

"Not yet, but it's only a matter of time."

"I've been trying to get his permit revoked, but Kirk has three lawyers working for him, and they're proving difficult and threatening to sue. There's nothing I can do to stop this from happening."

"Dazielle! It looks like Kirk's going shifter hunting. He could kill someone. Let him sue you. He can't do this."

"He won't." Tate's voice was a low grumble as his werewolf side peeked out. "If that guy lays a finger on any of the shifters, he'll have me to answer to."

"No! I don't want vigilante justice going on here," Dazielle said. "My angels are monitoring the situation."

"I feel so much better for knowing that," I said. "We should run Kirk out of the village."

Tate passed Wiggles another slice of pizza. "I'm happy to lead that project. He can take his nasty silver cage and get lost. If I have to apply my boot to his backside to make it happen, that's fine by me."

"No attacking him. Kirk's done nothing wrong," Dazielle said.

"Yet," I muttered. "If we give him enough time, he could cause serious problems."

"I have things under control." Dazielle frowned as boxes were carried up the hill toward the huge marquee being set up.

"How about the angels monitor Kirk and we keep an eye on the shifters?" I said to her. We had an uneasy alliance when it came to law enforcement. Dazielle had grown to tolerate my interference, as she called it, in her cases, especially since I'd gotten good at solving murders. And I just about tolerated being around a self-righteous angel, who shed feathers everywhere and ordered me about as if she owned me.

"That's why I was looking for you," Dazielle said. "Kirk has a big crew working for him, and I need some extra muscle."

"I always knew you enjoyed having me around," I said.

"I want to be involved too," Tate said. "I've got plenty of muscle, and the shifters trust me. They'll listen if I tell them to keep a low profile while Kirk and his goons are in the village."

"What about the pizza?" Wiggles said. "You can't shut down Mystic Mushroom."

Tate chuckled. "You think pizza is more important than keeping our shifters safe?"

Wiggles' furry forehead wrinkled. "If I say yes, does that make me a bad hellhound?"

Tate petted him on the head. "Don't worry about the pizza. There'll be plenty to go around."

Wiggles wagged his tail. "So long as you don't forget us hungry hellhounds, I'm up for a little creep monitoring."

"I overheard some of Kirk's crew joking about werewolves," I said. "That's their focus. Although all shifters will need a warning about him."

Tate growled again. "I'd love to know where he's getting his information."

"Stories crop up all the time about big cat sightings, yetis, and animals with glowing eyes out on the moors, but we've always kept those stories quiet so we don't attract idiots with weapons." I pursed my lips as I looked at Dazielle. "And we never give them permits to visit and shoot us."

Dazielle sighed. "I never said Kirk could shoot anything. I am trying to fix things."

"Try harder," I said.

"Most of the shifters around here keep their heads down and their noses clean," Tate said. "It wouldn't have been any of them causing a stir and getting noticed. Although some of the older guys can be eccentric."

"When you say eccentric, you mean they frequently get arrested for running around with no clothes on and baying at the moon," Dazielle said.

"We all get our kicks where we can," I said. "If that's the worst our resident shifters do, you should be grateful."

"I had toothless Brian in a cell for two days because he refused to put on any pants," Dazielle said. "That's not a sight any of us need to see."

I wrinkled my nose. Toothless Brian was a harmless, ancient werewolf with no teeth and blunt claws. He liked to hang around the thermal spa and scare tourists for kicks. Ancient werewolves often got quirky. When you've been around for a few hundred years regularly shifting into a werewolf, it tampers with your sanity and, seemingly, makes you forget about wearing pants.

"We'll team up," I said to Tate. "We'll handle the shifters. Dazielle and the rest of the angels can keep an eye on Kirk and his crew."

"That's fine by me," Tate said.

"I give the orders when it comes to law enforcement," Dazielle said.

I crossed my arms over my chest. "So, what are your orders?"

She looked at the truck as more boxes were unloaded. "I'll handle Kirk. I tried to speak to him when he arrived, but he brushed me off and passed me to his harassed assistant. He's not the nicest man to deal with, and I don't want you getting in trouble if he ruffles your feathers." She glanced at me.

I shrugged. I knew what trouble she was talking about. I was still having the occasional problem with my demon, Frank. He was as strong and annoying as ever, and neither of us liked dealing with jerks. It brought out our mean sides.

Tate cracked his knuckles. "If Kirk tries anything—"

"You tell me about it," Dazielle said. "I don't want to spend the next year dealing with lawyers because that... that poop head found a loophole in my permit."

I snorted a laugh. That was the strongest cuss word I'd ever heard Dazielle say. She must be angry. "Let's get rid of him while we can. I'll hex him, Tate can go all super wolf on him, and..." I gestured at Wiggles to include him in this plan.

He licked his muzzle clean of pizza crumbs. "I'll gas him with my unique hellhound aroma."

Dazielle shook her head. "We're doing this properly. We'll monitor the situation and see what Kirk has planned."

"And if he goes hunting shifters?" I said.

"We'll make sure he doesn't catch them," Tate said, "by any means necessary."

"No, not by any means necessary," Dazielle said.

I squeezed Tate's arm. "We'll make sure the shifters are safe and Kirk doesn't get his grubby little hands on them."

Tate heaved out a sigh then nodded.

I was glad to have a project to focus on. Aurora was away on another vacation with her new husband, Lex, I hadn't had a demon hunting job for weeks, and I still hadn't figured out my problems with my boyfriend, if he was still that. This was the distraction I needed to ignore my messy personal life.

"I'll try to speak to Kirk again," Dazielle said. "Figure out what he's planning."

"I can talk to the shifters," Tate said. "Make sure they know to keep a low profile until this jerk leaves."

"Keep me informed." Dazielle nodded at us before striding toward the trucks.

"It's a good idea to chat to your shifter buddies," I said, "but I also think we should talk to Kirk."

"Dazielle won't like that," Tate said.

I arched an eyebrow at him. "Are you scared of the angels?"

He chuckled. "Dazielle would kick my butt in a fight."

"I was wondering about that. An angel against a werewolf. You don't think you can take her?"

"I'd have a go, but it's not so much her wings that bother me. She gets to see the health and safety reports on the store. Dazielle could make my life difficult if I get on the wrong side of her. She could even shut down Mystic Mushroom."

Wiggles groaned. "Don't annoy Dazielle. Your pizza is the best. I'd be miserable if you got shut down."

"We won't annoy her. Besides, she can't get angry if she doesn't know what we're doing," I said. "Dazielle plays by the rules, and Kirk doesn't. If that's the case, I'm happy to bend them to make sure he sees sense and moves on."

"Works for me. What do you want to do first?" Tate said.

"We'll deal with the shifters while Dazielle does what she needs to with Kirk, then we'll have a chat with him to ensure he doesn't tear Willow Tree Falls apart in his shifter hunt or learn too much about our unique residents."

It was time to go find our shifters.

Craving of the Witch is available in paperback and e-book.